IRON TIDE RISING

IRON TIDE RISING

The Map to Everywhere: Book 4

By Carrie Ryan & John Parke Davis

Illustrations by Todd Harris

Little, Brown and Company

New York Boston

Copyright © 2018 by Carrie Ryan and John Parke Davis
Illustrations © 2018 by Todd Harris

Cover art copyright © 2018 by Todd Harris. Cover design by Sasha Illingworth.
Cover copyright © 2018 by Hachette Book Group, Inc.

Little, Brown and Company
Hachette Book Group
1290 Avenue of the Americas, New York, NY 10104
Visit us at LBYR.com

First Edition: February 2018

Little, Brown and Company is a division of Hachette Book Group, Inc.
The Little, Brown name and logo are trademarks of Hachette Book Group, Inc.

The publisher is not responsible for websites (or their content) that are not owned by the publisher.

Library of Congress Cataloging-in-Publication Data
Names: Ryan, Carrie, author. | Davis, John Parke, author.
Title: Iron tide rising / by Carrie Ryan & John Parke Davis.
Description: First edition. | New York ; Boston : Little, Brown and Company, 2018. | Series: The map to everywhere ; book 4 | Summary: "Fin and Marrill's final adventure takes them to the Mirrorweb, the heart of the Pirate Stream, where they must confront an old friend who has become their worst enemy"— Provided by publisher.
Identifiers: LCCN 2017030077| ISBN 9780316240932 (hardcover) | ISBN 9780316240895 (ebook library edition) | ISBN 9780316240925 (ebook)
Subjects: | CYAC: Adventure and adventurers—Fiction. | Pirates—Fiction. | Maps—Fiction. | Fantasy.
Classification: LCC PZ7.R9478 Iro 2018 | DDC [Fic]—dc23
LC record available at https://lccn.loc.gov/2017030077

ISBNs: 978-0-316-24093-2 (hardcover), 978-0-316-24092-5 (ebook)

Printed in the United States of America

LSC-C

10 9 8 7 6 5 4 3 2 1

For our parents,
that we may sail forever on seas of gold.
And for Corey, Robbie, and Jamie—
may your adventures be as boundless as the Stream.

Contents

CHAPTER 1
A Rocky Start + 1

CHAPTER 2
Smash Course + 14

CHAPTER 3
Things Obscured in the Mist + 24

CHAPTER 4
Flight-of-Thorns + 38

CHAPTER 5
War and Peace (but Mostly War) + 52

CHAPTER 6
An Exit + 62

CHAPTER 7
Without a Flame + 74

CHAPTER 8
The Space Among the Tallowtrees + 87

CHAPTER 9
Marrill Is a Dolphin + 104

CHAPTER 10
At Dawn, the Light Is Peculiar + 117

CHAPTER 11
A Genial Conversation at the Beginning of Time + 128

CHAPTER 12
MirrorwebewrorriM + 147

CHAPTER 13
The Woman in the Glass + 165

CHAPTER 14
Striking Distance + 179

CHAPTER 15
Iron. + 191

CHAPTER 16
Finding Friends in the Worst Places + 205

CHAPTER 17
The King of Molten Metal + 215

CHAPTER 18
Baby Steps + 226

CHAPTER 19
Remy Gets a Tattoo + 238

CHAPTER 20
The Lightning Net + 250

CHAPTER 21
Friends Who Were Enemies Fight an Enemy
Who Was a Friend + 260

CHAPTER 22
No Reflections + 271

CHAPTER 23
Black Mirror + 284

CHAPTER 24
Headwaters + 299

CHAPTER 25
The Last Port + 306

Epilogue + 318

HEDGECAW'S INDEX OF ORACULAR IMPLEMENTS

A GUIDE TO THE MANY THINGS REFERENCED IN THE MERESSIAN PROPHECY,

Collected and Protected by the Most Vigilant Meressian Order

GUARD AGAINST IT AND PREVENT IT

VOL. III: VERSES 180—495

Brine Butterfly (1), in a jar: Recovered from two of our own so-called guards just after the sinking of our Temple Ship at the Khaznot Quay. This butterfly, and an untimely sniffle, allowed a mysterious and unknown thief to slip aboard.

> Verse 199, lines 1–2: *The Master of Thieves, he needs no keys / just wings of salt, and simple sneeze...*

Status: *FULFILLED*

Clock of Scarabs: Clock of a thousand hands, recovered from the Abandoned City of Avoraquorum, deep in the caverns beneath Flight-of-Thorns Citadel. The eyeless men of the caves speak of a time when all the Clock's hands lined up at once, and of the Great Pealing that forced them out into the dark.

> Verse 200, lines 4–5: *... whence the beetle's chime did sound / through towers tall, built underground...*

Status: *FULFILLED*

Shame of the Veiled Emperor: Bottled. **WARNING**: Do not mock.

> Verse 201, lines 14–15: *…his pride laid low, like starlight that sours / with a rustle of silk and the scent of dead flowers…*

Status: *FULFILLED*

Wickless Candle, Made from Mysterious Wax: Little is known about this artifact, save that it has melted and reformed more than once already.

> Verse 202, lines 3–5: *Let the unlit light, my way illuminate / to the web of mirrors, to the space beyond the Gate / with a candle unburnt, the token of She-Who-Waits.*

Status: *FULFILLED*

Candied Hearts of Yesterday: Sold on chains in the Calendar Delta, where the locals hunt wild days in a revolving bayou. Not as edible as one would think. This particular chain was wrapped around the wickless candle.

> Verse 202, lines 6–8: *Let yesterday's hearts, my path divine / that I might see the depth of time / and with a coat of sugar, they taste just fine!*

Status: *FULFILLED*

The Evershear: The legendary blade of Sir Emvigle of the Collapsing Court, enchanted so that there is nothing through which it cannot cut. Found lodged in the side of a serpent the size of a mountain. (or is it a mountain that crawls like a serpent?).

> Verse 203, lines 9–12: *Far beyond the Whimpering Lake / The serpent of many sizes wakes / There he sheds his epic Scale / A trade for a blade that never fails.*

Status: *FULFILLED*

CHAPTER 1
A Rocky Start

"Marrill...Marrill, honey..."

Marrill blinked twice at the morning light filtering in through the half-drawn blinds. Her mother's voice wrapped around her like a blanket, holding her warm and tight. The scent of distant rain was on the breeze, but as far as she could see, the clouds had passed; outside her window, the day was fresh and bright.

"Mom?" she whispered.

"Shhh," her mother murmured in her ear. Gentle arms

cradled her. One hand stroked her hair. No plastic tubes snaked from the back of that hand; no hospital monitor beeped beside them. Her mother's face smiled down, strong, healthy.

Marrill sank into the embrace. "Oh, Mom, I'm so glad you're here." Words tumbled out as her mother rocked her slowly back and forth. "I stayed on the Pirate Stream to save you, but everything just went wrong. We lost our friend Coll, and Fin's mother died, and Ardent—"

"I know, Petal," her mother cooed. She rocked her more strongly now, back and forth, back and forth. "But it's okay. It's all better now."

Marrill smiled. Her mom always did make things better. No matter how badly things went, her mom was so calm, so strong. So brave. Everything Marrill wished she could be, but wasn't.

"Look," her mother whispered. "Isn't the ocean beautiful?"

Marrill looked across the endless expanse of sea that spread out on every side. Her bedroom rested on a stone spire. Other than the one wall beside them with its cozy window, the whole thing was open—there was nothing but air between them and the sunrise-painted water.

Her mother rocked her harder now. So hard, it seemed like the whole stone spire was swaying. Back and forth, back and forth. The water grew closer then farther away, closer, farther. Fear welled up inside Marrill, but she bit it back. As long as she had her mother, she would be safe.

"Mom?" she asked. "Are we going to fall?"

Her mother laughed. "Only if you don't let go first, Marrill. Only if you don't let go."

Something wasn't right, Marrill could feel it. She looked up. An iron mask loomed over them, so huge it nearly filled the sky, the sun just a halo behind it. A sharp-fingered gauntlet rocked the whole room back and forth, furiously now.

Metal spread from the hand, running down the wall toward them. The spire pitched, plummeted. Marrill screamed, holding on to her mother for dear life.

"LET GO!" a booming voice commanded.

⊹ ⊹ ⊹

"Marrill, let go!" Fin gasped. Marrill's eyes popped open. He was leaning over her, face going red as she tugged on his collar. She let go.

Next thing she knew, Marrill was sprawled on the floor of her cabin as the *Enterprising Kraken* lurched beneath them. The cabin had changed again during the night. Its walls were as blue as the sky, in imitation of her dream, but the shimmering-water image beneath her sloshed violently with the motion of the ship.

"What's going on?" she muttered, still shaking away the

gap between dream and reality. The floor tilted bedward, sending her tumbling beneath it. Her cat, Karnelius, was braced there with claws anchored in the wood. He glared at her as she slid past, his one eye narrowed to a slit.

Fin leapt smoothly from bedside to bed to other bedside, bobbing with the rise and fall of the ship. "That's what I was waking you up for," he said. He hopped up on the bed and back down again, rubbing his throat. "Hey, did you know you strangle in your sleep?"

Marrill caught a bedpost as the ship tilted and she began to slide again. She clung to it for a second, letting reality filter back in. She was on the *Kraken*. She and Fin and the rest of the crew were on the trail of the wizard Ardent—transformed now into the Master of the Iron Ship. They had to find out why he'd unleashed the Iron Tide to menace the Pirate Stream.

And more importantly, how to stop it.

She gripped the bedpost tight as the ship shifted, then hauled herself to her feet. "Sorry," she said. "I was having a bit of a weird dream."

Fin grabbed her hand and yanked her toward the door. "Well, shake it off. We've got a weird reality to deal with!"

Marrill laughed as she chased after him to the great spiral staircase that ran up the middle of the *Kraken*. They bounced from side to side as they passed the Door-Way with its thousand glistening knobs; even the Promenade Deck made an appearance before vanishing off to some other ship (as it often did). For a moment it felt like old times—she and

Fin having adventures on the magical waters of the Pirate Stream, traipsing between all worlds in creation.

Still, Marrill couldn't forget the dream.

She'd been thinking about her mother more and more since the events on Meres. Her mother's face, her mother's warmth, her mother's voice, always knowing what to do. A pang of emptiness lanced through her.

She would have given anything for her mother to be here. The Stream had turned into a scary place now that Coll and Ardent were gone. The Master of the Iron Ship was out there, somewhere, spreading the Iron Tide wherever he went. Somewhere else, the living fire known as the Salt Sand King would burn anything that hadn't been turned to metal. And his unstoppable army, the Rise, would conquer anyone who got in the way.

"Ready?" Fin asked as they reached the main hatch.

Marrill took a deep breath. Her dreams would have to wait. At least until they dealt with...whatever was happening now. "Ready," she said.

And with that, they exploded onto the main deck. Just as the prow of a boat the size of a skyscraper crashed toward the *Kraken*.

"Tack, tack!" screamed Remy's voice from above. Marrill's babysitter-turned-captain waved like a madwoman from the quarterdeck, ship's wheel spinning between her hands. The *Kraken* surfed to one side, slipping around the massive vessel like a cheetah darting around an elephant.

Marrill tumbled into the starboard railing. As quick as she hit, she was back on her feet, knees loose the way Coll, their former captain, had taught her. By now she was used to rough rides. It would take more than a sharp turn to throw her.

"Look who deigns to show up," grunted a crusty old voice nearby. Marrill looked over to see the Naysayer, all four arms tangled in ropes, pulling and straining as the ship turned. He thrust one of the lines at her. "Take this. It's against my principles to work this hard before breakfast. Or after breakfast. Or at all."

Marrill snagged the line. "Wake, wake!" Remy cried. The first wave coming off the other ship hit them square in the side. The *Kraken* rolled.

Marrill clung to the rope as her feet left the deck. Suddenly, the railing was *below* her. Her insides turned. A loose bucket of prollycrabs tumbled over the ship's edge, bursting into a flock of white birds as it struck the magical water of the Pirate Stream.

"Awwwww, breakfast!" the Naysayer wailed. "Now what am I workin' for?"

The ship righted, spun, tumbled the other way as the next wave hit. This time, they took it at an angle, keeping the *Kraken* steady. Marrill quickly tied the rope around her waist, staggering from side to side, moving back and forth like a pendulum in a clock.

Just as she regained her feet, another huge ship plowed

into view. There were more, she realized. Many more. Hundreds, maybe thousands, of enormous ships all around them. Sails so large they nearly blocked out the sky. Hulls so massive that the tips of the *Kraken*'s masts barely reached the bottom of their deck railings.

The *Kraken* was racing through the middle of a giant fleet, darting back and forth between the oncoming ships like a mouse in a stampede of rhinoceroses. The mammoth ships churned the water into a roiling froth. The *Kraken* lurched and rolled, struggling to stay upright.

Marrill's feet skidded across the deck, the line around her waist pulling tight and swinging her out over the port railing as the ship tilted. Two others swung out with her on their own ropes: Fin to one side, and a girl she didn't recognize to the other.

"Well, this is fun," Fin said, raising his voice to be heard over the rush of the wind.

"This is what it's like when the full force of the Rise attacks," said the girl as the *Kraken* tilted back the other way. "I don't see them, though, so thaaaAAAAaaaa..."

They all shrieked as the ship rolled up on its starboard side. A wall of floating wood thundered past; the *Kraken* narrowly avoided smashing into the enormous hull.

"...at's good," the girl finished. "I'm Fig, by the way. I'm Fade; you've met me, probably a hundred times by now." She smiled.

Marrill smiled back. She didn't remember the girl at

all. But that was the thing about the Fade—no one remembered them. Fin's people were the perfect spies; attention slid off them, and their faces vanished from memory after a few minutes. Not long ago Fin had spurred his people into a rebellion against their heartless twins, the Rise. It hadn't exactly ended well, but it made sense that at least one of the Fade would still be around.

"Nice to..." Marrill paused as the *Kraken* lurched back, dodging another big ship. "Mee...

"...*eeeEEEEEeeee*...

"...eet you?" she finished.

"We have to steady ourselves!" Remy yelled from the quarterdeck. "I can't stay the course if we keep listing like this!"

Marrill looked around, trying to find something, anything, to help. The only reason they hadn't toppled over yet was because the Naysayer had anchored himself in the middle of the ship, and his huge bulk was enough to counterbalance everyone else's weight....

"Counterbalance," she said aloud.

"Marrill, what are you ta..."

"...*aaaaAAAaaa*...

"...lking about?" Fin asked.

Marrill laughed. That was the answer. "We need a counterbalance to stay upright and keep from capsizing," she told him. "And we already have one. Naysayer! Run to the opposite side when we swing!"

"Oh, sure," the big lizard shouted back. "You guys just hang out, and leave it to the ole Naysayer to fix everything. Ya lazy…"

Marrill didn't hear the rest over her own yell. But this time, just as they reached the end of their swing, the ship caught itself.

She looked across the deck. The Naysayer clung to the opposite railing, almost above them. For all his grumping, the old beast had actually done it!

"It's working!" Remy shouted as the ship began to right itself. "Keep going!"

"And wear out my knees like a sucker?" the Naysayer said. "Forget you, lady." Just as they started to swing back, he let go of the railing, throwing himself in the air. "Cannonball!"

Marrill, Fin, and the forgettable girl—*Fig?*—swung to starboard just as the Naysayer swung to port. Then back again. Then back again. Each time, the *Kraken* tilted less and less, slowly stabilizing. They were like swings on a playground, their arcs completely opposite each other.

As they fell into a rhythm, Marrill got a chance to examine the big ships thundering past. They were enormous; she had to crane her neck just to glimpse the lowest decks. People and creatures and plantimals and things she didn't know how to describe crowded against the portholes and outside railings. Every crash of the massive hulls against the water sent shock waves across the *Kraken*, tossing her like a toy in a bathtub.

The sight alone was dizzying. The smells were like an out-of-tune orchestra, spices tangling with the heady fragrance of overripe fruit and the odor of so many bodies cramped together.

But more arresting than anything else was the sound. People chattering and creatures chittering, voices babbling in panic as they leaned over the railings, staring back at the horizon behind them. It was that panic that puzzled Marrill. She tried to figure out what could cause so many giant ships to crowd the Pirate Stream, with seemingly no regard for the poor *Kraken*.

"It looks like they're running from something," she shouted. She looked to Fin. "Maybe we should get…"

They reached the peak of their swing. For a long moment, they hung motionless in the air.

Her lips formed automatically
the word
"Ardent."

Fortunately, the *Kraken* rocked back before the wizard's name came out. Marrill bit her tongue as they swooped down over the deck, her eyes catching the closed door to what had once been Ardent's cabin.

She braced against the twisting daggers of sorrow and betrayal that stabbed her heart every time she thought of him. Sorrow for losing him; sorrow for what *he* had lost: his love, the wizard Annalessa. Betrayal at what he had done— what he had *become*—because of his grief.

She couldn't wallow in the feeling, though, or it would paralyze her. The Ardent she knew was gone, she reminded herself as they neared the peak of their backswing. Even so, she couldn't quite bring herself to name their *new* companion, either.

"...the wizard?" she finished,
the words dangling
in the moment
of still.

Fin spun as he swung back to starboard. "He doesn't seem much like the helping sort," he called over his shoulder to her.

Overhead, tackle squealed as the Ropebone Man—the *Kraken*'s living rigging—shifted and moved. He tightened the lines that stretched from him in all directions, while the many-legged pirates scampered along the yards, adjusting the sails. The *Kraken* turned, taking advantage of a break in the onslaught to veer wide.

"Almost through," Remy shouted, tension lacing her voice. "I think we can skirt around the rest of these big ones."

Marrill's swinging slowed as the *Kraken* steadied into her new course. Her feet skipped lightly, tripped slightly, then gained purchase on the deck. She pulled loose the knot at her waist, dropping the rope and running with the last of her momentum to the port railing.

The remaining enormous ships smashed through the

waves toward them, but the *Kraken* was fast; there was plenty of room to slip around them. Up ahead, the big ships thinned out into smaller ones at the edge of the fleet. Beyond them were calmer waters the *Kraken* could handle with ease.

Marrill's breath caught. "Look!" she shouted, pointing. A ship smaller than the *Kraken* had gotten ahead of itself. It must have been sucked in by the wake of the remaining massive ships; it was caught between two of them, clearly struggling to turn and escape.

She gripped the rail, feeling the wood grain press into her skin. The little ship was about to get smashed to pieces, like a nut in a nutcracker.

"It's not going to make it," a girl Marrill didn't recognize whispered beside her. She sucked in a sharp breath. "They're caught in the recirculation."

Marrill felt ill. "Remy!" she cried. "Turn in! We have to help them!"

"You're crazy," the captain replied calmly.

Fin leaned dangerously far over the port railing beside her. "Remy, Marrill's right," he said. "That's not just any ship." He pointed to the black flag flapping from the tip of the mast.

Marrill hadn't noticed it before, but now that she did, she recognized the ship instantly. After all, she'd seen a flag like that before, on a ship shaped just like this one. Twice, in fact. Once had been the *Black Dragon*, the ship that nearly destroyed the Pirate Stream. Then again on the

Dragon's smaller replacement, the *Purple Serpent*. She and Remy had hitched a ride on it after a flood of Stream water had picked up their car from an Arizona parking lot and turned it into a fish.

This ship was even smaller yet, but in nearly every other respect, it was identical.

Marrill spun toward Fin. He looked back at her with the same tense concern in his eyes.

"Stavik," they said as one.

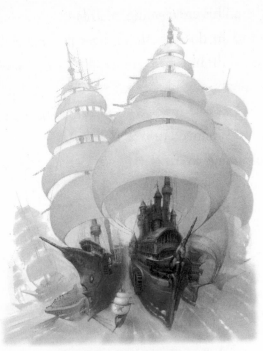

CHAPTER 2
Smash Course

Fin leapt onto the railing, eyes wide as the two gargan-
tuan ships tilted toward each other with no regard for
the smaller boat between them. In a few moments,
she'd be crushed to timbers, and any survivors would go
straight into the Pirate Stream. The magical waters might
change them into monsters, or memories, or a million other
things he could think of, and a million he couldn't. But
whatever they became, one thing was for sure: If they went
into the Stream, they wouldn't be "survivors" anymore.

Stavik and his crew would be killed.

They had to do something. Stavik had been the most important adult in Fin's life growing up aside from his adopted parents, the Parsnickles, the Pirate King had been a mentor and a role model, albeit one with a penchant for thievery, and Fin loved him for it.

Now, Fin only knew one thing: Whoever he was, he was the *opposite* of Vell. And that meant there was no way he was going to let Stavik get squished.

"Quick," he yelled to Remy, "we have to go in after them! We have to save them!"

She gave him a sad look. "I wish we could, Plus One," she called back, using the only name that she knew him by: the other kid on the ship—Marrill plus one. "I want to save them, but I don't see how. If we get between those two ships, we'll just end up crushed as well."

Fin exhaled. His shoulders fell. She was right. But he couldn't give up. "There has to be a way."

"Welp," the Naysayer grunted, "ya *could* just ram 'em a quarter tilt off their bow, pushin' 'em around and out the recycle while still maintaining enough momentum to carry us clear of the collision area."

As one, Fin, Marrill, and Fig turned and stared at the old lizard. Fin could practically hear Remy's jaw drop.

"Course ya could just stand there gaping like your brains fell out; that's fine, too," the Naysayer sneered. He casually tied off the three ropes he'd been holding and lurched toward the hold. "Anyone needs me, I'll be downstairs cobblin' together a life raft."

Fin looked back at the struggling ship, mentally mapping out the Naysayer's plan. "I think it'll work," he breathed. He bounded up the stairs to the quarterdeck without missing a beat. "I think it'll work!" he yelled to Remy.

"Hmm, maybe." Worry creased the older girl's forehead. "I can get us in, probably fast enough to get us out again. *Probably*," she stressed. "But it'll be hard to line up unless they know what we're doing."

Fin glanced toward the floundering ship. She was too far away to hear them, too far away to catch a signal. He'd have to have wings to reach her in time. His fingers twisted in the strings on the arms of his skysails. A smile crooked across his mouth.

"Leave that to me," he told her. "Just go, now!"

"Fine," Remy said through gritted teeth. "Hope you know what you're doing."

She turned the wheel sharply. The *Kraken* swooped a half-moon through the water, lining up to run straight down the middle of the rapidly closing gap between the two massive ships.

"Full sails!" she shouted. Up above, the Ropebone Man flexed his knotty muscles, snapping the sails to life. The *Kraken* sped toward the opening, even as the big ships raced on, oblivious. Their giant hulls grew closer until their sides almost kissed as they smashed through the waves. The *Kraken* would barely have room to scoot through.

Fin took a deep breath. Showtime.

Before he could talk himself out of it, he leapt off the quarterdeck railing, hit the main deck at full run, vaulted the forecastle, and darted toward the bowsprit.

"Fin, what are you doing?!" Marrill cried after him. He didn't have time to stop and explain. He snagged a loose rope just as he hit the tip of the bow and swung out to one side.

A breathless second and his feet touched the hull of one of the big ships. He kicked, clinging to the rope as he ran sideways along it. And then, just as gravity started to catch up, he let go of the rope, yanked the strings on his sleeves, and jumped.

The skysails in his jacket burst to life. The howling wind created by the towering ships buffeted him, threatened to roll him. But it buoyed him, too. Below, the waters of the Stream shimmered and roiled, practically whispering all the things he might turn into if he crashed. He struggled to keep his arms out, to keep his back straight and head up as he swooped toward Stavik's boat.

A few harrowing heartbeats later, there was dullwood beneath his feet. He staggered to a stop, his hand clenched in the thieves' sign and a "Hello, fellow shady-fellows" on his lips. Confused stares surrounded him. *Better than sword blades*, he thought.

Shadows dropped across the pirate vessel. Overhead, the ships' towering walls closed in, blocking out the sun. They'd be smashed to splinters lick-straight.

"No time to tooth-rattle, bloods," he said, darting through the stunned crowd toward the ship's wheel. "Helmsman," he called to the quaking pirate manning it, "turn quarter on, let that ship hit us just by the bow." The pirate opened his scaly snoot of a mouth in confusion.

"Do it!" Fin commanded, grabbing hold of the railing to brace himself.

The helmsman nodded, stunned, and did as he was told. The ship turned, lining up just as the *Kraken* bore down on them. Pirates screamed, clutching each other in a very un-pirate-like manner.

The ships collided. Timber cracked and snapped. The deck rocked. Fin's gut heaved; he tasted bile rising up the back of his throat.

At first, he thought they were wrecked for real, sunk and dead. But the Naysayer had known what he was talking about. The angle was just right; the ships glanced off each other. The pirate ship turned, shoved backward. Its figurehead, a coiled lavender salamander, shattered apart against the wooden wall beside them, but the ship itself washed free.

The massive boats thundered on, leaving the smaller crafts spinning in their wake. A moment later, the two vessels crashed together, obliterating the space where the pirate ship had just been.

A cheer went up from the pirates. Before Fin had time to think, hands slapped his back and lifted him high in the air. He laughed, soaking in the pirates' admiration. Being the center of attention wasn't an experience he had too often. And besides, he knew it wouldn't be long before they totally forgot about him—everyone did, eventually.

The pirates lowered Fin to the deck as the *Kraken* sidled up beside them. Fin had already started toward the railing when a heavy hand landed on his shoulder. The pirate looming over him was more scar than skin, his frame lanky and angular in its dragon leather vest and pants.

"Stavik!" Fin cried happily. Then he cringed at his own excessive friendliness. He'd forgotten—Stavik *hated* friendliness.

But the Pirate King surprised him. "I don't know ya, kid, but ya did good." The scars on his brow struggled against each other in a show of admiration. "I owe ya, and I'm not a man to forget his debts."

Fin felt his throat tighten. He wished it were true, but he knew it wasn't. On multiple fronts, really. He thought about the time Stavik had taught him to jimmy open a window latch while hanging from the eaves by his toes, or when he'd shown him how to skin the rings off the feeler-fingers of a merchant arch-nid without it so much as noticing they were gone. Those were good times. But Stavik would never remember Fin. That was just the way things were.

He placed his hand over the Pirate King's, watching the

old thief's eyes widen in surprise. "No, Stavik," he said. "You don't remember, but the debt was mine."

Stavik considered him for a moment, then nodded. "Call us square up, then."

Beside them, a rope dropped down, securing the *Lavender Salamander* to the side of the *Kraken* for Fin to climb up. "So," he said, hoping to linger in Stavik's attention for just a little while longer. "Mighty big fleet, not like you all to be in the middle of it. Were you...um, running from something?"

Stavik snorted. "Don't run from much, kid." A sharp dagger slipped out from his waistband. Fin's heart skipped a beat until the Pirate King started picking his teeth with it. "But yeah, this time. Yeah. Creeping metal."

The Iron Tide. Fin grimaced. It was a little weird to think the Tide could be in front of them, being as how they'd left it behind in Meres. But then, the Stream wasn't exactly flat; it didn't flow like other rivers.

"Must have washed in on some weird current," Fin said aloud.

Stavik nodded. "And just keeps coming," he murmured, "like a spreading plague. Anything it touches gets infected, turns into a statue. And I mean *anything*. Ground, Stream, flesh—dullwood, even."

Above, Remy popped her head over the side of the *Kraken*. "Hi!" she chirped cheerily, waving. At the sight of the teenager, half the pirates cringed and took an involuntary step back.

"Ah, for the mercy of the moonless night, not that one again," Stavik groaned. Fin started to say something more, but it was no good. The Pirate King's attention was broken; Fin was forgotten. Remy had apparently made quite an impression on the pirates the last time she'd been on their ship. They'd taken her hostage briefly. By the end of it, the pirates would have paid a ransom themselves, just to get rid of her.

Fin felt the warmth of the sun on his neck as he watched straggling ships race past the *Salamander*. The big ships were long gone, but the smaller ones still swarmed by like locusts. They cut a light spray of Stream mist in the air, filling it with a scent like cinnamon and rain.

All of them fleeing the Iron Tide. Fin swallowed, thinking of the places the Tide had taken. And of one in particular. The Khaznot Quay. The place where Fin had grown up, learned to be a thief, lived most of his life.

Dread coiled around him, tangling his arms and snaring his legs, threatening to drag him away from himself. He tried not to think about the unstable old house on Gutterleak Way. He tried not to worry about sweet Mrs. Parsnickle or her grumpy husband, Arler, two good people just doing their best to get by and make other people's lives better along the way.

Surely they were safe. Surely the *Quay* was safe. But then, it wasn't like Stavik and his pie shop pirates had a den in every port on the Stream. Sure, they *could* have been at sea when the Tide came, but...

To chase the thought away, he headed toward the *Kraken*. He didn't have all day, after all. The pirates were milling about, making sure the *Lavender Serpent* was ship-shape, but they weren't going to stick around long.

"...sure you don't want to come up and see *my* ship?" Remy was saying. "I don't bite. I mean, I know I *did* bite, but you had that coming."

Stavik rubbed his wrist. "Mmm, yes, I recall." He flicked his tooth-picking dagger against the *Kraken*'s hull to clean it. Remy wrinkled her nose at him in disgust. "Oh, sorry," he muttered. He pronounced the word like it was from a foreign language; Fin knew from experience that he didn't say it often.

Marrill's head poked up beside Remy's. "But where will you go?" she asked.

The dragon leather vest wriggled on the Pirate King's shoulders as he shrugged. "Well, that there's the problem, in'it? All I know for sure is we can't go home."

"You could come with us," Marrill offered. Fin smiled, imagining traveling with his old mentor. But as much as a part of him wanted that, he knew it wouldn't happen. Saving the world wasn't the pirate way.

"Pass," Stavik said, eyeing Remy cautiously. "But I owe you a debt for saving us. Name your price, and I shall repay it."

Marrill giggled and whispered in Remy's ear. Remy winked at her. Together, they pointed down at Fin.

"How about we just take that one crewman?" Remy said. A smile danced on her lips. "He looks like he belongs up here anyway."

Stavik glanced down at Fin. Not even a hint of recognition crossed his face. "Fine. On with you, boy." His voice dropped to a whisper. "Good luck, lad. Watch the blond one—she'll poke you right in the eye, no warning. Ain't civilized, that."

Fin jumped to the railing and scrambled up the rope ladder dangling down the side of the *Kraken*. Halfway up, he turned around. "Stavik!" he yelled.

The Pirate King grunted. "What?"

Fin swallowed, not sure if he was ready for this. But he had to ask. Even though he knew the answer.

"The Iron Tide…did it…did it really take the Khaznot Quay?"

Stavik squinted at him. The ugly red scar on his chin twitched. "Aye, lad. Every last drab and drillet."

CHAPTER 3
Things Obscured in the Mist

Marrill stood beside Fin at the stern of the ship, watching the golden water turn ruddy as the Stream narrowed into a black-water bog. A smell like leather and decay filled the air. Rafts of creeping moss bobbed by. Tendrils of it twitched unnaturally and waved toward them as they passed.

"I'm sorry," she said softly. She'd never seen his home on Gutterleak Way, never met the Parsnickles, his semiadopted family. But she remembered all too well the dream of her own mother. She remembered the feeling of fingers in her hair. The fear when her mother had first gotten sick. She knew how Fin must feel because the same feelings threatened to overwhelm her every time she thought about losing her mom.

A girl lingered beside them. Marrill knit her eyebrows in confusion, but the girl just pointed to Marrill's wrist. *Fig—Fade—Friend*, said a scrap of sail bound there. The handwriting was Marrill's. Above it was a sketch of the girl, also in Marrill's own hand.

"Maybe the Iron Tide isn't forever," the girl—*Fig, apparently*—said.

The rumor vines that twined around the ship's railing echoed her:

maybeirontideforevermaybeironforevermaybeforever

Fin's frown deepened. Marrill swallowed. Sitting here wasn't helping. "All the more reason for us to get moving and find out how to fix this," she declared, trying her best to sound confident. She pushed away from the railing, tugging Fin after her. "Come on," she said. "It's high time we find out exactly what the plan is."

"Remy!" she called, dragging Fin toward the ship's wheel. Mist leaked up from the bog around them. Something like a giant eyeball with bat wings flapped past. "Where are we going?"

Remy flipped her head, making her blond ponytail dance toward the main deck. "Ask him."

Just beneath them, for the first time since they'd left Meres, the door to Ardent's cabin lay open. Across from it, a gaunt figure stood at the forecastle, hands clasped behind his back as he studied the bog before them. White stars speckled the darkness of his robes.

"Look who's up," Fin said, laughing. It was a halfhearted laugh. But, Marrill thought, at least it was something.

Just looking at Serth gave her chills. This was the man who'd set the Gibbering Grove on fire, who'd brought about the destruction of the lost city of Monerva, who'd nearly killed them all *bunches* of times. Formerly the living host of the all-destroying Lost Sun of Dzannin; even more formerly the mad Meressian Oracle, driven insane by drinking pure Stream water and obsessed with bringing about the end of all things.

But he was better now, she told herself. And they needed him. He knew things no one else could know, had seen places no one else had seen. Plus, he'd been Ardent's best friend, back in the day. He understood better than anyone else the man who was now the Master of the Iron Ship, the bringer of the Iron Tide.

If they wanted to stop their former mentor, Serth was the only lead they had.

"Great," she whispered. "I'll, uh...I'll just go ask him

what the plan is, then." She paused a moment, just in case anyone else wanted to volunteer. No one did.

Marrill wiped sweaty palms against her shorts and walked down the stairs toward Serth. Her entire body hummed with the urge to flee; each step was a force of will. Several feet away from him she halted, keeping her distance. In the past, his robes had seared anything that touched them with frost. She could still practically feel it biting her skin from the time months ago when he'd held her hostage on the *Black Dragon*.

Serth turned slowly, deliberately, to face her. His presence felt like a sucking wind as his attention fell on her. His features were smooth, placid. His cheeks still bore the grooves from centuries of crying black tears, but his eyes were dry as they watched her.

"Hi" was all she managed to say.

"Hello," he replied.

Marrill swallowed. Somewhere out in the mist, something burbled. The bog air was moist and clutching against her skin. Nerves fluttered in her belly. "So..." she started.

"I have been communing with the Pirate Stream," Serth announced. His gaze pierced her straight through the middle.

"Oh," Marrill said. She looked down at her hands, not quite knowing what else to say.

"Or trying to, anyway," the tall wizard continued. "Ardent will no doubt have told you that a wizard's power comes from his relationship and rapport with magic." He let out a slow sigh. "The magic *hears* me as well as ever. But it is . . . a bit cross with me at the moment."

Marrill frowned. She didn't realize magic could *be* angry. "That sounds bad," she offered.

He raised an eyebrow at her. "Only if one is a wizard who relies on magic to perform various tasks."

"Right." Marrill fidgeted uncomfortably. "I was going to ask where we're going," she said at last.

Serth barely moved. "Ah."

For a long moment, neither spoke. Cool fingers of mist brushed through Marrill's hair, sending goose bumps down her arms. There was a frantic splashing somewhere off the port bow, then stillness.

She realized Serth was waiting for her to actually ask the question. If she weren't so intimidated by him, she would have rolled her eyes. Instead, she clasped her hands painfully in front of her. "So where are we—"

"Flight-of-Thorns Citadel," he said before she could finish. "It is the last home of the Meressian Order, founded long ago by the acolytes who attended me in my madness and first wrote down my Prophecy." He paused and then added dryly, "They were *supposed* to stop it from happening, but we all saw how well *that* turned out."

"Oh," Marrill said. She waited for him to say more.

He didn't.

She bit her lip. Serth wasn't big on volunteering information, apparently. "So," she said, "why are we going there?"

His face was impassive. "They still have my things."

And with that, he turned back to studying the bog.

Marrill's mouth gaped. She didn't know exactly how to respond. This wasn't at all how this conversation was supposed to be going. The last time he'd spoken, Serth had told them that to stop the Master, they would have to follow him back in time, to the birth of the Stream. He'd said he would guide them. And now they were just going to some random citadel to pick up his old junk?

"Hold on," she said. She chose her words carefully. Talking to Serth was like walking on the edge of a knife: slow, painful, and always just one slip away from disaster. "You're supposed to…I mean, is this really…I mean, we're supposed to be stopping the Iron Tide."

Serth did not turn around. "I am aware of the situation."

Sudden anger welled up in Marrill. It blasted away her sadness and overwhelmed her fear. "Then do something!" she snapped.

The wizard stayed still for so long that she wasn't even sure he'd heard her.

A scraggly skeleton of a tree brushed past, its branches dragging lightly across the *Kraken*'s deck. The tips of them had fingernails. They scratched weakly at the dullwood, trying but failing to find purchase. Pirats scrabbled down from the rigging to cautiously lift them away.

A terrible thought occurred to her. "You don't know how to stop the Iron Tide, do you?" Marrill finally whispered.

The wizard said nothing.

Her stomach sank. This was all useless. Everything was useless. Serth was useless. Maybe she should just have the ship take her home to Arizona so she could spend time with her mom and dad before the Iron Tide swept across her world, destroying it along with everything else. She turned slowly to walk away.

"I do, actually," Serth said behind her.

She paused halfway across the deck and looked back. The wizard was facing her once more. Only now his fingers were tented together before him. He raised an eyebrow at her, inviting her to listen.

A spark of hope lit in her chest, but she didn't dare acknowledge it, for fear of it guttering and going out. "You do?"

Without warning, Fin jumped down the stairs to land beside her. "Oh, for love and salamanders, just tell us already!" he cried.

"Seriously," said a girl—*Fig*, according to the sail-scrap drawing on Marrill's wrist. "Enough with the drama. Just tell us what the plan is."

A hint of a smile played across Serth's lips, then dropped and died away. "The Iron Tide and the Master are one and the same. Stop the Master, and you stop the Tide. Simple."

"Well, that clears that up," Fin said, with a roll of his eyes.

Marrill cleared her throat, hoping to cover up his sarcasm. "And the way to stop the Master is..."

"In his effort to save Annalessa, Ardent has encased

himself in impenetrable metal and imbued himself with incredible power," Serth declared. The tips of his fingers drummed together as he spoke. "But he is still human. The answer is relatively straightforward. To stop him, we only need one thing: a weapon sharp enough to cut through the metal armor and reach the man underneath."

Marrill frowned. The plan was way more straight-forward than she'd been expecting. She was used to convo-luted, multiple-step tasks.

Fin had apparently been thinking the same thing. "That's it? To stop the Iron Tide we just need to find a sword sharp enough to cut the uncuttable?"

"It's a knife, actually," Serth said. "The Evershear. I used it years ago to sever a scale from the side of the Slithering Moun-tain." His lips curled. "The Scale to the Map to Everywhere."

Marrill's eyes widened. She'd always wondered where he'd found that. Then she smacked her forehead as realization dawned. If Serth had used the Evershear to get the Scale, that meant it was tied to the Meressian Prophecy. And if it was part of the Prophecy…

"The Meressian Order has the knife," she said out loud. "*That's* why we're going to Flight-of-Thorns Citadel."

The young deckhand standing next to her—*Fig, Fig, Fig*, Marrill reminded herself—frowned in confusion. "I'm not sure I follow."

"The Meressians were obsessed with Serth's prophecy," Fin explained quickly. "They spent centuries collecting anything and everything that was mentioned anywhere in it—and it's a *long* prophecy. If this knife thing still exists, they'd definitely be the ones to have it."

For the first time, the pale wizard's smile seemed genuine. "Just so. In part anyway. There are other things we will need there as well, but I wouldn't let that concern you."

The spark of hope began to burn more brightly in Marrill's chest. But it was short-lived. "Of course then we'll have to *use* the Evershear," Serth continued. "Which, admittedly, makes things a bit more complicated."

Marrill had thought it sounded too easy. "Complicated how?" she asked, pretty sure she didn't want to know the answer.

Serth began to pace. "The wish orb that Ardent used to become the Master contained the power of the Lost Sun of Dzannin, merged with the pure waters of the Pirate Stream. The magic of the Stream water is what held the Lost Sun in check. But that would never have lasted. The Lost Sun was too powerful; the orb couldn't hold it for long."

He pressed his fingertips together under his chin. "When Ardent made his wish, he brought both forces—Sun and Stream—into himself. In a sense, *he* became the glue that holds them together. The being we know as the Master of the Iron Ship is a combination of all three: Ardent's passion and intelligence, the power of the Lost Sun and its drive for destruction, and the magic and malleability of the Pirate Stream."

A girl beside Marrill shook her head skeptically. "Sounds like he just made himself super powerful."

Serth stopped, wheeled on them. "In a way," he said. "But in another way, as the glue binding it to the Pirate Stream, the Master is holding *back* the power of the Lost Sun. And if we take him out of that equation..."

"Then there's nothing to hold back the Lost Sun," Marrill gasped.

Serth nodded slowly. "Indeed. Once we strike the man beneath the metal, the Lost Sun will be free once more."

"And we're right back to it burning a great big hole in the world," Fin finished.

Serth snorted. "We would be fortunate if it left us something to burn a hole *in*."

"Great." Fin sagged against the railing. "Because we all know how easy stopping the Lost Sun will be," he grumbled. "That worked out *sooooo* well the last time."

"Last time you failed to lock the Lost Sun in its proper prison," Serth said pointedly. "Only the Pirate Stream itself can contain the Star of Destruction."

"We tried that already," Fin protested. "At Meres. But the only way to trap it in the Stream is through the Map to Everywhere, and that's broken, remember? Even Ardent couldn't fix it."

Serth waved a hand dismissively. "The Map isn't the only way into the heart of the Pirate Stream."

He said it so matter-of-factly that Marrill's brain ground to a halt.

Fin stared at him, mouth agape. "Then why did you spend all that effort trying to find the pieces to put it together?" His voice grew more heated. "The Key to open the Gate, remember?! If there was another way to unleash the Lost Sun, why didn't you use that instead?"

Serth smiled. "Because assembling the Map was the easy way."

Fin let out a moan of frustration. Marrill understood how he felt, but they had to focus. "So, if there's another way into the heart of the Stream, where do we find it? And how do we trap the Lost Sun there?"

"To answer your second question first," Serth said, "the Master is already inside the Stream. We just have to get in there *with* him."

Fin cracked his knuckles. "Well, that should make things easier. If we defeat the Master inside the Stream, the Lost Sun will already be trapped!"

But Marrill had a sinking feeling. Nothing was ever that easy on the Pirate Stream. "Okay, then, how do we get in there to reach him?"

The corner of Serth's mouth turned up imperceptibly. "We do what he did: travel back in time and enter the Pirate Stream at the dawn of its creation," he said simply.

Fin barked out a laugh. "Oh, *that* old trick. Travel back in time."

"Exactly." Serth seemed pleased Fin was keeping up. "A touch more complicated, certainly. You can see why I felt that using the Map to open the Gate seemed a simpler solution."

Marrill threw up her hands. "So when you said we only need one thing to stop the Iron Tide, what you really meant is that we have to crash the Meressian Citadel so we can grab the Evershear, travel back in time so we can enter the Pirate Stream, and *then* find the Master so we can stop the Iron Tide and trap the Lost Sun once again?"

Serth nodded. "I did say it was *relatively* straight-forward."

Marrill didn't know whether to laugh or cry. Whether to let the ember of hope inside her bloom or to stomp it out for good. She closed her eyes, struggling against a tide of over-whelming fear. "It sounds impossible."

Fin leaned against her, his arm warm against hers. He took her hand and squeezed it. "This is the Pirate Stream, Marrill. Nothing is impossible."

He smiled, and she felt something inside her begin to brighten. Another little spark of hope igniting in the ashes. Fin was right. They'd faced tough odds and impossible tasks before and succeeded. More or less.

At least they had a plan. No matter how crazy it seemed, it was a start.

They would find the Evershear, follow the Master— apparently back in time—confront him in the heart of the Pirate Stream, and . . .

Then what?

She looked out across the bog.

The dark current flowed, slow and gentle; the rafts of moss still tangled with each other, stalks shaking hands lazily as they passed. But somewhere in the distance, beyond the screeching of tongueless birds, a dull roar was rising. A roar that could have been the wind. Or a waterfall.

And then what? Her brain asked again.

The thought echoed in her head, like the looping calls of the birds. Like the growing roar in the distance. Because somewhere beneath all that iron, there was still *Ardent*. Regardless of what he'd done, somewhere in there was the goofy old man she loved like a grandfather. If everything went exactly as Serth said, what would happen to him?

Would the Evershear kill him?

Marrill closed her eyes, her heart squeezing tight. She wasn't sure she wanted to know the answer. They didn't have a choice about stopping the Iron Tide—they had to in order to save the Stream.

Even if that meant losing Ardent in the process.

And hadn't they already lost him when he'd chosen to become the Master? She still didn't understand how he could have done that. Abandoned them and let loose the Iron Tide. A familiar sense of betrayal began to clutch at Marrill's chest, burning its way up her throat.

She shook her head, forcing thoughts of Ardent from her mind.

"I thought we said no more dramatic pauses?" volunteered a deckhand. (*Fig*, Marrill reminded herself. *FigFigFig...*)

"An excellent point," Serth said. He slipped around them almost effortlessly, headed toward Ardent's—*his*—cabin. "Captain!" he called up to the quarterdeck. "Prepare for some tight rapids. The Flight-of-Thorns Citadel is heavily guarded, so we'll be sneaking in. The way is a bit treacherous."

"Yeah, sure," Remy called back. "Rapids, rough, got it. Done it before, no problem."

Marrill looked ahead, squinting through the fog. The roar was getting louder. The air smelled of damp wood and regret. Whatever was coming, it was going to be big.

"Get some rest," the wizard told them. "By tomorrow morning, we will be nearing the Citadel, and I'll need you all to be ready. The Meressians are unlikely to be welcoming. And once we are done with them, things will really start to get tough." With that, he ducked into the cabin and closed the door.

"He's charming," the girl beside her offered.

Fin shrugged. "At least he's knows what we need to do to stop Ardent. Right, Marrill?"

Marrill didn't answer. Instead, she looked out into the mist, listening to the rush of the water picking up speed. Terrified of where this current might be taking them.

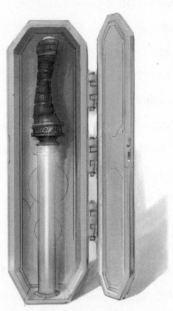

CHAPTER 4
Flight-of-Thorns

Fin held tight to the railing, even as Ropebone wrapped a line around his waist, holding him tighter still. Serth hadn't been kidding about the rapids. The *Kraken* surfed on a drizzle of water that ran down the outside of a stalactite hanging from the roof of a massive cavern. Remy pulled them into a spiraling path, looping around the stalactite fast enough to defy gravity—at least until they reached the big drop at the bottom.

Below them, Flight-of-Thorns Citadel hung like a great

barbed bat from the ceiling of the enormous cavern. Bridges of narrow steel fanned out from it into the distant darkness. Even from up here, Fin could see that each one was secured by rows of gates, stockades, and checkpoints. He had a strong feeling there were no guardrails. Crossing through the barriers would be nearly impossible if you weren't wanted.

Close to the Citadel, the bridges came together in a huge ring, itself joined to the main fortress by even narrower, more dangerous-looking bridges. Below *them* hung yet another ring, this one cupped and filled with Stream water. It was a hanging moat, Fin realized, that ensured anyone falling from the outer bridges wouldn't be climbing back up ever again.

"The water running down this stalactite falls into the heart of the Citadel itself," Serth shouted over the shrieking wind. "It's how they get their drinking water. It is also, incidentally, the only unguarded way in."

As they skidded closer, Fin caught sight of movement along the far bridges. He squinted, trying to get a better look, just as a belch of fire enveloped one of the guard posts. The bridge was alive with fighting and flame. The Citadel was under attack!

"What's going on down there?" he shouted over the whoosh of the wind.

Serth looked back at him immediately. There was no confusion in his eyes—no moment of hesitation while he struggled to place Fin in his memory. Serth simply remembered him, just as he always had. As terrifying as the wizard was and as much as Fin missed Ardent, he had to admit that it was nice not being forgotten.

"I'm . . . not sure," Serth admitted. The stony look on the wizard's face faltered for just a moment. "I'm not used to being unsure."

Fin felt a tug of sympathy as he gripped the rope tighter. It must have been difficult for Serth. Not long ago, he'd known the future, everything that would happen crammed into his head by the Stream water he drank. Now, all that was gone. He was back to normal. If that term had ever really applied to the wizard.

Then again, this *was* the same Serth who'd set free the Lost Sun of Dzannin. The same Serth who'd used the Wish Machine of Monerva to create the wish orb that transformed Ardent into the Master of the Iron Ship. In a sense, literally *everything* that had happened was his fault—up to and including the Iron Tide taking the Parsnickles. Fin could only feel *so* bad for him.

"Nearly at the bottom!" Remy shouted, breaking him out of the thought. "Get ready!"

Fin held on tight. The tip of the stalactite was just below them. And below it, nothing but empty space between them and the hanging Citadel. He looked to Marrill, who nodded, then back to Fig, who gave him a thumbs-up. Cold wind whipped at his hair. His struggled not to get dizzy as the ship's spirals tightened.

"Ready," he confirmed.

"Cut the mizzen sail free, now!" Remy yelled. Above, brave pirats, tied to their masts with twine, reached out and snipped the bindings holding one of the aft sails in place.

Immediately, the wind grabbed it, whipping it up into a balloon shape. Each corner was still tied to a rope, however, and Fin's eyes traced one of them down to where it looped around his waist. The slack in it began to disappear, getting ready to snap taut as the balloon-sail billowed up and off of the ship.

"Here we goOOOOOOOOO!!!!" he yelled. The rope yanked him into the air. Marrill and Fig lifted up with him, Serth on the far corner. The four of them dangled from the makeshift parachute, drifting away from the *Kraken* as the wizard muttered and waved his hands. Fortunately, unlike Ardent, Serth and the wind seemed to be on good terms.

"Mainsail, now!" Remy shrieked behind them. Sails flared as the *Kraken* hit the end of the stalactite, popping off at just the right angle to send the ship flying. Several seconds later, the *Kraken* splashed safely down into the dangling moat below.

Cold cavern breezes sent shivers up Fin's arms as the makeshift parachute winged them downward toward the hanging Citadel.

It was like dropping into the bloom of a thistle—if that thistle were under attack. Shouts from the battle drifted toward them, but so far it seemed as if the invading army was confined to the outer bridges.

Fin was too far away to see much more than swarms of

soldiers crashing against each other and bodies plummeting from the narrow bridges toward the Stream-water moat below. He couldn't exactly tell which side was winning, but the front of the invading army seemed to be shifting closer and closer to the Citadel.

From the look of things, it wouldn't be long before they overtook the hanging fortress itself.

Fin swallowed uneasily. He hoped Serth was a quick packer; they wouldn't have much time to gather his things once they landed.

Beneath them, Flight-of-Thorns grew larger and larger. Its hard stone surface stretched before them, stuttered with sharp edges, unbroken but for a single square of light—the entrance they were aiming for. A steady drizzle of water streamed into it from the stalactite above.

Fin eyed it dubiously. The entrance was small—smaller than Fin had figured. Just barely large enough for one person to fit through. Maybe. He didn't see any way all four of them could parachute into it.

"Prepare yourselves," Serth warned them.

"Prepare ourselves for what?" Marrill yelled.

Before Fin could even yelp, Serth flicked his hand. A massive gust of wind blew up beneath one side of the sail-parachute, sending it off kilter. All at once, it collapsed, sending all four of them plummeting.

The little opening passed in a blur and a scream. Fin tumbled, tangling in the parachute. He saw light,

the white of the sail,

a brief flash of unhappy faces.

And then

S P L A S H!

He was soaked, surrounded by water, wrapped in sail, tangled in ropes, fighting, pummeling, struggling to get free. Hands grabbed at him. His feet struck bottom. The rope from his waist came free. The sail slid away.

His head broke the surface, and he hauled in a mighty gasp.

"Fin!" Fig's voice sounded in his ear. She tugged at his arm. "Come on, fast."

Fin blinked. They floated in a mat of white sail, bobbing in a pool in the middle of a huge chamber. Columns were everywhere. Overhead, a massive marble statue of Serth loomed over them. The whole place was horribly familiar.

Behind him, someone cleared their throat. Fin twisted, finding a crowd of *very* unhappy-looking people, all dressed in the distinctive purple robes of the Meressian Order, standing around the edge of the pool. One of them, a big ox of a man, snorted and shook his head in disgust.

"Hey, Bull Face!" Fin cried, recognizing the big brute who'd chased him through the Meressian ship back at the Khaznot Quay so long ago.

"Shhh!" Fig hissed, pulling him into the shadow of the

statue dominating the far side of the chamber. She slipped up and over the rim of the pool, keeping herself flat. "They're distracted," she whispered. "Come on. Let's hurry up and find that magical knife so we can get out of here."

Fin swallowed a laugh. As forgettable as he was—and Fig, too—he had a hard time believing the Meressians wouldn't notice *that* entry. Then again, he realized, they were mostly looking up past the statue. And he quickly saw why. Serth, dark robe waving around him, floated down like a leaf on the breeze, landing gently on the opposite side of the pool. He folded his hands together calmly, as though a falling sail full of children hadn't just plummeted into the room ahead of him.

A tall, thorn-skinned Meressian stepped forward from the crowd. Fin recognized him, too, from the ship in the Khaznot Quay. He'd only briefly laid eyes on the spiny Meressian then, but here there was no doubt he was the leader.

"The Oracle," said a voice like crushed glass. His barbed skin flexed dangerously. "And I was just saying things couldn't get worse."

"Okay, maybe they *are* distracted," Fin whispered. "And it looks like they may be a while." He didn't want to stick around any longer than they had to, but first he had to check on Marrill.

He found her clinging to the rim of the pool just behind Serth. She caught his eye and smiled. He pressed his fingers to his lips and then fluttered them in front of him, their secret sign language for him sneaking away while everyone forgot about him. Or, as Marrill called it, "going all Fin on them." She nodded, giving him a subtle thumbs-up.

"Hello, Hedgecaw," Serth said, sounding imperious, his chin lifted high. "So good to see you again. How long has it been?"

It was the perfect cue to get moving. Fig took the lead, sneaking around one of the folds of the big stone robe. Fin slipped out of the pool and followed, throwing a cautious glance over his shoulder. There must have been fifty Meressians filling the chamber. Beyond them, the great doors to the cavern outside were propped open, with more Meressians standing guard. Each was armed to the teeth, all beetle-shell armor, long trip-glaives, and a string of shriek-slingers ready to go.

From the other direction, a steady stream of Meressians flooded in through hallways, racing out from the depths of the Citadel to join the battle. But as they reached the great statue, they ground to a halt. Suddenly, the assault on their fortress was forgotten. Instead, they, like everyone else in the chamber, seemed completely fixated on Serth. Which made it a perfect distraction for two Fade kids.

Fin grabbed Fig by the hand and made a quick dash into the crowd. A Meressian frowned down as they pushed by her, but Fin immediately whirled around, craning his neck like he, too, was gawking at Serth. Fig did the same, letting out only a quick giggle. Together, they slowly walked backward, casually making their way through the maze of bodies, before darting into the nearest hallway.

They soon found themselves in a much smaller side chamber that was blessedly empty but for a purple banner strung along the far wall. The Meressian motto was emblazoned across it: GUARD AGAINST IT AND PREVENT IT.

Good work with that, Fin thought to himself. Despite the Meressians' efforts, every bit of the Prophecy had come to pass.

He popped his head into the corridor, hoping to spot a break in the traffic. But the flow of Meressian soldiers seemed pretty constant. "Looks like we'll have to keep sneaking our way through the rest of this place."

Fig gave him a wink. "Maybe not." She checked both ways, then reached up and yanked the banner from the wall. With a swift move, she tore it down the middle and draped half around her neck.

"Ta-da!" she announced. "Instant Meressian!"

Fin laughed, wrapping himself in the other half. It wasn't the best disguise—for most spies, running around with a torn flag on your shoulders was probably *worse* than nothing. But for forgettable kids in a fortress under full alert? It was perfect.

"Spiff!" Fin said. "That's one problem solved." He looked around, thinking on the next big problem—how to find the Evershear. It wasn't like there were signs reading THIS WAY TO KNIFE THAT CAN CUT ANYTHING.

Of course, it occurred to him that a knife that can cut anything would be pretty useful if your fortress was currently under attack. It might be exactly the type of thing you'd want to have on hand.

He waited until a Meressian passed by who fit just the right profile—youngish, with the look of authority, but an uncertainty that said he was new in the ranks. Then Fin struck.

"Did you bring it?" he demanded, jumping in front of the Meressian. The boy, barely out of his teens, went wide eyed, like a scared beaver. "The Evershear." Fin held out a hand. "You brought it, didn't you?"

"I—uh, I, wha—" the boy stammered.

Fin let out an exaggerated, exhausted sigh. "You've *got* to be kidding. Hedgecaw needs the Evershear *now*! The Oracle is here. He trusted you to get it!"

The kid looked both ways, seeking help or reassurance, but finding neither. "I, I don't..."

Fin rolled his eyes in the most exasperated fashion he could imagine. "Fine, *I'll* do it. Just tell me where you left it. I'll even tell him you sent me because I like you, you know? You're not mean like the other—" He paused, making a guess at what Meressians might use for ranks. "Seekers?"

"Oh, th-thank you," the boy gushed. "But, I didn't have the Evershear. It's still in the outer galleries, far as I know."

"Right," Fin said. "The outer galleries, which are thaaaaat waaaay?" He slowly trailed one finger across every possible direction.

The boy nodded as he reached the right one. "Yes, yes. Fourteenth row up, looking out over the archway bridge." He stiffened, falling into the role of commander giving an order. "Be quick now!"

Fin gave what he hoped looked like a military salute, then quickly ducked away. Fig slipped out after him, and together they darted deeper into the Citadel.

Flight-of-Thorns was a maze of interconnected cells; there was no way they could have navigated it on their own. Fortunately, the same trick seemed to work without fail on other Meressians; seven interviews, sixteen flights of stairs, and a long looping hallway covered in displays later, and Fin found himself in a empty room, a single glass display case between him and a rose-stained window. He approached the case carefully. Inside, an ornate bone handle perched gingerly between two pediments. Beneath it rested a glass cylinder.

Outside, the shouting and sounds of battle had reached a crescendo. The invading force must be getting close. Whatever was going on, Fin was pretty sure he and Fig didn't want to get caught in the middle of a siege. They needed to grab the Evershear and get out, fast.

"Security's slack," Fig said, examining the case for a moment before popping it open from behind.

Fin laughed, remembering the traps the Meressians had used in their Temple Ship. "Sneeze Breeze again?"

"Nope." Fig held up a little pink crystal. It shifted oddly in the light, forcing Fin to squint. Without thinking, he took a step toward it. Fig clapped her hand shut around it, breaking him out of the trance.

"Eyecatcher," he groaned to himself. A little bit closer and he would have been in the market for a patch. He breathed a sigh of relief and studied the now-open case. The bone within certainly *looked* like the hilt of a knife, and the glass cylinder beneath looked like a sheath. But where was the blade?

Fin held out his hands, shaking his arms to limber them. If this really was the Evershear, he kind of doubted a single eyecatcher was the only guard on it. "Keep watch," he told Fig. "I'll perform the extraction."

While she checked the doorway, Fin gingerly reached into the case. Carefully, he lifted the bone handle a few centimeters and paused, every nerve humming, prepared for a trap. But nothing happened.

"Huh," he said. He stared at it, waiting for some sort of alarm, while Fig paced back across the room to the window. Still there was nothing. "Well, that was uneventful," he said, turning the handle sideways as he withdrew it.

There was a sharp *schnik*, and the display case fell clean apart, right along the path where his hand had moved.

Fin stared down at the bone hilt. A thin sliver of silver stuck out from it now, an edge so sharp that it seemed to cut the very air itself, causing a slight haze whenever he moved it. He turned it to one side, and the blade practically vanished.

Fin let out a deep breath. "We'll have to be careful with this," he murmured. He tossed the bisected display case until he found the glass cylinder that had been resting beneath the knife. Sure enough, it was designed to attach to the handle and flare out, so the blade would never touch it. It took Fin a fair amount of concentration to slip the blade inside. One twitch the wrong way and the Evershear would cut right through the glass scabbard.

When he had the blade sheathed, he spun toward Fig to show off the new toy. "Hey, check it out!"

But Fig didn't move. She stood frozen, her shadow dark against the red stained glass.

"Fig?" Fin asked. Outside, shouts and clangs of battle raged onward, growing closer by the minute. The invaders, Fin realized, must have almost breached the Citadel.

"It's them," Fig whispered. Slowly, she looked at him. Her dark hair fell across her face, but it only half masked the terror in her eyes. She pointed out the window.

"Fin," she said. "It's the Rise."

CHAPTER 5
War and Peace (but Mostly War)

Marrill coughed, sputtering water out as she struggled to get her bearings. She was floating in a fountain in the middle of a huge chamber. Angry purple-clad soldiers surrounded the pool. Serth drifted down from the air in front of her, his feet coming to rest on dry stone.

"The Oracle," said a voice like rusting metal. "And I was just saying things couldn't get worse."

Marrill kicked to the edge of the pool, her feet finding the bottom at last. She looked around. On the far side of the chamber, under the shadow of a huge statue, she caught sight of Fin. He winked and gave her the sign that said he was about to go all Fin on them. She smiled, subtly giving him a thumbs-up.

"Hello, Hedgecaw," Serth said, regaining her attention. "So good to see you again. How long has it been?"

The man Serth addressed—if he could be called that—had green-tinged skin and light purple eyes. More notably, he was covered in sharp thorns from his throat to the tip of his bald pate. More thorns pushed through the back of his velvet gloves, which flexed with the crack of his knuckles.

He looked like the definition of unhappy.

"A hundred and thirteen years," he snarled. His eyes fell on Marrill. She swiped the waterlogged hair off her forehead and did her best to smile. He did not smile back. "I see you've brought a friend. Branched out to kidnapping children?" He shook his head sadly. "Funny, I don't recall that being part of the Prophecy."

Serth quirked an eyebrow. "Don't know why. I did it in four separate verses," he muttered. "But this isn't one of them." His back straightened. "The Prophecy has ended, and I'm here to gather my things you've so assiduously collected. Hand them over, and we'll be on our way."

The Meressians glared at one another warily. Their hands lingered by strange weapons. There was a deadly look in their eyes.

Marrill shivered, and not just from the cold water

trailing down the nape of her neck. Somewhere beyond the crowd, she could hear the clang of metal on metal, the yelps of fighting. An increasing stream of armed soldiers poured through the chamber. Some stopped and joined the crowd around them; others pushed through to join the battle outside. The guards at the door yelled regularly, and more Meressians reluctantly peeled away to join the fight.

Marrill sensed the Meressians had been on edge *before* their sworn enemy had dropped in through the sunroof. At any minute they could decide that Marrill and Serth—or as they called him, the Oracle—were too much trouble and attack. Someone had to do something to break the tension. She took a deep breath, thinking about what her mother would do.

Just dive in with both feet, her mother's voice sounded in her head.

Before wizard and walking rosebush could continue their verbal sparring, Marrill sloshed forward and hauled herself out of the pool. "What my friend *means* to say is, good news, everyone! The Prophecy has ended and we won! Go, Meressians!" She paused, fist pumped in the air, a huge smile glued on her face. "And also we kind of need your help?"

Hedgecaw snorted. He didn't make a move. But he didn't make a *hostile* move, either, so that was good. "Go on," he said.

As quickly as she could, Marrill explained the situation. She made little *whoosh* sounds as she described how they'd beaten the Lost Sun and captured its essence in the wish orb. Her voice caught as she described how Ardent, their former friend and crewmate, had used that same polluted orb to become the Master of the Iron Ship, their mortal enemy. She posed as a statue to illustrate the destructive power of the Iron Tide, and clapped her hands together pleadingly as she explained—as best she could—that they needed the Evershear, among other things, to stop all this and save the Pirate Stream.

At first, the Meressians appeared skeptical. But as Marrill talked, she could see them leaning in to listen, could feel them warming to her. Only Hedgecaw remained unmoved. It seemed like every word she said to him was a pebble flung at a solid brick wall. But as she neared the end of her speech, even *he* finally nodded.

"Very well," he said at last. He glared at Serth out of one narrow eye.

"So you believe us?" Marrill asked hopefully.

"Of course," Hedgecaw said. His voice was an iron file dragged across rough stone. "Word travels fast these days. If we didn't already know of the Lost Sun's passing, I'd have cut you down the moment you dropped through the roof."

Marrill let out a nervous laugh. But Hedgecaw held up one purple-gloved finger. "I believe *you*," he clarified. "But can we really trust *him*?" He swung his spine-studded finger toward Serth.

Marrill took a deep breath. This she understood. Serth had done a whole lot of terrible things. Almost *all* the terrible things, actually. And it didn't help that he looked exactly like the villain in a cartoon story. Cloaked all in black, straight-backed and unperturbed, black-tear trails etched into high, arrogant cheeks—it was hard to see him as anything other than awful.

But then, the *evil* Serth had been nothing like this. He'd been stooped, constantly sobbing, endlessly reciting scenes of a future that had been shoved fully formed into his head. *Evil* Serth had never done anything to try and *stop* the destruction of the Stream. She wasn't sure she liked the new Serth a whole lot better, but one thing was clear: He'd changed.

And there was one other thing. She looked the thorny Meressian dead in the eye. "He saved our lives," she said. "We can trust him." *At least for now*, she reminded herself.

Hedgecaw seemed to ponder this, but only for a moment. Another round of shouts broke out from the main entrance. Marrill strained to see what was happening outside.

"Master Hedgecaw, they're nearly on us!" cried a panicked guard, racing through the crowd to the thorny leader. "We have to shut the main gates!"

"They just keep coming," Hedgecaw muttered. "I've never seen anything like it." He wheeled immediately, whipping his hand through the air. "BRING IN OUR FORCES!" he shouted at the top of his lungs. "SEAL THE DOORS AND PREPARE FOR SIEGE!"

The other Meressians jumped to action, racing to the big gates, securing arms and armor. Hedgecaw barked more orders to various guards and couriers, sending them scrambling to one task or another.

Marrill bit her lip as she watched the massive doors swing closed, effectively trapping them inside. She hoped Fin had already gotten ahold of the Evershear because it sure didn't look like they had a lot of time.

"Don't worry," Hedgecaw told her. "Flight-of-Thorns Citadel has never fallen." He placed a hand on her shoulder reassuringly. Even through her shirt and his gloves, Marrill could feel the muted points of briars on the palms of his hands.

"Who are they?" Marrill asked.

Hedgecaw gritted his teeth and shook his head. "Not really sure. They just showed up and started marching on us. Only thing we know is they call themselves the Rise."

Marrill's heart seized with dread. She stumbled back a step, feeling the blood drain from her face. No wonder the Meressians kept falling back. The Rise were invincible. Unbeatable. At birth, their weakness was cut away from them and used to create their Fade twins. So long as their Fade still lived, a Rise soldier was *literally* unstoppable.

It was only a matter of time before the Citadel fell. With them inside it.

Serth sliced a hand sharply through the air, cutting away any distractions. "There is a candle with no wick, made from wax that smells like whispered secrets. A string of red, heart-shaped pearls that are sweet to taste and feel like you ought to remember where they came from. A blade that can cut through anything—I imagine that will stand out. And an ornate mirror that reflects everyone who looks in it as a fox." His words were quick, insistent. "We will need all these, and we will need them *now*."

Hedgecaw's lip curled, ever so slightly. "The candle and pearls are in the spiral galleries, below. I'll have them fetched for you." He flicked his hand at a big, bull-faced Meressian beside him, who nodded to two others. All three walked over to the edge of the fountain and knelt, two of them working to draw out the still floating sail.

"'Scuse me," Bull Face grunted, ducking down beside Marrill. He made a sign with his hands that she couldn't quite follow, then touched the fountain with a thin metal rod. To Marrill's shock, the water drained away, revealing a spiral staircase. Bull Face skipped down the steps, quickly disappearing.

"The Evershear is in the galleries above," Hedgecaw rasped. "You'll have to get it yourselves. And the Vulpine Mirror, I'm afraid, sank with our Temple Ship at the Khaznot Quay...thanks to you, I believe." His tongue flicked across the ends of chiseled teeth. Even *it* was barbed with thorns.

Serth sighed. "We'll make do without it, then. Frankly, I only wanted it because I like the way I look with fur." He glanced down at Marrill with one eyebrow arched wryly.

Marrill gaped at him. *Did Serth just make a joke?*

She shook her head, focusing. "No worries about the Evershear, either—we've got it taken care of."

She'd barely finished speaking when another guard raced over to them, saluting Hedgecaw. "Our gates are closed and sealed, Master Hedgecaw. But the enemy just keeps on coming. They'll breach soon."

"What?" Hedgecaw spat. "Already? How is that possible?"

The guard gulped. "They just...they just don't *stop*, Master. They brush aside our blows like we're tickling them. At this rate, I fear they'll be battering our doors down any—"

Ka-THOOM!

The whole chamber shook. The whole Citadel even. Suddenly, the clamor of the Meressian army went silent.

Marrill gulped. The Rise were upon them.

It'll be okay, she told herself.

Ka-THOOOOOOM!

Hedgecaw scraped a barbed thumb over the tip of his thorned chin. "No one has ever breached Flight-of-Thorns," he said. "Ever. That's why we brought the last of the Prophetic relics here."

Armed guards fell into place.

Every breath held, waiting.

We'll just explain to them we're here to stop the Iron Tide, Marrill reasoned.

Ka-THOOOOOOOOOOOOOOOM!

Hedgecaw looked to Serth. "If you truly have changed, wizard, we could use your help about now."

But Serth merely shook his head. "I fear I don't have much to offer against the enemy you face."

Marrill squeezed her hands together, willing the doors to hold just a moment longer.

Even the Rise have to be in favor of stopping the Iron Tide. Right?

Ka-RAAAAAAAAAAAAAAAAAAAAAAAAAAAAAAAASH!

The great doors at the end of the hall smashed and splintered. Marrill covered her face, half expecting to be hit by flying shrapnel. Fortunately, there was nothing. Nothing but shouts and the stamping of feet as the Rise rushed in, quickly filling the already crowded chamber.

"Hold!" shouted a familiar voice. Too familiar. It was Fin's. Only harder, colder—sharpened.

Carefully, she peeked between her fingers. A contingent of Rise stood stock-still, like terra-cotta soldiers, arrayed in a neat military column. On either side, they held banners bearing the sigil of their leader: the living, all-consuming fire that was the Salt Sand King. The Meressians held in a circle around them, weapons leveled. Fear and uncertainty flashed in their eyes.

A figure swept down the pathway created by the rigid

figures of the invading army. It was Vell, Fin's Rise. He was Fin's mirror image, if Fin had been shipped off to a military school at birth and then raised to have no feelings. Vell was cruel where Fin was kind, arrogant where Fin was self-conscious.

And he was the Crest of the Rise—the leader of this unstoppable army.

"They're here," declared a dark-haired Rise girl next to Vell. Marrill didn't recognize her. But something about her made her look down at the scrap of sail still tied to her wrist.

There, smeared and waterlogged, was a sketch of the girl. *Fig—Fade—Friend*, read Marrill's own handwriting beneath it. She looked back up. The features were the same, without doubt. Crueler, harsher, perhaps, but still the same. With one major difference: This girl was definitely *not* a friend.

"Which means our Fades won't be far," the girl said. Something was wrong with her, Marrill realized. Half her face was duller than the other, mottled with the gray of tarnished silver.

"Indeed," Vell agreed. "Go and fetch them."

Marrill mustered her courage. As awful as the Rise were, she reminded herself, they would understand the danger of the Iron Tide. Who knew, they might even help!

She stepped forward. "Listen," she started.

Vell turned to look at her full on. But just like the girl, something was wrong with him. One of his eyes was dull, lifeless. Silver streaked down the side of his face.

The word caught in her throat. Not silver, she realized. *Iron.*

CHAPTER 6
An Exit

Fin tucked the sheathed Evershear through his belt next to his thief's bag, then took off. Fig charged ahead of him as they tore down the corridors. The whole Citadel rocked under the force of the Rise. They had to get back to Marrill and get out before it was too late.

"It's too late," Fig gulped, skidding to a halt just inside the main chamber.

Fin stopped beside her. Beyond the big statue of Serth

the Oracle, the massive doors hung open. The Rise filled the room. Vell stood at their head.

The situation looked bad. But they couldn't just turn and run—Marrill was still there somewhere. He clenched his hands into fists. He refused to let the Rise take his best friend prisoner.

"Okay," he told Fig under his breath. "We've faced Vell before—we can do it again." He counted the rows of Rise soldiers. Five, ten, fifteen. Twenty soldiers per row. That added up to... a *lot*. He mentally recalculated.

Beside him, Fig cleared her throat.

He knew what she was going to say, and she had a point. "I know: Last time we had a whole army of Fade helping us, and this time it's just you and me. But I think we can still make it work, if we... hmmm..." He paused, contemplating the exact amount of force it would take to push the big stone Serth off balance, and exactly where it might fall.

"Fin!" Fig hissed. He looked over at her. And then at the hand on her shoulder. And at the arm attached to that hand. And the body behind that arm.

The girl was identical to Fig in every way. Every way except for the cold eyes, the humorless smile, and the lifeless metal streaked across one cheek.

"Hello, Brother Fade," the girl said.

"Karu, this is Fin," Fig said through clenched teeth.

"Fin, this is Karu, my Rise. She is…apparently going to take us prisoner now."

Fin waved weakly. In the back of his head, his plans smashed to pieces, right alongside his hope. He shifted the Evershear on his hip, tucking the handle of it under the hem of his shirt so no one could see it.

Four seconds later, Karu marched them to the front of the Rise group.

Vell looked Fin over. "Brother Fade." He spoke the words the way someone might spit out a sip of sour milk.

Fin frowned, but not at his Rise's attitude. Dull metal marred his face and when he raised a hand, steel glinted beneath the cuff of his glove. "Shanks, what happened to you?" Fin asked.

"It's all of them," Marrill said behind him. "They're all part metal now."

Fin's eyes flicked over the Rise troops. Sure enough, everywhere he looked, iron mottled the formerly human Rise. Iron fingers on flesh hands, iron ears on flesh heads. It melded with the skin so perfectly, it almost seemed like they'd been born with it.

"The Iron Tide," Serth pronounced. "It can't cover them completely because they are by definition unstoppable. But they can't completely resist it, either. Fascinating, really."

Fin shot an exasperated look at the tall wizard. Apparently, Ardent wasn't the only one who found the wrong time to appreciate the dangers of the Pirate Stream.

"Well, it is," Serth said with a shrug.

All at once, Vell laughed. It sounded weird, like someone who'd never laughed before imitating what he thought one should be like. "Too true," he said. "Which is why we must get these two *Fade* to safety."

Hedgecaw snarled. "And what happens to the rest of us?" All around, his guards gripped their weapons more tightly.

But Vell flicked his wrist. The column of Rise shimmered with motion. "Our King demands conquest. This place is conquered. The Rise are done. What happens here is up to *him*."

From the rear of the Rise ranks, a figure appeared, seemingly floating over the heads of the soldiers. As it drew nearer, though, Fin could see that it was no flying wizard. It was a statue, slightly smaller than a man, held aloft by the Rise, who passed it forward between them.

When the statue reached the front, four tall Rise carried it to Vell. Once beside him, they knelt low, bringing it down nearly to his level without allowing it to touch the ground.

Up close, Fin recognized the hunched, beaked figure. It was the Salt Sand King in his nonburning form. Only he was made entirely of iron.

The Iron Tide, he realized, had taken the Salt Sand King.

Fin didn't know how to feel. Part of him—most of him, honestly—was happy to see the Salt Sand King turned into metal. At least they wouldn't have to fight a living fire today. And very little of him felt bad for the Rise. But there was something sad in the way Vell stroked a hand across the iron beak.

"You were right, my liege," Fin watched his twin whisper. "They came, as you said they would. The old broken wizard can't stay away from his things."

Marrill stepped forward. "Vell," she said. "Clearly you know better than the rest of us what the Iron Tide can do. If you help us, we can stop it—"

A whistle of steam cut her off. Fin felt sweat begin to bead across his brow. Suddenly, the room grew warmer. The iron fingers belonging to the beaked statue appeared to soften, to move. The iron edges began to glow.

"Blisterwinds," Fin muttered. He'd spoken way too soon. The statue was melting. Somewhere within it, the unquenchable fire still burned. The Salt Sand King was *alive.*

Vell held up his hand. "The King passes judgment!" he cried.

"All right, no time for this," Serth declared. "Children, down!"

The wizard didn't have to tell Fin twice. He grabbed Marrill with one hand and Fig with the other, and together they dropped to the ground. Suddenly his back felt like it had been licked from heel to head by a stinging icicle. The tips of his ears burned with cold.

He looked up. A wall of ice stood before him, so thin he could see right through it, but reaching all the way to the ceiling. On the other side, the statue of the Salt Sand King was solid once more, frost spreading over what had been hot metal moments before.

"That won't hold. Let's go," Serth commanded. "Now!"

The kids scrabbled backward, tripping over their feet as they went. Hedgecaw motioned them frantically toward the fountain. To Fin's shock, it was empty now, save for a staircase leading into its depths.

"This way," the thorny Meressian commanded, ushering Fig and Marrill downward. "There's a secret exit at the far end of the spiral galleries. If we're lucky, we'll make it."

Fin glanced back through the wall of ice. Vell sneered at him, shaking his head in disgust. Then his lips curled into a cruel smile, and he crooked an eyebrow as if in a challenge. Fin's pulse skittered. He knew what that look meant, and it wasn't good.

"We should hurry," he urged the others. But he kept his eyes on Vell. Looking through the ice was like staring into a twisted mirror, seeing himself in another life. The other him dropped his hand sharply, and the Rise holding the statue of the Salt Sand King let it fall, heavily, to the ground.

The second the iron touched the floor, Fin understood why the Rise carried it themselves. A dull darkness spread out from its base. The darkness crept outward, across the floor, up the ice, through it. Petrifying it.

The Iron Tide. Other than the Rise themselves, everything it touched became metal, and everything that turned to metal became a part of the Tide. The Salt Sand King, living fire or not, seemed to be no exception.

He couldn't hear Vell's voice through the ice. But the words his lips made were clear: "Surrender, before the Tide takes us both."

Fin sighed. This day hadn't started well, and if he was being honest, it wasn't getting much better. "Bad news," he called to the others as he raced after them down the spiral staircase. "Iron Tide is coming."

"Then hurry up!" Fig shouted back.

Fin flew down the passage beneath the fountain, quickly catching up to the others and bolting past to lead the way. Ahead, the tunnel made an abrupt turn, and he zipped around it, crashing headfirst into Bull Face.

"Oh, hey, I got your *waaaaaah!*" The big Meressian shrieked, stumbling backward, throwing a string of what looked like jewels in the air. Fin regained his balance easily and reached up to snag them.

Serth beat him to it, snatching them and shoving them into a hidden pocket in his robes. "Thanks so much," the wizard said, grabbing the candle from Bull Face's other hand as he pushed past.

"Run, run!" Hedgecaw cried, bringing up the rear.

Together they raced through the passage as it curved

and arced downward. They skidded around corners and slid down ramps, and then all of a sudden the corridor opened up into walls of glass.

"Whoa," Fin breathed. He paused for just one moment to take it in. They stood at the top of a broad open spiral. Its walls and floors were made of stained glass. He could see out to the underside of the fortress above and the dangling circle of Stream moat below. Throughout the spiral, inside and out, a hundred different boxes dangled from the base of the fortress by long chains. Each, he imagined, containing some artifact of the Prophecy.

"Whoa," Marrill echoed next to him. But she was pointing up. Overhead, a dull blotch formed on the bottom of the Citadel and began spreading outward. The Iron Tide was coming.

"Move!" Hedgecaw shouted from behind them.

They sped down the glass spiral, the Tide swallowing everything above as it ate its way toward them. They had a head start, but the Tide spread in all directions. They had to run around and around, while it could just ooze straight down. It would catch them, eventually.

They needed a new strategy. Fin ground to a halt, ignoring the grunts of Fig and Marrill almost colliding in an effort to avoid plowing into him.

"Fin," Marrill hissed, "what are you doing?" She grabbed his arm, tugging him forward.

But he held his ground, scanning their surroundings. Through the window he saw the *Kraken* circling in the moat below. If there was anything he'd learned as the Master Thief of the Khaznot Quay, it was that sometimes you had to make your own escape route.

His eyes skipped across the long chains and their display boxes strung throughout the glass spiral. An idea snapped into place. "We need a chain that lines up with the *Kraken*," he shouted. Without asking why, Fig and Marrill both started craning their necks, searching.

"Over here!" Fig yelled a moment later. "Check it," she said, pointing. "It goes all the way down."

She gave him a big smile. Fin felt oddly warm. It was nice having someone like himself around.

He gripped the Evershear tightly, sliding it from its sheath and making sure to keep the blade away from his body.

Then he slashed it through the air, *ker-snick, ker-scnak!* A pane of glass dropped away, falling into the darkness of the chasm below. All they needed to do was slip through the hole, grab the chain, and slide down to the *Kraken*. They'd have to be quick about it, though—the Iron Tide was already spreading along the chains themselves.

"Okay," he said with a grin, carefully resheathing the Evershear. "Who goes first?"

One by one, they shimmied down the chain, then swung to the ship. Serth went first, since he could save himself if the chain ended up breaking, then Marrill, then the two

Meressians—mainly because they forgot about Fin and Fig and cut ahead of them in the line.

Then it was just the two of them. Fin grabbed the chain, readying himself for the leap. It occurred to him that as awful as all of this was, he'd really enjoyed having a partner in crime. "You know," he said, "before Marrill, I didn't know what it was like to have a friend. Now I have two, and…well…"

He felt himself blushing. He still hadn't gotten used to this "being genuine" stuff.

"Me too," Fig said, grinning wide. "Now go!"

A minute later, Fin hit the deck of the *Kraken* with a flourish. "Tralada!" he declared as he landed. "Day saved, again. Naysayer, add that one to my score."

"Oh yeah," the big lizard grunted, repositioning Karny on his shoulder. "Let me just find my some-kid-barely-manages-to-not-get-us-all-killed scoreboard…and yep, that puts you at four who gives a clam, a dead tie with whatser-name."

"Also a bit premature," said Fig's voice. Fin looked up. Standing on the quarterdeck next to a visibly furious Remy was Fig's Rise, Karu. Serth and the Meressians surrounded her, but for some reason, none of them moved.

"You're a clever little Fade, I'll give you that," Karu pronounced. "But you should know you can't outsmart the Rise. We're the better parts of you, if you recall. And now we have you."

She held up one hand. Cradled in it, dull and glinting,

was a shard of iron. Fin let out a breath. That was why no one was doing anything.

"You brought the Iron Tide," he said.

Karu laughed. It wasn't as bad as Vell's, but it didn't sound quite natural, either. "It would have come on its own," she said. "The only thing that can stand against it"—she swept an arm down and across herself —"is the power of the Salt Sand King."

"Now," she said to all of them, "where is *my* Fade?"

"Right here!" Fig shouted from above. Fin looked up. Fig was halfway down the chain. She'd pulled the other half up and held the end in her right hand. Then she let go with her left.

The chain swung down past Fin, Fig at the tip of it. She swooped over the deck, flying wildly.

Not wildly, Fin realized. Dead on course.

"Fig, no!" he cried.

But there was nothing to be done. Fig slammed into Karu, snatching her Rise up and carrying both of them off the *Kraken*. Fin's heart skipped a beat. Everyone raced to the side of the ship, watching the twins twirling together out in the air.

For a moment, just a moment, all eyes were on forgettable Fig.

"This is childish!" Karu shrieked. "You can't stop me, Sister Fade!"

Fig caught Fin's eye as they spun around, heading on an arc back toward the *Kraken*.

"I don't need to stop *you*." She grabbed Karu's hand, prying at the piece of iron in her fingers.

Fin gaped in horror. "Fig, *no!*" he screamed again.

But it was too late. The Iron Tide had reached her. It crawled up Fig's arm, across her back, over her. In moments, she was gone.

"Sail, Captain, sail!" Serth commanded, begging the wind with his hands. The ship lurched forward, just in time to dodge the end of the chain with its deadly cargo.

Karu shrieked once, then shrieked again, struggling to jump free. But she remained clutched in Fig's iron-coated arms. The silver that had streaked the side of her face spread out, covering her. There was no escape. Her Fade was gone now. Karu was mortal. Immune to the Iron Tide no more.

Fin's heart caught in his throat as the *Kraken* set sail. Ahead, Serth guided the ship toward an eddy that would dump them back onto the Stream. Ahead was salvation. Ahead was the path to the Master. Ahead was the way to put a halt to this creeping doom.

But behind them, the screams had stopped. There was nothing left, save for two statues dangling at the end of a very long iron chain.

CHAPTER 7
Without a Flame

That evening, rust red flecked the gold surface of the Stream. Clouds stretched like veils across the drowning sun. And for the second time in as many days, Marrill stood next to Fin, consoling him over the loss of someone he cared about. She grabbed his hand and squeezed tight.

"This is starting to be a habit," Fin said. "One I really don't like." His voice broke, giving away the deep pain his flippant words were struggling to hide.

Marrill couldn't have agreed more. They'd lost too many friends. And with this one, she didn't know what to say. She hadn't really known Fig, after all.

It was hard to really know someone you couldn't remember.

"Hey," she said, thinking back to the last time they'd been in this position. "Remember what Fig said before? Maybe the Iron Tide isn't forever."

Fin eyed her suspiciously. "Hold up a tick. You *remember* Fig?"

"Of course I do," Marrill declared automatically. Then she laughed as the reality of what she'd just said sank in. She hadn't even thought about it—Fig had slipped *into* her mind just as easily as she used to slip out of it. "She saved our lives," Marrill told him. "How could I ever forget that?"

"Huh," Fin said. He nodded, once, twice to himself. "Worse comes to worst, she'll be remembered."

"No doubt."

For the first time since leaving the Citadel, he smiled. "Well," he said, "maybe that alone is enough." But his eyes fell back to the light playing on the golden water. "She was a good friend," he added softly. "To both of us."

"She was," Marrill agreed. "And thanks to her, we've got the Evershear. And Serth's stuff. And now that we've dropped off Hedgecaw and Bull Face, all we have left is a little light time travel before we're able to stop the Master of the Iron Ship." She nudged him with her elbow and smirked. "We're practically done already."

Unfortunately, her attempt to lighten Fin's spirits didn't work. He shook his head sadly. "What if we can't? What if the Iron Tide is irreversible? What if everyone it's taken, all those worlds…what if they're just gone forever, like all the things the Lost Sun destroyed?"

Marrill couldn't think about it. Wouldn't. Otherwise, the fear would paralyze her. She shook the doubt from her head and plastered a smile on her face. "Look, Ardent said the Pirate Stream is pure, endless possibility, right? Which means that somewhere out there is the possibility that we stop the Tide and fix everything. Right?"

"Sure." He wasn't very sincere. But clearly he wanted to believe it just as much as Marrill did. And she needed him to.

She grabbed the idea and ran with it. "So there's definitely magic in the Pirate Stream more powerful than the Iron Tide."

Uncertainty coiled in Fin's eyes. "How do you know?"

She leaned forward. "Because if the Iron Tide were all-powerful, it could take the Rise. It could stop the Salt Sand King."

Fin straightened suddenly. His eyes widened. "Marrill, you're right! The Salt Sand King was alive, even after being turned to iron…."

"So Fig might be, too!" Excitement flooded through

Marrill. She hadn't actually expected to come up with a good answer, but the more she talked, the more she began to believe. "And not just Fig—everyone and everything else touched by the Tide as well."

"The Parsnickles." Fin's voice cracked. "And the Khaznot Quay."

Marrill nodded. "If the magic of the Stream can protect the Rise and the Salt Sand King, then it *must* be able to reverse the Iron Tide, too." She smiled at him. "We can still save them."

The next thing Marrill knew, she was wrapped up in a huge hug.

"I've said it before, I'll say it again," Fin whispered in her ear. "Marrill, you're a genius."

Marrill laughed. Together they rocked with the force of the moment. It was amazing. The Iron Tide really *could* be stopped and its damage reversed. And they were on their way to do it.

But later that night, as Marrill lay in bed with the walls around her shimmering with starlight filling an infinite sky, she couldn't keep the doubts from creeping back in. She'd stayed on the Stream because she was determined to find a way to make her mom well again. And if the possibility existed that she could fix the Stream, then the possibility *had* to exist that she could fix her mom as well. Didn't it?

Even if those possibilities existed, though, what were the odds of both happening? Even if she and Fin did fix the

Stream, even if they did undo the Iron Tide's damage, she still might not find a way to make her mom healthy.

Marrill rolled onto her side, pulling Karny tight and burying her head in the fur of his neck. She squeezed her eyes against the burn of tears. She missed her mom. And she was terrified that she might never see her again.

＋ ＋ ＋

The next morning, it was hard to believe the Iron Tide existed at all. The sky above was an arc of blue. The Stream was shimmering gold, laid out before them like the yellow brick road. Overhead, sails snapped in the wind, and the deck swayed softly beneath their feet, rhythmically rocking as the *Kraken* cut through gentle waves.

The Naysayer sat in his usual spot at the stern, simultaneously fishing for prollycrabs, tending the rumor vines, and petting Karny. Remy stood by the wheel, stifling a yawn while Marrill and Fin perched on the forecastle railing, kicking their feet in the breeze and watching the horizon for signs of their destination.

Not that any of them had any clue what they were looking for. None of them knew what their destination actually *was*. Serth had been just as cryptic about this stop as he'd been about the last one.

But now that they had the Evershear, it was on to step

two of their plan: time travel. Marrill had no idea how that was even possible. And Serth hadn't bothered leaving his cabin since they'd fled the Citadel, so she hadn't been able to ask him.

"If we can go back in time, why not just go back early enough to stop all of this?" Marrill wondered aloud to Fin. "Keep Serth from drinking the Stream water. Stop Annalessa from turning into Rose. Keep the Master from..." She waved a hand in the air.

Just then, the door to Ardent's cabin burst open, startling them all. Karny bolted from the Naysayer's lap, darting down the stairs and past Serth's feet as he strolled onto the deck.

"Not possible," said Serth, stretching as though he'd just woken from a nap.

Marrill and Fin exchanged a confused glance. "What isn't possible?" she asked.

"What you just said about stopping me from drinking Stream water." He didn't even bother glancing her way. "Prophecy is inevitable. Even if you changed that one moment, the Prophecy would still come true. Somehow, some way."

Marrill frowned. "But how did you hear what I was say—"

He didn't wait for her to finish before he strode past them toward the bow, effectively dismissing her question.

Serth, Marrill was learning, wasn't one to continue conversations that no longer interested him.

He seemed to reach an arbitrary point on the deck and stopped, looking around. "Almost there, I see," he pronounced.

Marrill nearly dropped the chunk of potatofish she'd been gnawing for the last hour. There wasn't a single object between the *Kraken* and the horizon. No ships, no islands. Not even a sign, like there'd been for the Khaznot Quay. Things had a way of popping up on the Pirate Stream, but usually there was *some* indication that you were *somewhere*.

"Almost where, exactly?" she asked.

"Nowhere *exactly*," he told her. "Here, more or less." He took two steps across the deck, looked down at his feet, licked a finger and tested the wind, then took a long, deep sniff of the air. "Captain," he called, "take us two degrees to starboard."

Remy nudged the wheel wordlessly. Marrill took the opportunity to ask the question she hadn't been able to ask the last time Serth showed his face. "Speaking of time travel," she tried again, "how exactly is it possible to, you know... travel back in time?"

Serth held out an arm, twisting slowly until his shadow lined up. "Time is just another current on the Stream," he explained. "Slow and strong—so strong, in fact, it is virtually impossible to fight against. But a current nonetheless. With enough strength, and the right line, one can travel upstream."

Remy's ears seemed to perk up with that. "So it's a navigational challenge?"

He looked over at her sharply. "No."

She scowled. Fin swallowed a laugh.

"Besides," Serth continued with a dismissive wave of his hand, "there's no possible way you and I could ever hope to muster enough power to actually follow a current of time upstream. It's essentially unheard of."

"Oh." Marrill slumped. So time travel was technically possible, it just wasn't something *they* could do. "So how are we…"

"We'll cheat," Serth said simply.

Fin straightened. "Now you're speaking my language." He slipped from the railing and sauntered across the deck. "What're we talking here, the old loopty-eyeballs trick? The nottaday-nottamarra head fake? A salmon drop with a Webonese switch?" He snapped his fingers. "I got it: the Manomarion tea party. Point me at the mark and let's go!"

Serth's eyebrow twitched, but he said nothing. Instead he turned to Remy. "Another two degrees if you will, Captain." From where they were standing, Marrill could *just* make out the unhappy curl of Remy's lip as Serth directed her.

"*We* cannot possibly muster the power to travel back through time. But with both the Lost Sun and Pirate Stream at his fingertips, the Master has already done exactly that," the wizard continued. "If time is a current, think of the Master as one of those massive ships we so deftly navigated around two days back, just smashing its way across the Stream. What did those create?"

He waited patiently, like a schoolteacher calling on a student. It reminded her of Ardent. Marrill wondered if it was a trick they learned in wizard school.

She pondered his question. The ships hadn't *created* much of anything, other than a huge mess, and very nearly a wreck. She closed her eyes, visualizing the ships crashing toward the *Kraken*. She could practically feel how the deck pitched wildly as they passed.

Then it came to her.

"A wake," she declared, remembering how the two big ships had dragged Stavik's ship along with them.

Serth nodded. The hint of a smile played across his lips. "Precisely," he said. "Another two degrees, Captain!" He looked down at Marrill as the *Kraken* changed course, so slightly she could barely tell. "That's exactly where we're headed. To a place where we can catch the Master's wake through time." He frowned at Remy. "I said two degrees, not one and three-quarters. Where did you learn to pilot a ship?"

Remy made a big production of barely tapping the wheel with the tip of her finger, grumbling under her breath the whole time. Marrill couldn't make out what she was saying but was pretty sure she caught the word "keelhaul."

The ship shifted again, or so Marrill assumed. To her

there was no difference. Fin leaned toward her. "Is now a good time to go back to the whole should-we-be-trusting-the-evil-wizard conversation?"

Before Marrill could answer, Serth froze and raised his hand, as though pausing for a sneeze.

"Aaaaannnnnnnnnddddddd…" He held the word for a moment longer than it seemed like he should. "SWING TO PORT!"

Remy reacted instantly, spinning the wheel hard. The ship tilted. All at once, the wind died, the sails falling empty and limp. The ship coasted a few yards more before momentum drew it to a dead stop.

"Here we are," Serth declared, holding his hands wide.

Marrill looked around. They were in the middle of a big, empty ocean. Same as before. Except now they were at a complete standstill. She exchanged a glance with Fin, who seemed just as confused as she was. "But I don't see anything."

Serth nodded, reaching into his robes. "Obviously not. I haven't lit the candle yet." He knelt, producing the candle they'd retrieved from Flight-of-Thorns.

Remy snorted. Marrill caught the word "maroon" as the older girl stepped away from the wheel and leaned against one of the masts, arms crossed, waiting.

Marrill moved closer, trying to see what was so special about the candle. It looked perfectly normal as far as she could tell. Seemingly regular wax, white and clearish.

Shaped just like any other candle. Unexciting. There was only one thing about it that was unusual at all.

"There's no wick," she pointed out.

"Good point," Fin said. "How are you going to light it?"

With the very tips of his fingers, Serth carefully adjusted the candle to one side, then the other. "Technically," he murmured, "it will light itself."

Marrill squinted at it again, wondering if she'd missed something. "But...it's just wax."

The wizard shook his head. "It's not the wax that's important. It's what's *in* the wax that we want. Just have to find the right spot...."

"But—" she began again. Serth turned toward her, and Marrill felt the protest stick in her throat. Her body still automatically cringed at the sight of him, the black grooves down his face from centuries of crying inky tears still causing her heart to trip with fear.

Then all of a sudden, the candle burst into flame. And the lights went out.

Night dropped on them like a stage curtain. The bright light of day simply...*stopped*. No stars glimmered overhead, but a hundred thousand seemed to have gathered upon the surface of the Stream in the distance. They danced and shimmered in the sudden blackness.

Marrill blinked. Not stars. Candles. A hundred thousand candle flames. Lit across the face of huge wax towers—candles themselves, Marrill realized. Some were tall, some were small, as if they'd burned at different speeds. But an intricate lattice of wax bridges and buttresses strung them together, connecting them into a single whole. Elegant but melty, like a drip-sand castle.

Beside her, Fin let out a breath of wonder. "I've never seen anything like it."

"Tallowtrees," announced Serth. He faltered, seemed almost to stumble. Instinctively, Marrill reached out to steady him, stopping herself just before grabbing his arm. Even if his skin no longer froze, she couldn't bear to actually touch him.

"Are you okay?" she asked instead.

Serth nodded. "Yes. Yes, it's just...not as I remembered." He placed a steadying hand on the railing. "I am not used to things being different than I remember." He shook his head, regaining himself. "See how there is a great clearing in the heart of it?"

Marrill nodded. Even in the dark, she could tell that the candle towers formed a ring around a large open area.

"That is the place where something old and awful clawed its way up from the dawn of time. When it emerged, it tore a hole through the Stream itself. A hole where the time currents flow fast and free and closer to the surface. That hole will give us access to those currents." He waved the ship forward. "Incidentally, you may hear something calling to you in the voice of lost friends or dead family members. Just ignore it, and it won't eat your emotions."

Marrill gulped. She liked her emotions. "But—"

Serth didn't wait for her to finish. "Take us in, Captain," he ordered.

CHAPTER 8
The Space Among the Tallowtrees

At first, it felt like bugs.

A bug crawling on the back of his neck. He swatted at it.

A bug behind his knees. He shook his leg violently.

A bug on his ear—

a bug *inside* his ear.

Fin jumped and shouted, pawing at his head. He stopped, realizing the others were staring at him. The feeling was gone. Had it even been there in the first place?

"Sorry," he muttered.

Ahead, Serth resumed their trek, Marrill and Fin trailing in his wake. Fin glanced back to where the *Kraken* lay moored, a beacon of safety growing farther away as they continued their journey on foot.

Wax seemed to wrap around them, dull and white yellow in the candlelight, as they made their way through a tunnel toward the clearing in the middle of the Tallowtrees. Sound echoed oddly here, as if it were somehow unaccustomed to the place. If Fin listened just right, he swore he could hear someone crying.

"So, what can we expect when we get to the middle?" Marrill asked.

Fin tried to focus on her. But the walls around them appeared to have melted and re-formed; their surface was smooth and strangely ridged all at the same time. The shadows looked almost like faces. Almost.

Serth ducked his head around a sagging arch that seemed to be reaching out to touch them. Even *he* stepped cautiously in this place. "A lake of crystal blue, floating on a sea of gold like a drop of water on a saucer of cooking oil. Through it, we can pass into the current of time."

A shiver stole down Fin's back. Whether from their creepy surroundings or what Serth had said, he wasn't sure. He quickened his pace to stay close to the wizard. "And that will take us back to where...er...to *when* we need to go?" he asked.

"Absolutely not," Serth replied. In the flicker of candle-light, the wax ceiling bowed. "But combined with the Hearts of Yesterday, it *should* take us deep enough to catch the wake of the Iron Ship. And *that* will take us back to the time of the Dzane, the original wizards, where the Master first entered the Mirrorweb...and where we shall follow."

Marrill stopped dead in her tracks. "Mirrorweb? I thought we were going into the Pirate Stream?"

Serth paused a few feet ahead of her and spun to face them. "The Mirrorweb is the heart of the Pirate Stream," he explained. "The place *inside* the Map to Everywhere, where all possibilities come together at once. It is the Master's destination. And, hopefully, it will become the prison of the Lost Sun of Dzannin once again."

Fin frowned. He'd never wondered what was actually *inside* the Pirate Stream. "So this...Mirrorweb...is that where you went when you walked through the Gate in the Map? It's where you were trapped?"

Serth nodded, face solemn. The wizard's eyes took on a faraway look as though lost in a memory. "The Mirrorweb is a place where every possibility exists, each contained within its own mirror. An infinite sea of them, every single one a different reflection, a different choice, a path not taken. Or taken. Or taken later. Or earlier."

"Is it scary?" Fin asked. Marrill moved closer beside him, pressing her shoulder to his for comfort.

A haunted expression passed over Serth's face. "It is everything."

"I'll take that as a yes," Fin murmured. He took a deep breath, trying to picture it. "Are there spiders in this web?"

"Spiders are included in 'everything.' So yes."

Fin shuddered. "Another point in the scary column, then."

He glanced toward Marrill, but she didn't laugh at his joke. Instead, furrows of concentration marred her forehead, as if she was trying to work something out. "Are the reflections in the mirrors real?"

Serth shrugged. "As real as any possibility can be."

His answer left her silent, apparently deep in thought.

Fin, meanwhile, focused on the important part. "Are we talking like *giant* spiders?"

Serth stared at him. "All spiders. Literally all of them."

Fin thought he might have seen a twitch at the corner of Serth's mouth as he spun and continued down the path. It wasn't very reassuring at all.

In the silence, the echo of Serth's words twisted around, becoming something else entirely. All of a sudden, Marrill let out a shriek and spun into the air, as though someone had dropped a live eel down her shirt.

"Sorry," she whispered, hurrying to catch up with the quick-moving Serth.

Fin snickered.

Down a dark side passage, the wax turned his snickering into a slow, incessant drip...

drip...
      drip...
            drip...

Something with wings brushed against his cheek.

Fin jumped, racing after the others. He caught up to them just as they neared the end of the passageway. Ahead, through the tangle of arches that wove the candle-towers together, he caught sight of a gaping emptiness, marked only by the guttering of the flames on the far side.

Serth's steps slowed slightly. When he spoke, he spoke almost reverently. "This is where the light of the Lost Sun of Dzannin once burst forth, a column like a burning spear aimed at the heart of heaven. It shone through the waxen walls, rendering this whole place nearly transparent."

The wizard peered at the paraffin walls around them. His pale features seemed disturbed—fearful, even. "There were shadows in the wax then," he whispered, as if afraid the wax might hear him.

Fin shivered, doing his best not to think of shadowed things. Of things with wings and long, many-jointed legs, sealed somewhere in the wax.

They reached the end of the passageway. Serth had

promised crystal-blue water floating on a sea of gold. Instead, Fin saw an unbroken expanse of wax, stretching from one side of the circle of towers to the other. With the tip of one toe, he poked at the smooth surface in front of him. It was firm, as he'd expected. Solid, slightly slick. Yellow-white in the glow of a thousand flickering candles.

Yep, definitely wax.

"So where's the entrance you mentioned?" he asked, craning his neck.

Serth frowned as he stood beside him. "This place has changed far more than I thought. When last I was here, this was a pool of Stream water, and the candles were even and unburnt." He motioned to the great Tallowtrees. The one they'd just passed through was tall as a wizard's tower, as they'd say in the Khaznot Quay.

The next one over, however, was low and squat, barely half the height. As it had burned, its melting wax had oozed across the ground, covering the lake like ice in winter. Judging by the size of the other Tallowtrees around them, there were probably several solid feet of wax built up over the water.

"Obviously we'll have to find a way to clear all this away," Serth said, tenting his fingers under his chin as he contemplated the situation.

Marrill hugged herself, her hands rubbing against her upper arms. "Can't you just magic it away?"

Serth shook his head. "That would be very foolish. I am

still re-forming my connection with the Stream, and I will need everything I have to preserve us once we enter the rift."

"Powerful magic," Marrill mumbled. "Powerful…"

Fin stared at her. Her eyes were unfocused. He reached over and poked her lightly. "Marrill? You're not going wax crazy, are you?"

Her head tilted to the side, ever so slightly. "Maybe…" Then she seemed to snap back. "No. No, this is real. Serth, you said there's a pool of Stream water under here, right?"

The wizard nodded. "Just as deadly as any, to the unprepared."

"So what if we push the wax *down* into it?" she suggested. "The Stream water will change it just like anything else. We would just need a way to cut it, but then the Stream would do all the work."

Fin laughed. She was right—even this stuff was likely no match for raw magic. He produced the bone-handled Evershear, carefully stored in its glass sheath so its infinitely sharp edge wouldn't slip and slice a leg off. "Well, we do have something that can cut anything…." he offered.

Serth clapped, slowly. "Excellent work, children," he said. "You two work well together."

Marrill beamed. Fin felt a surge of pride. But the feeling soured a bit when he remembered the source of the compliment. Once upon a time Serth had tried to destroy their friendship. Had tried to destroy *them*.

Fin shook his head. It seemed impossible to reconcile those two things: the Serth who used to be and the Serth who was with them now. The madness may have passed, but even in Serth's best moments, the old him was there—in the sweep of his cloak, in the iciness of his glances. Etched forever in the tearstains on his cheeks.

Fin glanced at Marrill and saw the same complicated series of emotions flit through her eyes as well.

But they didn't have time to dwell on it. Serth, after all, had already moved on. "Fin, begin cutting," he ordered. "Marrill and I will retrieve the *Kraken*. Make sure you cut a hole big enough for the ship to fit through."

Fin's face dropped. "Wait, what?"

But Serth had already turned on his heel. "Come along, Marrill."

Fin's insides squirmed. He glanced at the long expanse of wax, then back at Serth. He glanced at the tunnel through the Tallowtrees, then back at Serth. Neither of these things he liked. "You're going to leave me here?"

"Precisely," Serth called over his shoulder, already walking away. "Good luck."

Marrill shuffled her feet. "Maybe I should stay with Fin?"

Serth turned back, giving them an incredulous look. "What, and risk losing *both* of you to wax madness?" he scoffed.

"Oh," Fin said. That made sense. He guessed.

"Don't worry," the wizard said with a wave. "The thing

in the wax can't hurt you." He hesitated. "Well, it probably can. It can probably do far worse than hurt you. I imagine it can flay the very thoughts from your brain, and turn your body into, one assumes, more wax." He paused again. "Anyway, don't listen to it and I'm sure you'll be fine. Come along, Marrill."

Fin gulped.

Marrill gave Fin an apologetic look, and he gave her a halfhearted wave in return. Then she bolted after the wizard as he vanished into the paraffin tunnel.

Smart girl.

Fin sighed. He was alone. In a dark so deep he wondered if there was ever a sun, the candles barely cast enough light to guide him. The air was just warm enough to feel like it should be comfortable, but just cool enough to raise goose bumps with the slightest breeze.

He produced the Evershear, checked the blade, and slashed down into the wax. A low, distant moan sounded, somewhere far away but also, somehow, close. He swallowed, wondering if he'd been too hasty in sending Marrill away. Too late now.

Gripping the bone handle of the Evershear tightly, he started to draw the blade around the edge of the wax seal.

"Hey there, Fin."

Fin jerked upright. "Fig?" he whispered. It was her voice, no question. So close to his ear she might as well have been breathing on him. But when he turned, no one was there.

"Did you forget about me?"

Fin spun. He'd heard her, he was sure of it. On the far side of the clearing tiny flames winked at him, one by one.

He closed his eyes, took a deep breath. This wasn't real. He knelt down again, tugging the Evershear farther around the perimeter. The wax made a sound like ripping fabric.

"Come inside where it's warm, dear. I'll look after you."

"Mrs. Parsnickle?" Fin shouted, twisting. He held his breath, waiting for the voice to speak again. He was met with silence. He shook himself. *This is silly.* Mrs. Parsnickle was gone, taken by the Iron Tide. So was Fig. Whatever was talking to him, it wasn't them.

He took another deep breath, ignoring the scent of burning hair that came in with it. He bent back down again.

A face stared up at him from the wax.

He fell backward, scooting across the slippery surface. The face opened its mouth, then seemed to melt in on itself. Flies buzzed behind his head.

Fin's heart pounded in his chest. His gut told his heart to be quiet, not to move, or the thing in the wax might hear it. Panic pumped through him. The tallow squirmed beneath his palms.

"Let me eat your thoughts, dearie," Mrs. Parsnickle said, from a place outside of everything. *"You don't want those nasty old thoughts anyway, do you?"*

"Slash all this," Fin muttered. He needed to end this. Now. He thrust himself to his feet, snatched the Evershear, and started running. It was a loping run, bending down to drag the blade through the wax beside him. Ardent's voice begged him to stop; then Annalessa's asked him to come inside; then his own dead mother told him that he was a good boy and that if he would just lie down and take a big bite of the wax, she would love him and hold him forever.

Fin ignored them all. He ignored the feeling of worms in his shoes, of fingernails rolling up his eyelids. He ran and ran, pulling the Evershear in a wide circle around the edge of the clearing, slashing through the wax.

Finally, he completed the circuit, the Evershear coming to rest right before the spot where he'd begun. The whole wax seal held on by a single thin bridge, ready to break free.

A face pushed forward in the dull light, frowned at him, then collapsed in on itself. The echo of his name whispered over him. *"Have you given up on me so easily?"*

Fin stumbled back, his breath leaving him in a whoosh. It was his mother. He had to clamp his lips tight to keep from calling to her.

"You searched so long, honey. Here I am," she cooed.

He shook his head, but his feet remained rooted in place.

His mother's voice dropped into a tremulous whisper. *"Don't leave me here alone like this."*

Her words struck in the deepest part of his heart. Tears welled up, and he closed his eyes against them. It would be so easy to let the fight slip from his limbs. To sink into the wax and let it take him.

His fingers loosened around the hilt of the Evershear, and he felt it begin to slide from his grip. *The Evershear.* He blinked, remembering running through Flight-of-Thorns with Fig to retrieve it. Remembering the sound of her laugh as they dodged Meressians.

Remembering the way she'd saved them. So that they could save the Pirate Stream.

"*I will have you,*" his mother's voice hissed.

Resolve flooded through him, straightening his spine. He wrapped his hand tighter around the bone hilt, determined to ignore the wax's false promises.

"No," he said, shaking his head. "No, you won't."

Just then, there was a crack and a thud behind him. Fin spun to find the *Enterprising Kraken* bearing down on him.

"Fin!" Marrill shouted from the bow, waving with one hand while clutching Karny with the other. "Come on!"

He didn't need to be told twice. He shoved the Evershear in its sheath and raced toward the ship, slipping on the wax as it started to shift and break under the *Kraken*'s weight.

"Lift me up, Ropebone!" he shouted. Marrill echoed the command, and a line dropped from the rigging to circle his waist. He leapt from the wax, feeling it give way at the same moment the line snapped tight, yanking him into the air.

He landed on the *Kraken*'s deck with a thud and rolled to his feet. His momentum was still carrying him forward when Marrill grabbed his hand, pulling him into a quick side-hug before tugging him to the railing. Together they watched as the giant circle Fin had carved in the wax broke completely free from the rest of the Tallowtrees.

The wax plug slipped into the Pirate Stream with a splash. It fizzed and bubbled as it touched the raw magic. Parts of it burst into flame; parts of it burst into tears. A cloud of bats in full tuxedos fluttered up into the night.

"Great work," Marrill said, clutching her cat and bouncing with glee. "I hope it wasn't too scary."

Fin shoved his chest out, doing his best to look nonchalant. "Nah." He lifted a shoulder. "Just dark was all."

In moments, the whole plug had been consumed by the Stream. To Fin's shock, though, tendrils of something sickly and white waved briefly on the surface, then retracted, wiggling, into the wax of the Tallowtrees.

"What. Was. That?" Remy demanded.

Serth slipped noiselessly across the deck. "There are other"—he paused as though searching for the right word—"*things* on the Pirate Stream. Just as awful, in their own way, as the foes we face." He tilted his head toward the now-calm waters. "That was one of them. Fortunately, it is not our problem today."

Fin took a slow, halting breath, remembering the voices in the darkness. He was definitely glad he wouldn't be facing those again anytime soon. "So now what?" he asked.

"Now," Serth said, holding up the strand of red heart-shaped pearls he'd recovered from the Meressians, "we dive." He plucked the pearls from the string and began passing them out.

Fin's eyes bulged. "Whoa, hold up." He glanced at the water beneath them. Its edges shimmered as gold as the rest of the Stream, but its center was cool and blue in the light, just as Serth had originally described it. He'd already seen what happened to things dropped into it. The same thing that happened whenever you dropped something into the Pirate Stream: anything.

"Did you say dive? Into that?" he asked, pointing overboard. "Are you headsoft?"

Serth ignored the question, instead tossing him one of the pearls. Fin caught it reflexively and examined it. To his surprise, it was covered in what looked like red sugar. He had no idea what he was supposed to do with it.

"Place it in your mouth," Serth explained. "It will keep you focused on the past."

Fin caught Marrill's eye. She seemed just as alarmed as he did.

When he finished distributing the pearls to the rest of the crew, Serth stood before them. "One thing you all *must* remember: If you somehow get separated from the *Kraken*, keep swimming. When the water first hits you, you may transform. You may transform a *lot*, actually. But you will survive—you will still be you. The power of my magic will protect you. But only so long as you are focused on moving forward. If you stray, or if you tarry, you will be lost. And there will be nothing I can do to help you."

Fin's fear shrieked like alarms guarding a royal treasury. Were they really going to do this? Jump *into* the Pirate Stream? His whole life, Stream water had meant death. One touch and anything could happen. He'd seen sailors with arms made of whispering glass, whose legs were little gremlins that tore eternally at their hip, all from just the slightest touch of raw Stream water. There was a term for them back in the Khaznot Quay: the Lucky Ones.

Beside him, Marrill pressed her face against Karnelius's side. "Good thing you're Stream-proof," she murmured, referring to Karny's dip with the Wiverwane back when Ardent was still with them. "Though if you feel the need to start spouting out more of the Dawn Wizard's will, maybe you can just save it for another time?"

She started to hike him onto her shoulder, then paused and set him down. "Actually, with your history of absorbing other critters, maybe I'd better *not* be holding you," she said.

She slipped her hand into Fin's instead. He gave it a reassuring squeeze. What they were about to do was stupid, reckless, and insane. But whatever was going to happen, at least they had each other.

Remy cleared her throat. "This is great and all," she said.

"But how are we going to get the *Kraken* in? She isn't exactly a submarine, you know." She put her hands on her hips, eyeing them one at a time.

"I got this one," the Naysayer grunted.

Fin choked on his snort. "You? You've got this?"

He braced, waiting for the inevitable Naysayer stinging comeback. Probably something about what a *great* job the rest of them had been doing so far, or how many kids and a wizard it took to sink a ship. Maybe even just a simple "Nooooope."

But the Naysayer merely stared at him. "Yup," he said. With one of his four hands, he popped his sugar-coated red pearl into his lipless mouth. With two other hands, he grabbed one of the thick docking ropes and knotted it into a yoke around his girth.

As the big purple lizard lumbered to the prow of the ship, Fin watched Marrill hold up her own heart-shaped pearl and dart her tongue out to take a taste. Her face pinched for a moment. Then she shrugged and shoved it into her mouth.

Fin followed suit. His lips puckered. It was sweet and sour and burning all at once, like the memory of something wonderful that was gone and would never be back again.

"Reathy?" Marrill asked around a slurp of her candy. Her voice wavered. Clearly, she wasn't.

"Reathy," Fin lied.

The Naysayer snorted, looking down at the shimmering

Stream water beneath. "Maybe if I'm lucky it'll turn me into someone who never met any of ya," he grunted. "Catch you losers a jillion years ago."

Then, with a pirouette that seemed almost elegant, he dove straight into the Pirate Stream.

The *Kraken* groaned. The bow dove. Fin braced, sliding forward across the now-sloping deck.

The bowsprit hit the water. The ship was going down.

"Remember," Serth cried, "no matter what happens, keep swimming forward!"

Glowing water surged over the deck. Fin stumbled, slipped. He took a deep breath. Then he was tumbling straight toward the raw magic that for all of his life had meant instant death.

CHAPTER 9
Marrill Is a Dolphin

Marrill sucked in a deep breath as the *Kraken* tilted. Not that holding her breath would help. She stumbled and fell headfirst into the waves.

Plunging into the water was like dropping into a cloud during a thunderstorm. Everything was furious and fantastic and bizarre.

Light and sound surrounded her, but none of it quite touched her. She *was fine*, she *realized*. But then something was odd. **Off,** ABOUT everything.

She'd suspected something strange. Something spectacular, sinister, silly. Saltwater surged; sea smells surrounded. Suddenly she shuddered. *So*, she speculated. Something spectacularly strange surfaced—

"Don't get distracted!"

—after all.

Marrill shook her head, recovering. She tried to catch her bearings, but everything everywhere was liquid. The word for world was water.

Oh no, she thought, *not getting into that again.*

She forced herself to look forward, to where Serth hovered above the deck of the sinking *Kraken*, calling to her.

He floated on his back, but he was carved from stone like a statue. A team of phosphorescent seahorses carried him downward through the warm water. Marrill could taste the light coming off them, and it tasted purple.

A current washed over them, and

Serth vanished in a puff of pollen

And a spattering of light rain.

"Follow me, follow my voice!" Serth commanded, his words dissolving into birdsong.

Marrill was trying, but it was hard to keep up when he kept turning into springtime like that. Then again, she wasn't much better off. Her hands were webbed, her legs were a muscular tail.

Marrill moved smoothly through
  the fast and flowing waves
When for a treat she slowed to greet
  a friendly Finta-Ray.

She was not who she once was,
  she realized with alarm.
But then again, neither was Fin—
  he had wings beneath his arms!

This is weird, Marrill thought, and she felt her thoughts bending into a nursery rhyme. She focused on the water around her, on moving back in....

No, she told herself, swimming onward. She struggled, fighting the urge. *Stay calm, Marrill*, she told herself. *Stick to swimming. Don't make the rhyme. Don't do it.*

It was really hard not to, though. Her will was beginning to fade. She opened her mouth to speak, but instead she squeaked!

A dolphin-squeak she made!

Maybe it wasn't so bad, she thought,
  Maybe she'd made too much fuss.

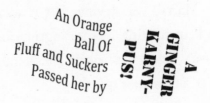

An Orange Ball Of Fluff and Suckers Passed her by

A GINGER KARNY-PUS!

"Staaaaay ooooɒ mmyyyy vooooooice!!!!"

Serth whistled, a whale call through the sea.

Up ahead the Naysayer swam,

In the form of a giant manatee!

"Keep following my voice," Serth called again.

Marrill blinked, her thoughts returning to *her* again. The water vanished suddenly, giving way to air. It was unbelievable, Marrill thought. The magic of the Stream was constantly changing them, transforming them. The *Kraken* turned into a beautiful, lush field.

"Almost there…" Serth cried, his voice lifting into a sing-song.

Keep swimming along
While singing this song
Deep in the Briiiin-ey stream

A tune struck up behind him, a light orchestral piece that accompanied his singing. Marrill felt herself altering now, the magic changing her yet again.

She tried to stay herself. She even had a thought about how.

But it popped out of her head and fluttered away on its own

Another piece of her followed it

and another.

and another.

and another.

and another.

and another.

Marrill burst into a million pieces as Serth sang them deeper into the heart of the Pirate Stream.

Just foll-ow my voice
as if you had a choice
deep in the Briiin-ey Stream!

Marrill
was wings
a of
cloud
of of
thoughts
flapping
flying
butterflies

In the midst of her meadow, Serth burst into view again, tapping his heels and waving an umbrella like an old-time movie star. The Buttermarrils flapped their wings together in cheer, fluttering urged on by the melody of his song.

Don't you drift away
Hear the words I say
Nothing good a-waits out there!

The music spun up, wild and fast now. Serth whirled on his heels, did a magnificent slide through the grass, and doffed a suddenly appearing top hat at a tree full of beautiful, bleeding blossoms that might once have been Remy.

BWAAAAAWWWHHHAAAAAAAA

A horn blasted through the song. The cloud of Butter-marrils fluttered together, their wings beating against one another, the tips of them slapping nervously.

"It's cooooooomiiiiiiiiiing!" Serth belted out, landing on the grass-green deck with a twirl.

BwaAAAAWWWHHHAAAAAAA

Reality rippled. A wave of force blasted through the Buttermarrils, and the next thing they knew they were a person again.

A sharp, black metal prow stabbed through the center of her vision. The Iron Ship tore past, blasting aside the world around them.

"This is it!" Serth shouted, his voice now his own. "Stay close!"

Marrill looked around. They were back on the deck of the *Kraken*. She was her, Fin was Fin, Octokarny was—just Karny. Everyone and everything seemed to have returned to normal. Well, as normal as it had ever been.

Not too far ahead of them, the scrap-metal stern of the Iron Ship thundered through a swirling hole in space, then vanished.

Marrill threw up her hands in anguish. "We missed it!"

Then reality rippled again, and they were somewhere else. They stood in the boughs of an enormous tree, on a platform hollowed out in the burl of a giant branch. The bark billowed, as though it were made from clouds.

"...I haven't worked out the math just yet, but I'm

pretty sure if you got too close, it would bite," said a familiar voice.

Marrill whirled about, her heart pounding. A thin old man tugged at the tip of his beard, kicking aside the length of his purple robes.

"Ardent!" she cried.

The wizard held up a finger to his companion. "Did you—feel something? It felt like fate."

Another wizard stood straight and elegant, laugh lines tracing the edges of her lips. "I only hear you, old fool," she chuckled.

Fin gasped beside Marrill. "It's Annalessa!"

"They can't hear you," Serth said. His hand fell heavy on Marrill's shoulder, holding her back. "We aren't completely here, after all. Just passing through on a surge of the Master's wake. He must have taken the straightest path backward—through his own past."

Marrill frowned. "I don't understand."

"This is Ardent's history we're trespassing in," Serth explained. "He's retracing his past; we're simply along for the ride."

Annalessa looked around. "I did feel something," she whispered. "It felt like...Serth."

Ardent snorted, crossing his arms. "Chasing after Serth will lead us nowhere," he said, a storm in his voice. "Nowhere good, anyway."

Beside Marrill, Serth let out a *hmph*.

"Well, he wasn't wrong," Fin said.

Marrill ignored them both. She was too busy studying the two wizards, trying to capture every last detail. She missed Ardent—*this* Ardent. And the last time they'd seen Annalessa, she'd followed Serth's example and drunk Stream water, turning into the Compass Rose of the Map to Everywhere.

That had been nothing but an echo of the past. Maybe it was fitting, Marrill thought, that they would see her here, when *they* were the echoes cast back from the future.

"This must have been the moment when she asked for his help finding Serth and he refused to go with her," Fin said softly beside her.

Marrill nodded. Other than their time out of time in Monerva, it was the last time Ardent had seen Annalessa. The moment that set his quest for her in motion.

"I love you, Anna," Ardent said, turning away. "But I cannot join you in this."

Marrill opened her mouth to yell. Maybe if she could just shout loud enough, they would really hear her. Maybe Ardent would wise up and not let Annalessa walk out alone.

But as the words left her mouth, reality rippled again. The wake of the Iron Ship pulled them deeper into the past.

Now they were standing on top of a hill at night. She spun and found Ardent and Annalessa lying on their backs in the soft grass nearby. Their heads tilted toward each other, almost touching, as they stared up into a midnight sky peppered with stars.

They were younger here, their faces showing fewer traces of time. Ardent's fingers danced in the air, and at his command the stars above swirled and coalesced into shapes. Animals and creatures danced and played out some story he'd just made up.

Marrill raced toward them. "Ardent!" she shouted as loud as she could. She wanted to warn him, but she didn't know what to say.

Ardent stiffened and the stars dimmed, the night growing darker. He started to push himself up.

Marrill fell to her knees in front of him, only inches separating them. Tears blurred her eyes as she choked out, "Don't let her go, Ardent." She reached for his arm but her hand fell through emptiness.

"You won't be able to reach him, Marrill," Serth said behind her. There was a hollow note to his voice, as if watching it hurt him, too.

But she shook her head, refusing to give up.

Annalessa's fingertips brushed against Ardent's shoulder, coming to rest on his arm. "Ardent?"

"I felt..." He stared down at where she touched him, frowning. It was the same spot Marrill had just tried to grab. His eyes lifted to meet Annalessa's. Eyes that were full of love and wonder and promise. "I'll never let you go, Annalessa."

And Marrill let her tears fall, because she knew it was a lie. Reality rippled again, ripping her from the scene, and she was grateful for the reprieve.

The memories continued, dizzying and overwhelming as the *Kraken* was dragged backward through Ardent's life.

Now they stood on the deck of the *Kraken*, the Stream a stretch of golden water, smooth as glass for as far as she could see. Overhead the sails hung limp, the ship so dead in the water that not even the smallest hint of a ripple lapped against her hull.

Ardent sat with his feet propped against a table, leaning his chair so far back that it was a wonder it hadn't fallen over. He studied a handful of cards and shrugged, tossing two onto the table.

Coll sat across from him, and Marrill felt her heart lurch to see him again.

But it was Remy who gasped. Remy who yelped "Coll!" as she raced toward him.

Ardent's chair fell forward, slamming against the deck. He peered around the ship. "Did you hear that?"

Brightness lit Remy's eyes. "Yes! Coll! Can you hear me?"

"Maybe it's the wind playing tricks," Coll said dryly. "Oh, wait, there is no wind."

Ardent sighed, kicking his chair back into its improbable lean. "The wind can't stay mad at me forever," he said, waving a hand. "Trust me. In a battle of obstinacy, I shall always prevail."

Coll sighed. "If only you hadn't—"

His words were cut short by another ripple. Another jolt to Marrill's gut as she was dragged from the memory and thrust into another.

They were on a balcony now, in what looked like a library. The walls were made of stone, and the windows were narrow. Glowing orbs filled the air, dancing and shifting to light the path of the wizards browsing through the towering shelves of books that spread in every direction.

Three college-aged wizards, Ardent, Annalessa, and Serth, sat at a table in the corner. They shook and twitched, and for a moment Marrill thought something was terribly wrong. But then she realized...they were laughing. All three of them. Annalessa had her head thrown back, and Serth's eyes were squeezed shut. Ardent snorted, which only caused the three to laugh harder.

"Oh, Ardent," Annalessa gasped. "Your stories..."

Behind her, Marrill heard a soft chuckle and she turned to see Serth watching the trio. "He could always make us laugh," he said, a smile ghosting his lips. But his eyes glistened with pain and regret, and when he drew in a breath, it hitched in his throat, almost as if he was holding back a sob. Marrill's heart twisted at the sight, but before she could say anything there was...

Another ripple. This time she was standing in the middle of a crowded market. Ardent crouched nearby, now a gangly teen. His fingers leapt, dancing a makeshift puppet before a child with tear-streaked cheeks, turning his cries into laughter.

Ripples. Memories. Ripples.

Then they were in a forest, and Ardent was even younger, his magic apparently fresh and new as he concentrated, straining to unbend the branches of a tree and release a brilliant blue-stained bird trapped within. His face lit with wonder as the bird soared free.

Marrill's eyes closed. A deep anxiety swirled in her belly. For everything awful the Master had done, he was still this goofy, wonderful, passionate, lovestruck boy. He was still the gangly, awkward, grandfatherly old man.

He was still Ardent.

If they used the Evershear to cut through his iron armor, what would happen to him? She couldn't bear the thought of actually hurting Ardent. Of maybe even killing him.

The ripples came faster now. Ardent aged in reverse, shrinking to an infant, then was gone.

Faster.

Trees shrank into sprouts and slithered back into the ground.

Faster.

Rivers sucked away and poured upward as rain.

Faster.

Old mountains roared upward, then leapt back down again.

Faster Faster Faster Faster Faster Faster Faster Faster
Everything swirled together into a blur.
Faster Faster Faster Faster Faster Faster Faster Faster Fast
Then the blur seemed to tear open,
erFasterFasterFasterFasterFasterFasterFasterFasterFaster
and the *Enterprising Kraken* emerged
into a world
of light.

CHAPTER 10
At Dawn, the Light Is Peculiar

I t's like sailing on the Pirate Stream, Fin thought.

It was *like* that, but it *wasn't* that.

Beneath them was molten gold. Not the golden water of the Stream, but thick, swirling gold. The sky above was another sea, stacked atop them like the bread of a sandwich. At every horizon, the two touched and blended. The *Kraken* was sailing inside a bubble in an ocean of pure, raw magic.

In the middle of it all, a spire floated in midair. Directly beneath it, the sea plunged into a massive whirlpool. Overhead, a stream of molten gold poured down from the golden sea above, disappearing somewhere inside the spire. It was as though the water below was pouring through a hole and somehow coming out above to drain into the spire.

Ahead, something moved through the air, soaring toward the spire. Fin blinked, trying to focus. He recognized the ship, and his heart began to thump. "It's the Master!" he shouted, watching the Iron Ship fly through the sky, as though it was light as a cloud. As if it were a ghost ship.

"Where?" Beside him, Marrill shook her head, clearly still recovering from what they'd just gone through. In her arms, Karnelius lashed his tentacle—*tail*, Fin corrected himself—furiously. Fin pointed, and she drew in a sharp breath.

"Ardent," she half whispered. There was a note of sadness in her voice. Fin ignored it. Nothing of Ardent remained in that ironclad creature.

"After him!" Fin shouted as he raced to the prow. Serth stood there, tall and dark in the all-consuming light, staring up at the pinnacle in the sky. Beneath them, the *Kraken* groaned and shifted course. She inched forward, but the molten gold barely parted as she went. The ship's motion came from the slow suction of the hole in the middle of the sea than from her own force.

"It's no good," Remy called from the quarterdeck. "This is like sailing through honey."

"We would have to be able to fly, anyway," Serth added quietly.

Fin squinted up at the Iron Ship as it slid to dock against the top of the spire. They had to get to it somehow. *That* was what brought the Iron Tide. *That* was what had taken the Parsnickles and Fig.

His heart squirmed, and he reached for the Evershear sheathed at his side. The bone handle bit into his palm, he gripped it so tightly.

Marrill came to stand beside them. "It's the Font of Meres," she breathed, wonder threaded through her voice. "The source of the Pirate Stream."

Fin tilted his head as he studied the floating spire. Now that she pointed it out, the dark rock *was* familiar. As were the mouthlike arches on its sides. When he'd seen it before, water had poured from those—first the headwaters of the Pirate Stream, but after Ardent's wish, the dark metal of the Iron Tide. Here, they were dry. But the shape of them was unmistakable.

"Yes," Serth said. "This is the birthplace of the Stream. This place—and this time—are where it branches off of the River of Creation." He looked at Marrill and Fin. "Up there," he said, "the Dzane will have just finished their battle with the Lost Sun of Dzannin. What we see around us must be the very last of the raw stuff of creation—the pure magic that will become the Pirate Stream."

"Let's get up there before the Master gets away," Fin growled. "After him!" he called to Remy.

"You may not recall, but this ship doesn't exactly have wings," she pointed out from the quarterdeck.

"Good thing we have a wizard with us, then," Fin replied. "How about you magic us up there, Serth?"

Serth merely lifted a scowling eyebrow. Fin clenched his jaw and wrung his hand around the hilt of the Evershear, impatient to catch the Master and finally be done with the creature who'd destroyed those he held dear.

Marrill glanced toward him, alarm in her eyes as her gaze fell on the knife clutched in his fist. Fin forced himself to release his grip, shifting his hands to the railing instead. The grain of the dullwood sent tingles through his palms. Even in this strange place, it felt normal—boring.

Somehow that thought reassured him. Things *would* be normal again. They just had to catch the Master and find the moment to strike. No matter what it took, they'd come this far; something would happen. The sails would fill. The *Kraken* would lift out of the water. He could practically feel it already. They would find a way to get up to that spire, even if it meant sailing on air.

And in that moment, he believed they *could* fly.

"We're lifting!" Remy shouted.

Fin blinked, looked down over the railing. Sure enough,

the prow of the *Kraken* had broken free of the molten waves. Liquid gold flowed off from all sides as the ship rose into the air.

Fin's eyes widened. He couldn't believe it.

And just like that, the *Kraken* sloshed back down.

"What just happened?" Marrill asked, clutching Karny with one hand and the railing with the other.

Fin could only shake his head. "I don't know. For a moment there, I really almost believed we could fly, but then..." He trailed off, thinking. All he'd done was believe the ship could fly...and it had. They were in the heart of magic, after all. Anything was possible.

And just like that, the *Kraken* rose back up out of the water.

"I don't believe it," Marrill gasped. The ship stopped, faltering in midair.

Fin laughed. "It's belief," he cried with a clap. "I believe it *can* fly. Stop believing it can't!"

Marrill looked confused. But Serth nodded, catching on immediately. "Yes," he said, "that's it. The magic is young here; in legends, the Dzane shaped it with their will alone. We may not be as powerful as they are, but if we all believe in something, together we may be able to make it real."

Marrill looked at Fin. He grinned as big as he could, nodding to reassure her.

"Okay," she said. "I believe it. We can fly."

The *Kraken* rose higher and lurched forward, headed for the spire.

"Guys," Remy yelled from the ship's wheel. "We're actually flying! I'm steering us through the air!"

"You better believe it!" Fin cried. Serth groaned. Marrill nudged him in the ribs playfully. "Sorry," Fin said, but none of them believed *that*.

Within moments, the *Kraken* floated up beside the spire that would one day be called the Font of Meres. She moved in as she went, rising past the dry culverts, toward the very top.

As they neared the pinnacle, a curious, high-pitched little voice drifted down to them.

"I can do nothing for you," it said. "If she has become one with the Stream, then she was always one with the Stream and always will be, so long as the Stream exists."

Fin's heart beat faster. He recognized that voice. It was the Dawn Wizard, the last and trickiest of the Dzane. He was the one who'd built the Syphon of Monerva, that great and powerful Wish Machine, and tricked the Salt Sand King into using it. His last will and testament, in the form of a talking Karnelius, had led them to try to repair the wizard's greatest work, the Bintheyr Map to Everywhere, to stop the Lost Sun from destroying the Stream.

Of course, all of that was in the future, Fin reminded himself.

"Very well, but I warn you, you mustn't do this," the

Dawn Wizard's voice said desperately. "The Lost Sun is within you, I can feel it. It's driving you—listen!"

The *Kraken* rose, reaching the top at last.

In the future, this would be a stone building, with walls and passageways and a giant counsel-room with windows. But here in the past, there were no walls. Only a wide-open platform. From the deck of the *Kraken*, Fin could clearly see the Stream water pouring down from above, an ever-running thread hanging from the golden heavens. It ended in the very center of the spire, disappearing into a deep bowl there.

Next to the bowl, a stooped little shape hovered, two hands holding a square of parchment. Fin recognized it instantly: the Bintheyr Map to Everywhere.

The casualties of the Dzane's battle with the Lost Sun surrounded him: a golem of stone half-melted; a woman with three faces wincing painfully; a clockwork griffin smashed to pieces. Others lay nearby, in shapes and forms of all imagining, each one looking shocked, stunned, terrified.

On the far side of the platform, the Iron Ship waited. Her Master stalked toward her, all cold metal and angles, a figure carved from jagged hate. From one hand dangled an iron cage with Rose, his prisoner, inside it. He was tall and cruel as ever, brutal and powerful with every step. And his back was completely exposed.

He was vulnerable.

Fin's fingers slipped to the Evershear. Nerves fluttered

against adrenaline in his belly. He unsheathed the knife, listening to the searing slip of it slicing through the air. He took a step forward, but Marrill's hand fell on his, holding him back.

"Wait," she said.

He shot her a confused look. This was what they'd come for. To use the Evershear against the Master and end the Iron Tide.

Her eyes glimmered. "What if this kills Ardent?"

The thought punched him in the gut. But he wouldn't be deterred. "Marrill, it's the only way to stop the Iron Tide."

He started to pull away, but she tightened her grip. "We can't. Serth said we have to use the Evershear inside the Mirrorweb. It's the only way to imprison the Lost Sun again."

That caused Fin to hesitate. He gnawed his lip, his insides twisting as he watched the Master board his ship. With a sharp sigh he resheathed the blade and crossed his arms.

As they watched, the Iron Ship pulled away from the spire. The shrieking of bending metal tore through the air. The ship rolled, twisted, and dropped out of the sky. It plummeted downward, then smashed into the golden sea below. In a moment, it seemed to melt, spreading all around. Turning, Fin realized, into the Iron Tide.

Before Fin could even sound the alarm, the Tide swirled into the whirlpool below the spire and was gone.

Fin gasped, confused. He didn't understand.

"Ardent!" Marrill choked. She spun toward Serth. "What happened to him? Where did he go?"

The wizard didn't answer. Instead, he kept his eyes fastened on the thread of molten gold pouring into the bowl in the middle of the spire from overhead. A dark stain appeared, tarnishing the edge of it. It grew thicker, darker as it swirled toward the bowl below.

The Iron Tide, rising once again.

As they watched, the Dawn Wizard pushed the Map to Everywhere, faceup, into the center of the flow. Its sides unfolded, transforming it. The Gate within it swung open. The water, dark and gold alike, flowed into it and vanished.

Fin shook his head, disbelieving. "What—" But he didn't have time to finish the thought.

"Hey, little help down here!" came a gruff voice from below. Fin leaned over the railing and found a big purple form clutching the side of the ship.

He cringed. The Naysayer. They'd totally forgotten about him!

"Great grouper gravy, what kinda indecisive incompetents we got on this ship?" the Naysayer growled as they hauled him up. He smacked the deck with a thud and shook his greasy mane. Gobs of molten gold spattered off it. One droplet smacked against a bucket of crab shells, which got up and waltzed together down into the main hatch.

That settled one thing—the water here was at *least* as deadly as it was on the Stream. But the big grumpy lizard seemed unharmed. "Naysayer," Fin said, stunned. "You're... still you?"

Marrill gasped. "Wait—you really *are* immune to Stream water?"

It must have been hard for a creature without lips to sneer, but as usual, the Naysayer managed. "Oh, right." He patted himself down. "Good work, kid detectives. I'll give ya three points for statin' the obvious, and take off five for not being sure."

"Well, well," said a shrill voice from the spire beside them. "If it isn't the Contrarian. Hardly expected to see you here."

Fin turned. The little creature that approached matched the Dawn Wizard's voice perfectly, though he wasn't exactly what one would expect an enormously powerful wizard to look like. Grayish fur barely covered a body an indiscriminate shade of blue. Golden-tinged whiskers sprouted around his nose like a cat, but his ears hung low on his head. His eyes were uneven, definitely different sizes, and they glowed a pale orange as he looked past Fin. Straight at the Naysayer.

"Wait," Marrill said, swiveling back and forth. "You... *know* each other?"

"Me and Dawny go way back," the big beast grunted.

"Being older than the Pirate Stream and all. I'm one of the Dzane. Did I forget to mention that?"

Fin's mouth hung open. He couldn't believe what he was hearing. "*You're* a Dzane?"

"That's right," the Naysayer said. "Oh, and I could remember you this whole time, too." He leaned in, right by Fin's ear. "Acted like I couldn't, though." His breath reeked of prollycrabs. "'Cause it was funny."

CHAPTER 11
A Genial Conversation at the Beginning of Time

On the spire's edge, the Dawn Wizard twitched his catlike nose, making his whiskers dance in a flickering rainbow. "The Contrarian is not now, nor ever will he be, one of the Dzane," he assured them.

Marrill shot the Naysayer a withering look. Unsurprisingly, he'd lied to them.

The scaly monster heaved with laughter. "You shoulda

seen the looks on you suckers' faces. Swimmin' back through time was totally worth the trip just for that." He slapped his knees with his lower two arms. "But seriously, I *am* older than the Pirate Stream. And the thing about remembering the kid but pretending not to just to get my jollies—that was true, too."

The Naysayer laughed again, then lumbered off the ship, heading toward the center of the spire. Marrill stared after him, her mind stuck in a state of disbelief.

"I've long suspected," the Dawn Wizard said, "that he is a spirit of elemental orneriness. But he would never cooperate with my tests." He let out a good-natured *hmph*. "The nature of the beast, I suppose."

The little creature then looked them up and down, inspecting them with care. "More ghosts from a gray future, are you?" He straightened his cloak and nodded approvingly when he came to Karnelius. When he reached Fin, he cocked his head to one side. "Here to follow the last, I expect? Stop him, maybe?"

Marrill was relieved that he seemed to already understand. "Yes, exactly. He was our friend," she gushed, "but now he's started a tide of iron that's turning everything to metal, and we have to—"

Serth cleared this throat, interrupting her. "Marrill," he said slowly. "Recall that our friend here just *helped* our quarry escape."

Marrill froze. Her spine straightened. Right, of course.

She'd forgotten that the Dawn Wizard wasn't exactly trustworthy. She'd been talking to one of the most powerful beings who ever existed, one who was known for his tricks and riddles. She couldn't assume he'd be friendly to their cause.

The Dawn Wizard waved a tiny clawed hand. "Oh, whale-skates, don't let *that* bother you." He raised a finger to his chin. "Hmm, I think I just invented roller whales. Do they have those in the future?"

As one, the crew of the *Kraken* shook their heads.

The Dawn Wizard shrugged. "Guess they don't take off. Well, I'm going to invent them anyway, so there."

"You didn't explain why you helped the Master escape," Marrill pointed out, trying to get the conversation back on track.

The Dawn Wizard peered at her. She could practically feel the power radiating from him like an electrical field. There was a hardness in his eyes that made her want to turn and run, but she forced herself to hold her ground. "You didn't ask," he said.

She let out an exaggerated huff. Why did wizards have to be so persnickety? "Fine. Why did you help the Master escape and where did he go?"

His whiskers twitched. "The Lost Sun of Dzannin just stripped the Dzane of our immortality. I'd been able to die for all of five minutes when your friend showed up. Think I was ready to try it out?"

"He's not our friend," Fin cut in. Marrill scowled at him. "Not anymore," he amended.

"Regardless," the Dawn Wizard continued. "He demanded I open the Gate to the Mirrorweb and allow him into the heart of the Pirate Stream. So I did."

Fin frowned. "So all we have to do is threaten you, and you'll help us the same way you helped him?"

Kaleidoscopic patterns danced in the Dawn Wizard's eyes as he looked Fin over. "You could *try*," he said pointedly.

Marrill suddenly felt like a million bees were pressing their stingers, gently, against her skin. Fin stiffened next to her, clearly feeling it, too. Apparently, the Dawn Wizard was not pleased with his tone.

"Maybe we should just ask?" Marrill suggested through clenched teeth.

Fin nodded tightly. "That sounds good," he squeaked. Carefully, he turned toward the Dawn Wizard. "Will you help us?" he asked with exaggerated politeness. "Please?"

The Dawn Wizard winked, and the awful feeling vanished. Marrill and Fin relaxed as one. "Maybe." He started back toward the center of the spire, waving them after him. "Come on, then," he said. "All of you. Have a seat. Let's chat."

Serth hesitated. "We would love to stay," he said. "I'm sure there's much we could learn here. But as my young friend mentioned, we are on a mission to stop the man who just left. We've come from many eons in the future to track him down, and we must do so before it's too late."

The Dawn Wizard bobbed his head. "Oh, absolutely," he said. "But in the Mirrorweb, time has no meaning. Follow him now, follow him tomorrow..." He shrugged. "If you come from many eons in the future and it wasn't 'too late' then, I expect we have time for a bit of sit-and-chat before the world ends, hmmm?"

He held out a little blue-skinned hand to Marrill. Tufts of fur stuck out at odd angles between the fingers. For a long moment, she considered what to do. The Dawn Wizard was mischievous and unpredictable, after all. For all she knew, this could have been *his* plan from the beginning.

On the other hand, he looked like a raccoon that had nearly drowned in a vat of grape Kool-Aid, and Marrill was a total sucker for sad animals. She reached out and took the little paw, allowing the Dawn Wizard to lead her off the *Kraken*.

"Hold up," Remy called after her. "I'm not so sure about this." She warily eyed the Dawn Wizard and the rest of the Dzane scattered around the spire.

Serth stepped forward. "No harm shall come to them while I am with them. I give you my word." His voice held no trace of jest or irony.

Marrill tripped over her feet and stumbled to a stop. No way she'd heard that right. No way had Serth—the former madman who'd tried to kill them on multiple occasions—just *vowed* to protect them. She glanced toward Fin, who seemed to share her confusion.

A flash of surprise crossed Remy's face, but it didn't last long. "Great!" she chirped, shrugging. "Have fun!" She'd already turned to a hammock strung between two masts. "Don't wander too far, be back before dark, don't get into any cars with strangers, et cetera, et cetera...." Her warning trailed out into a yawn as she stretched and then flopped into the hammock. "Best babysitter ever," she mumbled, thrusting a fist into the air. She then let out an *oof* as Karny jumped on top of her and curled into a ball on her stomach.

"Did Remy just appoint Serth as our babysitter?" Fin asked under his breath.

Marrill shrugged. Maybe they'd misjudged the wizard. She glanced toward Serth, who already strode across the platform, back straight and robes flowing around his feet. The usual fear that twisted her stomach didn't come. "Weird."

Fin laughed. "I think that sums up everything about this."

He was right—everything *was* weird. All around them, the Dzane were recovering from their fight against the Lost Sun. The three-faced woman straightened, stitching herself up with a wave of her fingers. The pieces of the clockwork griffin jumped toward each other and reassembled. The golem remained half-melted, but he moved more easily now, as though he was supposed to be that way.

Marrill felt an odd sense of déjà vu as she looked at them.

She'd seen them before, she realized, as echoes—ghostlike apparitions—in Meres. The power of the battle with the Lost Sun, recent here, had left an impression that would still survive in her time.

A shiver traveled down her back. Her eyes turned to the swirling magic above and below them and filling every horizon. In her time, the Pirate Stream was ancient and full of secrets so old that they'd been lost to the ages; here, it hadn't even been born yet. But sometime in the very, very far future, she would be back in this place, walking across this same stone floor, trying to defeat the same all-consuming evil.

"You okay?" Fin asked under his breath. She nodded and forced a smile, turning her attention to the now that was now now.

Ahead of them, the Dawn Wizard slowed. With a nod of his head, a table unfurled like a flower from the floor. They settled themselves on soft, tufted lily stools while delicacies they'd never heard of nor scarcely could have imagined appeared before them.

As they ate, Fin and Marrill did their best to explain what had happened, including everything they knew of the Master and the Iron Tide—give or take a few key details. Like the fact that it was the Dawn Wizard himself who would one day create the Wish Machine that, in turn, would create the wish that ultimately turned Ardent into the Master. It seemed rude, Marrill thought, to tell some-one about his own future like that.

"I just don't understand," Marrill said when she finished the story. She looked at her hands, thinking about Ardent. "Why would he try to destroy the Stream? Ardent is kind and good."

The Dawn Wizard cocked his head, his orange-fire eyes turning to platinum flecked with jade as he considered her question. "Not always, it seems."

"Ardent the Cold," Fin said, nodding.

"Indeed," the Dawn Wizard said.

Marrill opened her mouth to defend Ardent, but Serth held up a hand to stop her. "Ardent *was* kind and good," he said. "We fought great evils together, saved lives, achieved things that, before us, were impossible." His lips twitched into a smile—a real one. Like most creatures born into an inhos-pitable environment, it died quickly. "But there is a darkness to him, too," he said. "You've felt it. An unquenchable thirst for knowledge, a need to control the uncontrollable. It burns in him, and though he may have learned how to push it down, it never vanished."

Marrill hated hearing these things about Ardent. But she also couldn't deny them. She'd never forget watching her friend reach out and take the wish orb, knowing what would happen if he used it. He'd become the enemy, and he'd done so willingly.

And that broke her heart. "But he loves the Pirate Stream."

"Perhaps, then, there is something he loves more than the Pirate Stream," suggested the Dawn Wizard, the fur above one eye tufted in an arch.

"Annalessa," she breathed. Of course. She remembered the moment Ardent had taken the wish orb from the Master.

He'd just watched Annalessa sacrifice herself to save the Stream. He'd blamed himself, believing that he'd failed her. *I will save her*, he'd said, holding aloft the orb. *If I must undo all of the Stream to make it happen.*

And at his words the Iron Tide had flowed forth.

He'd done it for Annalessa. He was trying to save the woman he loved.

"He did it for her," she said.

The catlike creature grinned and nodded.

Fin didn't seem convinced. "That's just crazy."

Marrill shrugged. "I think it's romantic."

He pursed his lips. "Destroying the world is *not* romantic, Marrill."

She didn't argue. He had a point.

Fin turned back to the little Dzane. "So how does the Iron Tide have anything to do with Annalessa?"

The Dawn Wizard reached behind him, seemingly into a place that only he could see. Carefully, he unrolled the freshly minted Map to Everywhere. His eyes flitted over it, as new places bubbled into existence on its surface.

"This Map and the Pirate Stream are one and the same," he said. "By merging with the Compass Rose, Annalessa has become a part of the Map itself. That means she has become part of the Pirate Stream. Irrevocably intertwined in its existence."

He touched the Map's surface lovingly, a father stroking the cheek of a newborn child. "The Pirate Stream is all possibility. But the Iron Tide turns everything the same. And when all your possibilities are the same, well... there's really only one possibility, isn't there?"

All around, strange shapes gathered. The Dzane had drawn closer to listen. Marrill could feel the power of them vibrating in her teeth. It was the rich odor of ancient, the round flavor of wise. It felt like the sound of the wind coming down off old mountains.

When she looked up, the Dawn Wizard's eyes were deep purple crowned with carnelian, the color of clouds at sunrise. "If there is no possibility, there is no Pirate Stream. Your friend seems to believe that if there is no Pirate Stream, Annalessa will be released."

Marrill's heart roared in her ears as she struggled to understand. "So he's destroying the Stream with the Iron Tide—he's erasing all possibility—because he thinks it will save Annalessa."

The Dawn Wizard nodded.

"Will it work?" she asked, her voice barely more than a breath. "Will he be able to save her?"

"I don't imagine it matters," the Dawn Wizard said simply. "Do you?"

Marrill's eyes dropped. She felt tears clutching at the back of her throat. A hollowness seemed to open up inside her. She shuddered, thinking of everything turned into iron. Of a world without life, without color. Everything hard, nothing giving comfort. Even if Ardent was right, even if that would save Annalessa, what would be left of the world that would be worth living in?

The Dawn Wizard didn't exactly have lips that could smile. But his eyes turned a reassuring shade of blue, like the sky returning after a storm. "It's not all gloom. So long as there is one last possibility, there is hope. So long as one shard of potential remains, the iron can be thawed. The Stream can be re-formed."

Marrill perked up. Beside her, Fin straightened. "Thawed?" she asked. "As in, everything already turned to iron will be returned to normal?"

The Dawn Wizard nodded.

"So if we stop him now, the Stream and everyone the Tide has taken are saved," Fin said.

"Indeed," the little Dzane cheeped. "But when there are no more possibilities, when every last one is iron?" His voice grew softer. "Well, that's it."

Fin nodded. He leaned back on his tufted lily stool, his hand drifting to the hilt of the Evershear on his hip.

Marrill shuddered, torn between her love of Ardent and her horror at what he'd done and what he was trying to do now. At what they would have to do to stop him. She played with the edge of the table. "Is there any way to stop the Iron Tide *without* hurting Ardent?"

Fin pressed his lips together. His eyes were cold, determined. She understood why. He'd already lost so much to the Iron Tide: the Khaznot Quay, the Parsnickles, Fig. He was angry and upset—so was she. But that wasn't a reason to abandon Ardent.

She looked to Serth, waiting for him to say something— to back her up and defend his oldest friend. But he'd turned away, seemingly lost to his own thoughts and memories. Without a word, he stood and wandered across the spire, leaving Marrill to defend Ardent on her own. She clenched her hands into fists.

"Ardent's not a monster, Fin," she said to her friend angrily. He dropped his attention to his plate, where he'd been pushing around a bite of broiled chaos, which kept changing from solid to liquid to gas as he played with it.

"He's trying to save someone he loves," she added. Her voice cracked, and she looked away, her eyes misting. She bit her lip, memories of her mom coming unbidden to mind.

The Dawn Wizard came around the table and took her hand between his. He flicked at her fingers playfully. "We all love things, tomorrow's child. Sometimes, we define ourselves by them. Sometimes, when we decide that someone else makes us who we are, it seems like there is no point in going on without them."

He looked at her expectantly, like he was waiting for

her to figure something out. She frowned, thinking back through what he'd said. Then it hit her: He wasn't just talking about Ardent and Annalessa. He was talking about *her*. And her mom.

Marrill swallowed, trying hard not to get emotional as thoughts of her mother surged inside her. That was different, she told herself. All she needed to save her mom was a little Stream magic. It wasn't like *she* was the one about to destroy the world.

She could—she *would*—make her mom healthy again, and no one would get hurt in the process.

She drew a deep breath. "I just want to know if it's possible to save Ardent."

The Dawn Wizard cackled and spread his arms wide. "Of course it's possible. Everything is possible on the Pirate Stream." He tapped one claw against needle-sharp, black-tinged teeth. "Until it isn't, of course."

Marrill sat forward eagerly. "Then how do we save him?"

"You reach the man underneath the metal," the Dawn Wizard said, his gaze locked on hers. Again she could feel the energy dancing around him, buzzing against her skin.

"Cut through the metal and reach the man." Fin tightened his grip on the hilt of the Evershear. "That we already knew."

The Dawn Wizard's eyes drifted to the weapon. "Cut through the metal and reach the man," he repeated to himself. He twisted his lips. "A bit literal for my tastes, but it should do the trick."

Frustration bloomed within Marrill. They seemed to be missing the point. The question wasn't *how* to reach Ardent. It was how to do it without destroying him in the process. "Yes, but how do we use the Evershear *without killing* Ardent?"

"Hmm," the Dawn Wizard said. "That could be more tricky. But saving Ardent while stopping the Tide *is* a possibility. And in the Mirrorweb, where you're going, every possibility is a mirror. So I would suggest finding the mirror where you save your friend."

Marrill blinked, waiting for him to say more. "And then what?"

The Dzane rolled his paw in the air as though her question was unimportant. "Turn it into a reality. You'll know what to do when you get there."

Marrill gritted her teeth. She didn't quite understand how the creature could be both so helpful and yet so unhelpful at the same time. "So . . . how do we find the right mirror?"

The catlike Dzane stood tall, seeming to grow in size. The tips of his fur blazed, reflecting the shimmer of molten gold pouring in from the ocean that was below and above. For a moment it felt as though Marrill and the creature were the only two beings in the world.

Then he shrugged. "How should I know? I'm just an old trickster." His voiced buzzed like electricity in her thoughts, blocking out everything but the creature standing before her. "Find a guide or something."

"But..." Marrill started to protest, but the wizard's eyes began to swirl a darker ochre, and she remembered she was dealing with an insanely powerful creature. It would probably be best not to anger him too much. So instead she tried to give him her most pitiful "please help" look. The same look she gave her parents when she wanted extra dessert.

"Fine," he huffed. "It will be the final mirror." He held up a paw. "And before you ask, I know it will be the final one because once it's gone, the possibility of saving both Ardent and the Stream disappears. Ergo, up until that moment, that possibility will still exist."

Marrill tried to follow the logic, but her thoughts just ended in tangled knots. So she asked a simpler question. "How will we know which mirror is the final one?"

The Dawn Wizard looked at her for a long moment, then dragged a claw between his pointy teeth to dislodge a bit of food. He waited a moment longer and then said, "All the rest of them will be covered in iron."

Marrill's cheeks heated. "Oh. Right. But if we find that last mirror... that's it?" she asked. "Find the right mirror, reach the man under the armor, save Ardent?"

The Dawn Wizard winked his larger eye. "More or less." His whiskers danced with amusement.

Relief washed over her, hope surging in its wake. She jumped up and spun toward Fin, her heart hammering with excitement. "Let's go mirror hunting!"

When she turned back, the Dawn Wizard's muzzle was

mere inches from her face. His needle-sharp teeth nearly touched her skin. If he breathed at all, she couldn't feel it.

"But don't forget," he said, "you now stand between all creation and an unending tide of unyielding metal. When the time comes, you must not hesitate." His eyes turned from gold to midnight, flames seeming to dance beneath them.

"If you can't save him," he said, "strike him down."

⊢⊦ ⊦ ⊦⊣

"Check it out," Remy shouted as Marrill and Fin reboarded the *Kraken*. "The Brains-of-Neb here rigged this thing to fly permanently!" She nodded toward a Dzane shaped like a cloud of eyes hovering next to her.

As Marrill watched, the cloud resolved into a mouth and started speaking. "It's still fueled on belief, remember," it said. "Away from here, it might actually *eat* belief, so I would say use this capability sparingly."

"I can fly forever," Remy insisted. But then her shoulders drooped. "Wish Coll could see this." Her hands tightened into fists. "Stupid Sheshefesh," she growled under her breath.

The Dawn Wizard's whiskers twitched with amusement as he perched at the top of the gangplank. "Is the Sheshefesh still causing problems that far in the future?"

Remy's jaw tightened. "He stole our captain."

The Dawn Wizard let out a cackle. "What, that little

squid? Here," he said, beckoning Remy closer, "let me tell you something about him you might find...helpful."

Marrill couldn't hear what the Dawn Wizard told her babysitter-turned-captain, but when he stepped back, Remy was smiling.

Then the little Dzane's eyes landed on Fin. He paused, tilting his head. His finger pointed toward a torn scrap of parchment poking out of the thief's bag slung around Fin's hip. His voice shook a little as he spoke. "Is that... my Map?"

Fin glanced down. "Yeah... the version from our time," he said, pulling it free.

The Dawn Wizard's hands opened and closed by his side. "May I see it?" he asked. In his eyes, a pale wind blew, scattering away all trace of color.

"Oh," Fin said sheepishly as he held it out. "Uh...it's kind of broken, though."

The Dawn Wizard took the Map carefully in his hands, turning it over. The hole in the center was just as ragged as it had been when the Lost Sun had burned it there. Splotches of Sheshefesh ink and stained dream ribbon still clung to it—signs of Ardent's efforts to repair it at the Font of Meres.

The Dawn Wizard peered through the hole with one now-golden eye. "So I see," he said. With one claw, he hooked the dream ribbon and drew it across the torn surface. Then he flicked his hands, and the hole disappeared.

Marrill let out an awed breath, her eyes going wide. "You fixed it? Just like that?"

The Dawn Wizard lifted a shoulder. "I just stitched up the tear. But it still isn't whole. Without the Compass Rose, it's not much use, I'm afraid."

Marrill slapped her palm against her forehead. "Rose." Of course the Map wouldn't work without her. That's why it was still blank.

The Dawn Wizard handed the Map back to Fin with a wink. "At least it looks nicer now, don't you think?"

"Thanks," Fin said, tucking it back in his bag. "I think."

The Dawn Wizard started toward the spire. Marrill trotted across the deck to catch up with him. "So this is good-bye?" she asked.

The catlike mouth grinned. His teeth sparkled with a strange, inner light. "In a manner of speaking." He gripped Marrill's wrist. "Remember," he told her, "so long as there is one possibility, there are all possibilities." Then he was down the gangplank and gone.

"All aboard!" Remy called through cupped hands.

Serth glanced up from what appeared to be a jovial conversation he'd been having with a shaggy Dzane that looked like a cross between a small woolly mammoth and a golden retriever walking on hind legs. Laughter still played around the wizard's eyes as he clapped the Dzane on the back and bade him good-bye before starting toward the *Kraken*. Whatever had bothered him earlier seemed entirely forgotten.

The Naysayer lumbered behind him, pausing at the table

festooned with food to scoop up as many of the treats as he could. "Smell you later," he grunted to the Dawn Wizard as he shuffled past.

With everyone on board, the Ropebone Man cast off the last of the moorings, freeing the ship from the spire. Marrill watched from the bow as the *Enterprising Kraken* headed out, down toward the whirlpool below.

"Have fun in the Mirrorweb!" the Dawn Wizard called after them. "Good luck saving everything!"

Marrill waved good-bye reluctantly. Down below, a swirling funnel of gold waited to suck them into a place where even the Dzane refused to follow.

CHAPTER 12
MirrorwebewrorriM

The *Kraken* tilted. Fin gripped a rope as the deck slanted beneath him. The hole in the sea opened up around them. The thick magic made it less like being sucked down a whirlpool, and more like being swallowed by a snake. Slowly, bit by bit, they descended into a world of molten gold.

Fin couldn't pinpoint the moment when everything looked exactly the same. But in that moment he couldn't pinpoint, everything changed. At the bottom, which was really the top, which was really the middle, the Map to Everywhere yawned open. Fin couldn't see it, but he could *feel* it, a knowledge that pulsed upward through the raw magic and settled into his brain. The gold walls closed in...

...and time and place didn't seem to matter anymore...

....or even...exist. Everything seemed to...

...draw out...

At first, he was sure they weren't moving.

Then

   he   rising.

     was   were   .

       sure   they   .

         they   sworn   .

           were   have   .

             falling.   he'd   Weren't they?

            Then,

He was sure they weren't moving. At first.

Fin's thoughts stretched out and surrounded him. He read them like they were printed on a scroll.

All we need to do is sneak in, find the Master, swipe him with the Evershear and let nature take its course, his thoughts read.

He nodded. Smart.

And find the mirror on the way and save Ardent, too.

Fin frowned. That thought was Marrill's. He grabbed for another one.

Great, if we can. But we have to do what we have to do. We can't let ourselves get sidetracked, or the whole Pirate Stream may be lost.
We will probably have to kill Ardent but I shouldn't tell Marrill that.

Wait, can she read my thoughts too?
Uh-oh, this small type says way more than I meant to.

He grabbed for the next thought in frantic slow motion.

But we have to save Ardent! He's our friend, and deep down he's an amazing person. We have to save him!
I can and I can't believe you, Fin.
You can't just let someone go because if you can then what about my mom?

Fin felt the blood rising, drawing up his neck and into his face in a slow-motion flush of embarrassment. Another one of his thoughts stretched between them, its subtext snagging on one of Marrill's

Sorry, Marrill. You're right, of course.
I think I'm right but I don't want to hurt you. I want to save Ardent, but I want to stop the Iron Tide and save the Parsnickles and Fig more. I really hope you understand but it's easier to pretend to give up than to try and explain.

It's okay. We just need to find that mirror before we find Ardent, that's all!
I'd rather not fight. IhopeIhopeIhope. And then we never have to fight!
IhopeIhopeIhopeIhope.

Fin nodded confidently. The gold world swirled and stretched around them and inside them. Another final thought wrapped up and around him.

No problem, it read. *How hard could it be to find?*

And then time snapped back into place,

and they were in another place and time.

They were surrounded by an endless jungle, up, down, around, sideways. Everywhere he looked, everything was trees, leaves, branches, leaves, vines, leaves. Green on green on green, infinite and indistinguishable. Impossible and impenetrable. Yet at the same time, it all seemed to be off at a short distance, like the *Kraken* was somehow sailing in an empty space in the middle.

"Huh," Fin said. Not a mirror in sight. This wasn't what he'd been expecting. Beside him, Marrill appeared just as confused.

And then, with a horrible grinding crash, the *Kraken* ran aground.

Fin pinwheeled his arms, struggling to stay on his feet. The ship pitched to one side, only to smash into something *else*.

"What's going on?" Marrill yelled, grabbing his arm to steady herself. "What are we hitting?"

From the quarterdeck, Remy waved a hand wildly. Strange shadows speckled her face. "Full stop!" she screamed.

The sails eased. The ship lurched to a halt. Fin raced to the port railing, looking over to see what they'd run into.

Just below the main deck, a huge, angled corner of glass had scratched a line across the *Kraken*'s hull. Inside the glass, jungle trees waved in a breeze he couldn't feel. He looked up, watching the same trees wave in the same rhythm right beside him. But for the fact that he could see the glass gouging the *Kraken*'s hull, he'd have thought they were a single forest stretching out in an unbroken line.

Fin tilted his head, changing his perspective. It was a

reflection, he realized. He'd seen the trick before, when the *Kraken* had stopped once in the PrestidigiNations, where real magic was considered rude and sleight of hand was the height of fashion. Mirrors set at the proper angles could create illusions—set two mirrors a few feet apart, and a man could appear to vanish into thin air just by walking between them.

Ardent had been the one to explain it to him, Fin recalled, his stomach twisting at the memory. He shook his head, pushing the thought away, and paced down the length of the *Kraken*. As he moved, the angles between the mirrors surrounding them changed, allowing him to figure out where one ended and another began.

Unfortunately, they were everywhere. Up, down, all around. Sticking out like the jagged tips of icebergs; twisted around the *Kraken* in multifaceted strands. He squinted at the trees. Sure enough, they didn't just look alike—they were identical. One forest, reflected across a billion mirrors, stretching out all around them as far as he could see.

"It's the same thing over and over," Fin murmured.

"Variations on a theme, actually," Serth said, slipping up behind him. "Reflections of endless possibilities. Look closer."

Fin squinted. For the most part, the trees themselves were fairly uninteresting. Painfully boring, even. But then he saw a spot where the trees in the mirror shivered, their bark bristling like fur on an angry dog. In the next mirror over, the exact same trees waved, only now he was confident they were actually sculptures made from copper and gemstones. Next to *them*, the trees were real—with a colony of ruby-colored birds building a small city in the branches.

Above, the same birds were going to war with a troupe of howling monkeys. To the left, the very same monkeys were hosting the birds in a friendly sporting match, and everyone was being exceedingly polite.

"What is this place?" Fin whispered, craning his neck to take it all in.

"Welcome to the Mirrorweb." Serth held his arms wide, in a gesture eerily reminiscent of Ardent. "Refuge of the Master of the Iron Ship, prison of the Lost Sun of Dzannin, and the essence of the Pirate Stream made literal."

Marrill leaned in beside them. Carefully she reached toward the trees. Her hand stopped, and her finger traced down the edge of another mirror. Fin could see the surface now that she was touching it, a dagger tip jutting up from under the ship. But if he hadn't known to look, the maze of reflections would have rendered it nearly invisible.

"What are we seeing?" Marrill asked.

Serth strode slowly across the deck, his eyes flitting from surface to surface. "Possibilities," he said. "They are what was, what is, and, most importantly, what *could* be.

The Stream is the raw potential to be anything. Here in the Mirrorweb, all the things it can be are reflected."

Fin's eyes darted from one image to the next. In one mirror, the leaves seemed bright, practically shining with cheer. In another, they were shaded, dark, and dripping with menace. Here, the trees were on fire; there the trees *were* fire.

"Pretty spiff," he said, "but how come everything is trees?"

Serth snorted a laugh. "Because," he said, "we are looking at a reflection of the *Kraken*."

Fin whipped his head around. He searched all the images. With the exception of a small copse of wood far above them where the monkeys had apparently invaded the birds by the sea, not a single ship could be seen. He started to wonder if they'd been too quick to declare Serth recovered from drinking Stream water.

"I don't—"

"It's the wood," Marrill interrupted. She motioned to a huge tree, distorted to enormous size in what he could see now was a long, curved mirror. There was nothing really special about it. In fact, just looking at it made him want to yawn.

Understanding hit him in a rush. It *was* boring. So boring that even pure magic couldn't make it more interesting. It was the only thing that could stand up to the waters of the

Stream—the stuff streamrunning vessels were made from. "Dullwood!"

"Indeed," Serth said, smiling as though pleased they'd figured it out. "We are looking at the reflection of the *Enterprising Kraken* as it was when it was still a tree not yet harvested. Remember, the Mirrorweb is a place apart from the current of time. Past possibilities live here, too."

Fin continued studying the many mirrors. In one, the leaves shifted shape, twisting like hands forming sign language. Apparently, it was possible that even dullwood might have once been interesting.

Snorting at the thought, he noticed that in the gaps between the mirrors he could see more mirrors, and beyond them even more mirrors, and more and more, and all of them were trees. Every mirror he could see represented only what was possible for this one single stand of woods at this one single point in time, and it still stretched to infinity.

He almost staggered at the enormity of it all. And then he sucked in a breath as he realized the implications. To save Ardent, they had to find a single mirror in a labyrinth of mirrors that was literally endless. It wasn't just hard.

It was impossible.

Next to him, Marrill's shoulders drooped sadly, and he realized she must have come to the same conclusion. He tried to figure out what he could say to comfort her, but before he opened his mouth, her eyes filled with tears and she turned away.

He understood her reluctance. But the reality was that it was looking more and more like there was only one way to solve this problem.

The Master had to go—and Ardent, it seemed, with him. No more hesitating. No more wavering.

Of course, to do that they needed to first find the Master, which presented its own set of challenges. Fin peered out at infinite variations of one tiny place on one tiny island at one tiny spot in a river of magic that went on forever, hoping to spot a lead. "The Master's got to be out there somewhere...."

"Indeed," Serth said. "As is the Iron Tide. Creeping through these possibilities, turning the mirrors dark." He paused, letting the image sink in.

With a heavy heart, Fin scanned the reflected forest around the ship. Every mirror showed a world that was wondrous and strange and maybe sometimes scary, but unique. He didn't want to think about them all disappearing, one by one.

"Well," Serth said, clapping his hands together and breaking the gravity of the moment. "We should get moving. I will guide us. I've been here before, after all."

"Can you help us find the mirror that will save Ardent?" Marrill asked cautiously.

The tall wizard looked down at her, sympathy in his eyes. He raised a hand, and let it hover for a moment before tentatively patting her shoulder. "I could *try*," he said. "But it would be difficult, and I doubt we would succeed."

"Well then," Marrill said, bouncing up and down with renewed energy. "Like you said, we should get moving!"

Fin shook his head sharply. He'd heard what Serth had said. The Iron Tide was out there, turning mirrors dark. Taking possibilities, like it had taken Fig and the Parsnickles and would take the dullwood forests. "Slow your tailwinds," he told her. "This is about stopping the Iron Tide. We need to head for *the Master*, not waste time hunting for some mirror."

"But we said earlier—" Marrill started.

Fin could see where she was headed, and he leapt in to cut her off at the pass. They talked over each other in a jumble.

"That was *earlier*—"

"—we were going—"

"—things have changed—"

"—you can't just give up—"

"—you can't just *abandon*—"

Remy called their attention with a sharp whistle. She was standing right behind them. For some reason, she'd donned gloves and covered her face and forehead with bandannas, leaving not even an inch of bare skin.

"Uh, Remy?" Marrill started. "What are you wearing?"

The older girl cut her off with a sharp swipe of her hand. "I don't like the glare," she said.

Fin frowned. "On your whole body? Ouch!"

Remy jabbed him straight in the ribs. "No more questions." The look in her eyes practically dared either one of them to speak. When they remained silent, she nodded.

"Okay, first things first: How are we supposed to sail our way through this?" She waved toward the reflections. "We'll run into a billion mirrors and break the ship into pieces. Plus, our luck's not exactly that great already...."

As one, they looked to the wizard and self-proclaimed guide. He lifted a shoulder. "Last time I was here I was on foot."

Fin rolled his eyes. "Great," he muttered.

"Well, we better figure something out," Remy said. "Infinite shades of infinite possibilities or whatever these things may be to you, it all looks the same from my perspective. And if we can't move on, we're stuck."

"Fine," Fin said, stalking back to the starboard side of the ship and craning his neck up, down, and around. It really was impossible to tell where one mirror ended and another began. But they had to start somewhere.

He unfocused his vision, letting it blur, searching for any gaps large enough to sail through. He thought he saw one farther right. "Go that way," he said, pointing.

Remy narrowed her eyes at him. Or at least, he thought she did—it was hard to tell with all the wrappings covering her face. "You sure?"

No, he thought to himself. Instead he shot her his most confident smirk. "Of course," he said. "What kind of a question is that?"

The captain glanced to Marrill, who stood on the other side of the *Kraken*, chewing her lip. "Half sails," Remy called to the pirats. Several of the sails fell into place. The air around the ship may have been as still as death, but the sails overhead puffed to life. The ship began to shift forward, letting out a horrific screech as her hull scraped across the mirror they'd run aground on.

They'd gone about a dozen yards when another mirror clipped the top of the mainmast. The moonraker's yardarm splintered. Remy let out an angry growl, aimed firmly at Fin.

"Don't hit that," he offered. Her look was a knife blade. "Kidding," he muttered. "I meant, veer farther starboard."

"No, wait!" Marrill countered. "We need to go down."

"Why?" Fin scoffed with a shake of his head. He waved his hands behind his back in a *no* signal to Remy.

"So we don't—" Marrill was cut off by a long rip of a sail caught on a mirror's sharp corner. It was followed by exasperated squeals as pirats rushed to assess the damage. "Hit that," she finished.

Scowling at Fin, Marrill fisted her hands on her hips. Clearly their argument from earlier still simmered between them. "Like I said," she called to Remy, "you should dive. Dive!"

"This isn't a submarine, Marrill." Remy swung the wheel, and the deck tilted as the large ship slid sideways, slamming them against another mirror.

Fin lifted his eyebrows at Marrill in a not terribly subtle *I told you so*.

Her glower deepened. She spun back to the railing. Fin did the same. "Pull up and head straight," she called to Remy. At the same time Fin shouted, "Make a hard turn port!"

The ship groaned. The timbers stressed as the *Kraken* rose and banked to the left. The hull clipped another mirror just below the forecastle, shattering a few windows along the port side. "Guys, you're not helping!" Remy yelled.

"Down! Down!" Fin cried.

"No! Up!" Marrill shouted.

A horrible sound filled the air as the ship's keel scraped across the face of a mirror. Fin threw his hands in the air and spun to face Marrill. They both started in on each other.

"What are you—"

"I know what I'm—"

"Doing!"

"Let me—"

"Why don't you just—"

"Finish!"

"I'm telling you—"

"Seriously, though—"

Something shifted in the corner of Fin's vision. He turned his head just in time to see a massive mirror looming directly in their path. Marrill must have seen the same thing because her eyes grew huge. They glanced at each other, their argument immediately forgotten.

"UP!" they both cried at once.

Remy didn't hesitate. Fin felt his entire body grow heavy as the deck lifted, the force of their climb almost flattening him. He let out a long breath as the keel cleared the mirror.

"Should I go to my cabin, or are you about done killing us?" Serth asked, inspecting his fingernails.

Fin sneered, though mostly it was due to his injured pride. At least the Naysayer wasn't on deck to join the heckling.

"You could help, you know," Marrill snapped at the wizard.

Serth merely lifted a shoulder. "Meh."

She caught Fin's eye, and they shared a moment of mutual exasperation before turning back to the navigation. Up ahead and to the left, a clear break emerged between the mirrors. "Go that way!" Fin called. He thrust his finger in the air, and the ship tilted toward it.

But as they grew closer, the gap shifted and narrowed. No way they were going to make it through.

Before he could shout a warning, Marrill yelled,

"Starboard, fifteen degrees." The ship shifted, and they soared between the two mirrors with barely any room to spare.

Fin grinned at her. "Nice one, Marrill."

She smiled back. "It was an optical illusion. You just couldn't see it from your perspective."

Suddenly, it hit him. He couldn't see it—he'd been looking at it all wrong. "That's it!" he said, snapping his fingers. "It's all about perspective! What I see from my angle is completely different from what you see from your angle."

Her eyes widened with understanding. "Of course. And if we work together—"

"We can navigate through the Mirrorweb!" he finished. They beamed at each other.

"That's great and all, but—" Remy was cut off by the screeching splintering of another yardarm as they sideswiped a mirror.

"Port thirty degrees," Marrill called from her side of the ship. "Down about eight o'clock."

Remy spun the wheel. The reflections in the mirrors bent and twisted as the ship dropped past them. Fin saw exactly where they were headed—and that the angle between the two mirrors made the gap look wider near the top than it really was. "Down more like seven o'clock," he corrected.

His stomach lifted into his throat as the deck tilted and

they plummeted like they were crashing down a steep wave. "Pull up and turn ten degrees port on my mark," Marrill shouted. "Annnnnnnnnnnnnd now!"

The *Kraken* bottomed out and Fin cringed, waiting for a crash. But there was nothing—they slipped between the two mirrors with room to spare. Marrill laughed, and Fin realized she was right. This was kind of fun, now that they were getting the hang of it.

He'd forgotten how well they worked together.

Remy called for full sails as Fin and Marrill continued shouting directions. The ship gained speed, the images on the mirrors blurring as the *Kraken* sped past. They slipped in and around, up and over, under and behind endless mirrors. Some were larger than mountains, others smaller than Fin's pinkie.

"It's incredible," he said.

Serth nodded. "And every single one of them represents a possibility." He stood at the bow, arms folded, staring out at the flashing images. "A different life. A separate destiny. A thing that could be."

Maybe somewhere in this web, Fin thought, he wasn't a Fade. Maybe somewhere he was remembered by everyone he met. Maybe his mother was still alive, and she hadn't abandoned him, and he still lived with her. Maybe in a cottage by the sea.

But then, even if that mirror did exist, even if that

possibility was out there, it didn't matter. Not really. *Could be* or *might have been*; if they didn't stop the Master, every single possibility would turn to iron.

His jaw clenched, some of the fun leaching out of the adventure. Up ahead, their path narrowed to a gap. It looked, from his perspective, wide enough for them to slip through. He pointed it out to Remy, who slowed the ship as they glided toward it. Marrill didn't call for them to change course, so he shifted his attention to the next obstacle.

And was completely blindsided when the *Kraken* slammed into a mirror, catching the edge of it with the starboard bow not three feet from where Marrill stood. The deck buckled, the dullwood groaning in protest as the ship ground to a halt. Everyone was thrown from their feet.

On instinct, Fin tucked and rolled, popping back up almost instantly. He shot a look toward Remy, who was using the wheel to pull herself up. Serth floated for a moment just off the deck, before settling down again. Marrill, meanwhile, had pushed herself to her hands and knees. Beside her the railing was splintered, resting against the unyielding surface of a mirror.

Fin had no idea how they'd managed to crash into it. There was no way Marrill could have missed it, and he had no idea why she hadn't steered them away.

"Marrill, you okay?" he asked, jogging over to her. She didn't seem to hear him as she pushed herself to standing.

When he reached her, her eyes were glazed, glistening with tears. His heart seized. "Marrill, are you hurt?"

She raised a trembling finger to the mirror. A woman moved within the glass. An older woman, but with features that were undeniably familiar.

"Fin," Marrill whispered. "It's my mom."

CHAPTER 13
The Woman in the Glass

Marrill had recognized her immediately, though she looked different than she'd ever seen her. The laugh lines around her eyes were deeper set, her skin papery thin and creased with soft wrinkles. Her white hair was tucked up in a loose scarf with a few wisps drifting across her face in the soft breeze. She sat on a bench outside what looked like a museum, and she was smiling, her hands clasped tight against her chest as she tilted her head back in a laugh.

It was Marrill's mother. Alive. Healthy. *Old.*

Beside her sat Marrill's father, also much, much older than when Marrill had left them. He held a book, and his eyes twinkled as he read aloud from it. Then he paused and glanced up. Marrill couldn't see what had caught his attention, but he stood, grinning widely. Her mom opened her arms, beckoning someone Marrill couldn't see to come in for a hug.

That's when Marrill knew. It was *her.* Marrill herself. Right there, just out of sight.

Her eyes blurred with tears, and her knees wobbled, threatening to collapse. It was all so perfect. So beautiful. Her heart almost burst with the desire for it to be real. She reached out, desperate to brush her fingers against the scene. But her touch hovered millimeters above it. Because she knew all she'd feel would be glass, and it would be proof that this possibility was beyond her reach. She couldn't bear that.

A pang of longing splintered in her heart, so sharp it was practically physical. Beside her, Fin shifted. Marrill swiped tears from her eyes as she turned to him. "It's my mom," she said again, almost choking on the word. She could see the heartbreak and sympathy in his eyes. The sorrow.

"I'm sorry," he said softly.

Didn't he understand, though? There was nothing to be sorry about. A laugh bubbled inside her, and she let it escape.

"Fin," she said, "this is great news! It means my mother is still alive! She's...healthy."

"In this possibility, at least," Serth said quietly, coming up behind them.

Marrill's eyes drifted back to the mirror, greedily taking in the image of her mom as an old woman. "How do I make it real?" she asked.

"It can be done," the wizard told her. "With a great deal of effort, possibilities *can* become realities." A touch of reverence entered his voice. "That's what magic is all about."

Next to her, Fin chuckled. "Wow, look at you."

She shot him a glare, but he wasn't looking at her. Not *here* her, anyway. Instead he was craning his head, spinning slowly as he took in the mirrors around the ship. "Is that a two-eyed Karnelius as a kitten?" he asked, pointing.

She looked up. Sure enough, in a small mirror off to her left, a tiny orange kitten lounged on its back in a sun patch. As she watched, he stretched, back toes curling and arms stretching far overhead. With a *mrrrrp* he yawned, both eyes going wide as though surprised by the size of it.

She'd recognize Karnelius anywhere, but she'd never known him this young. Beside him, in another mirror, he bounded around her parents' bedroom, both eyes still intact but sporting a bobbed tail.

"Look at you!" Remy squealed. "So cute with pigtails!" The babysitter was looking at a mirror showing Marrill dancing with a baby chimpanzee. In the background a sign read BANTON PARK LIVE-IN ANIMAL RESCUE RESERVE AND PLAYGROUND FORTRESS. It's where she'd been planning to go before her mother got sick again, forcing them to stay in Arizona.

Marrill peered at this alternate self. She seemed happy, definitely. But there was still a small spark of loneliness in her eyes that she'd never realized was there. If they'd gone to the Banton Park Animal Rescue Reserve, she realized, she'd have never found her way onto the Pirate Stream. She'd have never met Fin, never found a best friend.

She shook her head, clearing the thought. Her eyes drifted back to the mirror with her mom as an old woman. A *healthy* old woman.

Remy touched her arm lightly. "Marrill, honey, we have to keep moving."

Marrill shook her hand off. "Wait, just a minute longer." The splintered railing pressed into her hips as she leaned against it, trying to get as close as possible to the scene in the mirror. As though she could somehow fall in and become a part of it.

After another moment, Fin cleared his throat. "Marrill—"

"Just hold on," she snapped.

The silence behind her was strained, but she didn't care. This might be the last chance she ever got to see her mother alive and healthy. To watch the laugh lines around her eyes crinkle, to experience the love in her smile. Tears blurred her vision. She swiped them away, wanting nothing to mar the perfect scene unfolding in the reflection.

But even after drying her eyes, the image of her mother appeared dull, blurred along the edges. The color seemed to drain away. The trees that had been blooming so brilliantly in the background grew limp, leaching to a monochromatic gray.

She pulled the hem of her shirt over her hand, leaning forward to wipe at the mirror's surface, thinking that maybe she'd gotten too close—that she'd smudged it or her breath had fogged it.

Just before she touched the mirror, long fingers wrapped around her elbow. "Don't touch it," Serth commanded, pulling her away.

She whirled on him, blood raging hot. But the words died in her throat when she saw the dead certainty in his black eyes. Saw the terror on Fin's face beside him. Saw Remy standing frozen, staring toward the stern.

A horrible feeling seeped into Marrill's stomach. In the distance, back where they'd come from, the Mirrorweb had grown darker. The light that had once blazed within the lush jungle behind them had dimmed.

Turning dull. Gray.

Marrill's heart froze. Not dull, she realized. Metallic.

The Iron Tide.

"I do not know if the Tide can take us in here," Serth said, "but I strongly suggest we not find out. Captain?"

Remy jolted into action, sprinting toward the quarter-deck, shouting, "Full sail, now!"

Serth waved a hand, and an unfelt wind filled the sails. Tackle squealed as the Ropebone Man tightened the lines. The *Kraken* began to shift, her hull shuddering as she scraped against the mirror beside them.

The mirror with Marrill's mom.

Already they were pulling away. "Wait!" Marrill wasn't ready to say good-bye. Not yet.

"I'm sorry, Marrill," Fin said, "but we don't have time."

She glanced back at the oncoming Tide. It washed across the mirrors behind them, coating everything with metal. Turning whole worlds to iron. Erasing possibilities.

Soon it would erase her mother—erase the possibility of Marrill saving her.

No! This was what Marrill had come to the Stream to find! This was why she'd stayed to fight the Master in the first place, instead of going home when she'd had the chance. If the Iron Tide took this mirror, then everything she'd done had been for nothing.

Another groan echoed from the bowels of the ship. The railing along the mirror splintered even more as the ship strained forward.

"I think there's a gap up there," Fin called to Remy, pointing. Marrill didn't even bother looking. She couldn't take her eyes off her mother. Even though the mirror had begun to tarnish around the edges. Even though the sky in the world had shifted from a deep blue to a menacing gray. Even though red lightning rippled through clouds as they closed in fast.

Marrill's heart screamed. The *Kraken* had started to inch forward, forcing Marrill to shuffle along the railing to stay with the reflection of her mother. She couldn't leave it—she wasn't ready to say good-bye. She wanted to pry the mirror from the web and carry it with her. If only there was some way to cut it free!

"Hold on!" Remy called. Without Marrill and Fin to help navigate, the *Kraken* banked against another mirror, and the deck listed hard to port. Fin grabbed Marrill as they stumbled to keep their balance. Their legs tangled and something solid whacked against her knee with a crack.

She winced, and when she looked to see what had struck her, she noticed the glass sheath at his hip.

Her eyes widened. The Evershear. A blade that could cut anything. Of course!

She acted before she even thought about it. She reached for the bone handle. Fin yelped, leaping back as she drew the blade free. She could hear the sails billowing, feel the ship gaining speed. The mirror with her mom was sliding away.

Marrill raced down the length of the ship after it. She was almost at the stern when she caught up. Already the

Iron Tide had crept into the frame. It oozed in the distance behind her mother, seeping toward her.

The blade practically sung as Marrill swung it through the air.

"Marrill!" Serth shouted.

The edge of the mirror burst in a shower of golden sparks. Energy vibrated up her arm, setting fire to the tips of her nerves. There was a shattering sound, so loud it sent a shock wave rolling through her. She swung again, the booming growing louder with each strike.

She was dimly aware of someone shouting her name. It was Fin, standing several yards away. Too afraid of the Evershear to come any closer. "Watch out!" he cried, pointing.

The rumor vines twined around the stern railing repeated his warning.

watchoutmarrillwatchoutmarrillwatchmarrillwatch

She looked up as the large mirror she'd been attacking let out a thunderous groan. It tilted toward her with a series of loud *pop*s, as if pulling free from the very fabric of reality itself.

The world around her seemed to slow. Marrill stood frozen with her head thrown back, staring at the reflection above.

Her mother pushed herself up from the bench, one hand

outstretched toward future Marrill, just outside the frame. A hand entered the picture, then a wrist and an arm. Marrill sucked in a breath, waiting to see herself. But the Iron Tide got there first. It took the figure standing outside the frame—freezing future Marrill's fingers into an outstretched iron claw.

"No!" Marrill cried. The rumor vines took up her call, echoing her plea:

No No Noooo No No Nooo No No No

"Marrill," Fin whispered, coming up on one side. On the other, she could feel Serth's shadow reaching for her.

The *Kraken* continued to gain speed even as the mirror continued to fall toward Marrill. About to crush her. But she didn't care. She only cared that her mother's hand still reached for her, her fingers still alive.

Marrill swung the Evershear one last time. In rage. In pain. In desperation.

The world exploded in a shower of golden sparks. The stern dipped, the deck twisted as the mirror crashed against the railing, splintering it. But the *Kraken* was moving fast enough, and Remy spun the wheel sharply enough, that the mirror only struck a glancing blow before falling away.

And then it was gone.

Marrill stood, the Evershear by her side, breathing hard

as she stared at the empty space that had once held the possibility of saving her mother.

She'd failed.

Serth's arm fell across her shoulder, its touch surprisingly tender. But he said nothing, just let her be. Gentle fingers brushed Marrill's hand as Fin took the Evershear and carefully resheathed it on his hip.

"It'll be okay, Marrill," Fin told her. "You'll get another chance to save her."

savehermarrillchancetosavehersavemarrill

Her throat burned too much to respond. She wanted to believe him, but in her heart she knew he was wrong. Even if the Tide hadn't taken the mirror, she'd cut it free of the Stream. Cut it free from the realm of possibilities. That future, the one with her mom healthy, holding her arms wide for Marrill to hug her, was lost now, forever.

Because of her.

A shudder rippled across the deck as the *Kraken* careened off another mirror, jolting sideways. "A little help?" Remy called, her voice strained.

"Come," Serth said, his arm falling from her shoulders. "We must look forward." He turned and left them. Fin moved to follow. But Marrill's feet felt leaden. She wanted to curl up, put her arms over her head, and hide from the world.

If she did, though, the Master would destroy everything else she loved. *Including* Ardent. She couldn't let that
happen.

"Hey," Fin said, his voice nearly silent. "You coming?"

Marrill tried to force a smile, but couldn't quite manage.
"Right behind you."

behindyourightyoubehindright

Fin nodded. As if knowing she needed to be alone for a
moment, he scampered toward the bow to help navigate.

Marrill remained where she was, looking back. Watching as the Iron Tide swept across the gap that had once held
her possible future. Watching it swallow all the other possibilities as well.

Marrill let out a long sigh, then turned and started
after Fin. Her foot struck something, sending it skitter-
ing across the deck. Light glinted from its surface as it
spun.

A shard of glass. She crouched to get a better look.
And her heart lurched. Because there was her mother. Still
laughing. Still alive. Still healthy and old. No trace of the
Iron Tide anywhere.

"Mom," she whispered.

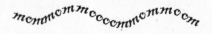

Marrill snatched up the sliver, turning it in her hands, trying to understand. She must have cut it free from the mirror as it was falling toward the *Kraken*. It didn't seem to matter that it was just a fragment of the whole; the possibility contained inside was still complete in every way. Every piece of a broken mirror was a mirror in and of itself, she realized.

Marrill closed her eyes, breathed deep. For a long moment, she allowed a fire of hope to blaze inside her. She'd succeeded. Her ideal future was safe in her hands. They just needed to stop the Master, and then she could make this possibility real.

She'd found a way to save her mom after all.

She was so focused on the shard and what it meant, Marrill didn't feel the hair along her arms begin to stand on end, or the tingle at the nape of her neck. Not until it was too late.

The world around her exploded in a flash of red, knocking her off her feet. A thunderous roar shook the *Kraken*, rattling the mirrors strung throughout the web. Marrill had just enough time to shove the shard in her pocket before the *Kraken* lurched, sending her tumbling.

She clutched at the stern railing, her stomach roiling as the deck pitched and rolled like it might in the worst of storms. She almost expected to hear the crash of waves and feel the drenching rain. But the Mirrorweb was devoid of such things.

A streak of crimson split the air behind them, arcing from one mirror to the next. It was followed by another and another, a web of red lightning dancing between the mirrors. The bolts blasted across iron and glass with an energy so intense Marrill's teeth hummed.

She held her breath. She knew what was happening, even before the lightning web parted. Even before the iron prow hove into view, or before her ears rang with the clanging of the chain-mail sails.

He was here.

The Master of the Iron Ship had arrived.

CHAPTER 14
Striking Distance

Alarm sent Fin's heart into overdrive. The Iron Ship bore down, its razor-sharp hull towering above them, poised to sever the *Kraken* in two. The Master stood at her stern, legs braced, the iron cage holding Rose clutched in his hand.

Remy screamed.

"Brace yourselves!" Serth shouted.

The next thing Fin knew, he was falling. The entire ship barrel-rolled, turning upside down. Lines sprang from the rigging, Ropebone Man grabbing items and crew and pirats as they tumbled free. But as usual, Ropebone wouldn't remember Fin. He was on his own.

He fumbled for his skysails, frantically tugging the strings and throwing his arms wide. The material caught, slowing his fall. But there was no wind in the Mirrorweb—at least none that Fin could feel—which made it next to impossible to steer.

At least he was no longer plummeting to his death, he thought. Even if he wasn't quite sure how he'd make it back to the *Kraken*. She'd continued forward, completely upside down. The Iron Ship crashed past her, their keels scraping against each other with a grinding screech.

"Not so fast, Plus One! No kid goes missing on my watch," Remy called. She cupped a hand around her mouth. "Man overboard, Ropebone!"

A line shot from the ship and snaked around Fin's ankle. He'd barely let out a relieved breath when it pulled tight, snapping him forward. He tumbled, dragged behind the *Kraken* as she slalomed through the maze of mirrors.

Beside him, Marrill dangled from a rope of her own. "YooooOoOoOoOu ooOoOkAaAaAYyYy??" she asked.

Up ahead, a huge scaly face burst out of a porthole. "Hey, hey, *hey!*" yelled the Naysayer. "Ancient being trying to *nap* down here."

He looked back at Marrill and Fin flailing through the air, then over at the Iron Ship, smashing through the glass maze of infinite mirrors. "Eh," he said. "I can sleep through this." And just like that, he was gone again.

Fin tumbled through the air, trying desperately to regain some control. Beside him, Marrill wrestled herself upright. She took the rope between her hands, leaning back with her feet splayed out beneath her. She wasn't exactly standing on anything... but then again, the ships weren't exactly sailing through anything, either.

"It's like waterskiing," she shouted, eyes bright.

Fin shook his head, struggling, and failing, to copy her stance. "Not much of that on the Pirate Stream."

She laughed. "Guess not." She scrunched up her nose, thinking. "Remember when you taught me to skate down the gutters of the Khaznot Quay? It's like that!"

Fin smiled at the memory. He twisted himself around, grabbing the rope so he could try to stand. He wobbled a bit at first, but after a few tentative moments, he got the hang of it. Together they skied behind the *Kraken* as Serth shouted directions from the front. The ship turned, arcing away from the path of the Iron Ship. Ahead, though, Fin could see the black vessel swooping, changing course as if to follow. He sure hoped the *Kraken* could outpace the Master.

"It's fun, right?" Marrill asked. The melancholy that had clung to her just moments ago seemed to have vanished.

Fin laughed. "Yeah, when you don't think about what's chasing us!"

Marrill rolled her eyes. "There's *always* something chasing us. If we don't have fun when we can, we'd…pretty much never have fun at all!" She dug her feet into the empty air, skidding closer to him and bumping his shoulder playfully.

Fin shrugged. "I guess you're right." Still, he was amazed at how quickly she'd gotten over the mirror with her mom in it.

On the other hand, burying pain was something he knew well. He'd taken more than a few blows recently. Ones he still felt in a place so deep down that he hadn't even known it was there until it hurt. But a Quay kid knew how to make a rough landing. *And* how to pop up again, smiling like nothing had happened.

Some days, the person you most needed to fool was yourself.

Up ahead, Serth appeared at the stern of the *Kraken*, a shard of black amid the green leaves of the rumor vines furled around the back railing. His hands fluttered, beckoning.

"Children," he shouted back to them, "I command you—to come *up!*"

childrenupchildrenupchildrenupchildrenupupup

The next thing Fin knew, they were swinging through the air.

"No, don't listen to the *vines*," Serth shouted as they shot past.

don'tlistentothevinesdon'tlistentothevinesthevinesdon'tlistendon'tlisten

The rope carried them in a broad arc, up and over the *Kraken*. Just as they passed over the mainmast, Fin reached out and snagged the very tip of it. He held a hand to Marrill, pulling her after him. They wobbled for a moment, perched on the top of the moonraker's yard, high at the top of the mast.

"Do you see the Master?" Remy called up to them.

Together they clung to the mast, scouring the Mirror-web for any hint of the Iron Ship. But there was nothing.

Marrill let out a laugh, her cheeks still flushed and eyes bright. "I think you lost him," she shouted. "Nice job!"

Remy slumped with relief. "Keep an eye out," she told them. "Just in case."

"Aye, aye, Captain," Marrill said with a salute.

Fin let out a long breath as he slid down to sit on the yard, his feet dangling. His heart slowed as Marrill settled in beside him.

Overhead the mirrors were filled with possibilities that looked like galaxies and far-off worlds, bright pinpricks of light shivering in the darkness. It was almost peaceful.

Almost. Fin glanced around, still wary of the Iron Ship. But it was gone. Somehow it had vanished.

Marrill sighed, craning her neck back, admiring their surroundings with an expression of wonder. "Sometimes it's easy to forget how amazing the Pirate Stream is." She waved a hand at the mirrors around them, worlds lush with plants and alive with animals of any shape and size imaginable. "All of this is possible. They're not just dreams or make-believe.

"It's like"—she chewed on her lip a moment, thinking— "it's like magic is nothing more than imagination made real. That's what this place is."

She shook her head, a flicker of sadness crossing her face. "I just can't believe Ardent would destroy it all."

Fin squirmed. He couldn't keep quiet any longer. "But he will, Marrill. He already has. That's why we have to kill the Master. To save the Stream. We can't wait any longer. We can't risk it."

Her face went dark. "We talked about this," she said, the wonder and awe in her voice gone. "The Dawn Wizard said we could save the Stream *and* Ardent."

He laid a hand over hers, hoping to get her to understand. He loved Ardent, too. But he loved the Stream more. "He chose to become the Master. He knew what he was doing."

She jerked her hand out from under his and started to climb down the ratlines strung between the high braces.

"People can make bad decisions," she said angrily, stomping from line to line.

Fin snatched a rope from the rigging and slid down it, giving a nod to the bobbing paper face of the Ropebone Man as he went. A second later, he dropped to the next yard. They were face-to-face again. "You have to let him go, Marrill."

Her cheeks flushed red as she glared at him. "I'm not giving up on him."

Fin was about to press the argument, when a shadow cut across them both. He looked up just as the Iron Ship broke into view, so close that the bowsprit almost clipped the mast where they'd been perched moments before.

Fin wobbled. Marrill reached for him, grabbing hold. The Iron Ship dipped as it bore down on them.

"Come on!" Marrill cried, dragging him toward the ratlines.

He glanced between her and the hull of the Iron Ship, cutting toward them. The Master standing at her stern.

Almost within reach.

He pulled free from Marrill. "You go." Instead of heading down, he started back up toward the moonraker's yard.

"Fin!" Marrill called after him. "What are you doing?"

He didn't look back, didn't respond. He didn't have time. The Iron Ship banked around them, cutting closer and closer. Rose's shrill cries rang out, her scribbled wings beating uselessly against the iron bars of the cage still clutched in the Master's hand.

Fin planted his feet, hand tight around the hilt at his hip. The Master swung into view. Only feet away. If Fin jumped, he could land inches from his face. His timing would have to be perfect.

But he was the Master Thief of the Khaznot Quay. His timing was *always* perfect.

Marrill continued shouting at him, but he ignored her. He slipped the Evershear from its sheath. He judged the speed of the *Kraken*, the speed of the Iron Ship, the tilt between them.

He leapt.

And then—

—he swung.

His blade arced through the air, straight toward the Master.

It would have been a direct hit. It *should* have been a direct hit. In one swing Fin would have pierced the Master's armor and saved the Stream.

If not for Marrill.

She grabbed his leg, pulling him off balance. The Evershear swung through empty space, its tip barely skipping across the Master's breastplate. Just enough to leave a jagged scar. Not enough to penetrate.

Kicking in midair, Fin tried to compensate. Tried to bring the blade around for another swipe in the split second before gravity pulled him down. But he'd missed his chance. The Master twisted away. The Evershear sliced past him, missing him completely.

But in dodging Fin's attack, the Master rolled his other shoulder forward, compensating for the loss of balance. The iron cage holding Rose swung like a pendulum on its chain, arcing forward as the Master himself fell back.

The Evershear collided with it as Fin fell, slicing cleanly through the bottom and shearing it in two. A ball of scribbled ink burst forth as Fin plummeted from the rigging. Drawn wings stretched wide above him, black squiggles frenetic with newfound freedom.

Fin snagged a line on his way down. It nearly yanked his shoulder out of its socket, but at least it kept him alive as he crashed to the deck. Fortunately, the Evershear didn't cut him *or* the ship. He quickly resheathed it before it could cause any damage.

Overhead, the Master let out a roar of fury. Rose banked sharply, diving. She gained speed, putting distance between herself and the Iron Ship.

The Master's eyes fell on Fin, two blue-hot coals wreathed in crackling flames of red lightning. Energy burst from his fingertips, streaking in every direction. Fin cringed, bracing for the sear of it blasting his body to cinders.

Instead, it splintered and vanished in midair. Serth stood at the railing, both hands raised, blocking the Master's assault as best he could. But more lightning followed it, and more after that. It was obvious the Master was too powerful.

With Ardent, the match had been nearly even—which made sense, now that they knew the Master *was* Ardent. But with Serth, there was little comparison. The black-robed wizard stumbled back, his face awash in pain.

"Sail, you fool!" Serth shouted to Remy.

"I'm working on it!" She spun the wheel hard and pushed them into a dive. For a minute, Fin was weightless. The deck dropped beneath him. He scrabbled to grab hold of a nearby bulkhead, letting out a whoop as the ship carried him down, down, down.

Ahead, Rose twisted, slipping easily between the mirrors. "Follow her through that gap," Fin gasped, trying to talk around a stomach that had lodged in his throat.

Remy shot him an anxious glance. "What if it isn't wide enough for us?"

Fin didn't have a good answer. "Brace for impact?"

Remy scowled at him. Or at least he assumed she did beneath her mask of bandannas. One had slipped to the side slightly, he noticed. An odd shadow seemed to twist on the exposed skin underneath.

The ship hurtled forward, still gaining speed as she dropped. Rose zipped and wove, the *Kraken* right behind her. And then the bird dove again, disappearing between two massive mirrors that faced each other, creating a glass canyon with no bottom, barely the *Kraken*'s width apart. It was too late for Remy to pull out of the dive, or veer off. They were going too fast.

Fin's eyes widened as the narrow gap loomed. "We're not going to make it!"

"Like fun we aren't," Remy snarled. She stood with her feet braced wide, her hands clutching the wheel.

"Aaaiiiiiiii!" Beside him, Marrill dropped from the rigging, just in time to shriek and drive her face against his shoulder.

They shot into the corridor, the walls so close Fin could practically hear the whisper of the railings brushing against the mirrored surfaces. The force of their descent caused a thrumming sound to echo around them, the air between the *Kraken* and the mirrors so narrow it vibrated, sucking the ship forward.

They were going so fast that the mirrors on either side became a blur, nothing but color and light rushing past with dizzying speed. Fin held his breath. The slightest twitch to the side, the smallest brush against one of the smooth glass walls, and the ship would crash, momentum tearing her apart.

Up ahead, Rose broke from the corridor, wheeling and whirling. The *Kraken* followed, bursting into openness. Fin spun toward the stern, craning his neck as he scanned behind them. There was no sign of the Master.

He slumped against a mast and let out a trembling breath. "I think we lost—"

But before he could finish the statement a streak of red lightning broke from a mirror off the starboard side, the Iron

Ship right behind it. The ship struck them broadside with a sickening crunch. They were thrown sideways, toward an iron-coated mirror. Overhead Rose spiraled, cawing madly. Fin grabbed hold of Marrill and cringed. Watching as the mirror loomed. Waiting for the crash.

CHAPTER 15
Iron.

Aaaaaiiiiiiiiiii!!" Marrill threw her arms over her head, even though she knew it was useless. The Iron Ship was forcing them sideways into a mirror that was now a sheet of metal.

Overhead, Rose let out a piercing cry. On the bow of the Iron Ship, the Master's ice-blue eyes snapped upward. Red sparks crackled.

Marrill's heart thundered hard, threatening to break free from her chest. Fin grasped her hand, and she squeezed tight. In moments, the *Kraken* would be smashed into pieces—or turned to iron. Whatever happened, she just hoped it would be quick.

"Hold on!" Remy shouted.

Marrill braced for impact.

Just then, Rose tucked her wings and dropped into a sharp dive. She flew past them in a *whoooooosh!* By the time Marrill's eyes could follow, Rose was about to collide head-first with the iron mirror.

Red lightning streaked, blazing an ozone smell through the same path Rose had just taken. Instead of hitting her, though, it struck the mirror. The surface reverberated with crimson energy. It cracked, and shattered.

What happened next was a blur. A cold wind, sharp and powerful, blasted through the Mirrorweb. The air condensed into fog. Lightning slashed through it in all directions.

"Hold tight, children!" Serth yelled.

Marrill thought she saw the shadow of the shattered mirror's frame pass over them. The wood of the deck groaned. The Iron Ship scraped free, pushing them aside. The sails whipped as the *Kraken* spun wildly into the heart of a furious storm.

Wind tore at them. Lightning growled at their presence. Marrill's stomach threatened to come out her eyes, then headed for her toes. She wasn't sure where down and up were, but she was pretty sure they were falling.

Marrill screamed. Fin screamed. Remy screamed. Somewhere deep in the ship, even the Naysayer screamed.

She couldn't see Serth, but she could hear him calling to Remy. "Hold her steady!"

"I'm trying!" Remy cried.

"Don't fight the power of the storm," he shouted. "Use it."

"How about you use your magic instead?" she spat, sounding almost on the edge of panic. The ship continued careening wildly, tossed like a toy in a violent sea.

"Because you're far too skilled a captain to need my magic," Serth told her, his voice a steady beacon in the chaos.

Remy froze for just a moment. Then she loosened her grip on the wheel, letting it slide through her fingers. No longer fighting the wind, but turning with it, letting it fill the sails.

And just like that, the *Kraken* stabilized, pulling out of its tailspin and righting. Moments later, they burst out the bottom of a giant thunderhead, flying smoothly once again. Remy looked to Serth. "I, uh...thanks," she said. The wizard nodded wordlessly.

Marrill sucked in a deep breath and took stock of their situation. They weren't in the Mirrorweb anymore, that much was obvious. The sky spread out before them beneath a roof of storm clouds. Below, a world made from metal stretched from horizon to horizon.

She immediately spun, bracing herself for another attack by the Master. "Anyone see where he went?" she called.

Serth pointed one long finger. "After his lost love." In the distance Rose whirled through the air, a slash of black against the clouds. Behind her the Iron Ship gave chase. "I suspect we may be safe for the moment."

Marrill bit her lip, her heart pinching as she thought about the young Annalessa and Ardent she'd seen in the Master's past. As she thought about the way Ardent's voice softened whenever he mentioned Annalessa's name. As she thought about his despair when he'd watched the echo of his love drink Stream water and morph into Rose.

Of course the Master would abandon them to chase after Rose. His entire existence was rooted in that one single purpose. He would tear the world apart just to save her.

The desolate landscape around them served as proof of that. The Iron Tide had taken everything for as far as Marrill could see. Wrought iron buildings, wrought iron land, wrought iron trees, wrought iron sea. Nothing had been left untouched.

Marrill gave a silent thanks to the Dzane who had enchanted the *Kraken* to fly. The Iron Tide was everywhere. If they touched it at all, it would take them in moments. And from this vantage point, they were the only living things left.

"What *happened*?" Fin asked. "Where are we?"

Serth pressed his fingertips together. "We are in the inevitable future of all things."

Marrill glanced toward Fin, who shrugged. He didn't seem to understand any more than she did.

"Huh?" she asked.

Serth had resettled into his natural pose—tall, unflappable, and decidedly scary-looking. The black-tear trails on his cheeks made him look evil and ominous. Like the weeping oracle he'd once been.

Except, Marrill reminded herself, that wasn't who he was anymore. During their journey he'd been helpful, protective, supportive. At times she thought he might even care about them, as bizarre as that sounded.

She still wasn't quite sure she was willing to trust him, though. After all, she'd trusted Ardent and look how that turned out.

"I believe the Iron Ship pushed us through one of the mirrors," he explained.

Fin snorted, inspecting a long gouge in the hull. "Guess that answers the question of whether or not we can touch the iron mirrors."

Serth shrugged. "The Mirrorweb operates by its own rules. All the same, I don't expect it will matter once the last of the mirrors is taken. At that point, every possibility will be exactly the same as this one."

Marrill frowned. "So we're inside a mirror right now?"

Serth nodded. "More like we are in the possibility that the mirror represented. More accurately, we are in a world *without* possibility. Nothing can change, nothing can grow. Nothing is possible. It is what will happen to every world the Iron Tide touches—every mirror will become like this."

He waved his hand over the metal wastes below. "This is what that end looks like."

Marrill shuddered. She looked down at the ground flashing by and thought of all that had been lost. The people, the stories, the dreams, the history.

Marrill dropped her hand into her pocket, squeezing the shard containing her mother. This is what would happen to her own world if they didn't stop the Iron Tide.

Fin must have had the same thought. He dropped his hand to the hilt on his hip. "We have to go after him," he said, eyes tracking the Iron Ship as it sailed away. He spun toward Remy. "Can you catch him?"

She let out a laugh. "Of course I can catch him." Under her breath she added, "Though why you'd want to..."

Marrill's stomach churned. "Fin—" she started, about to argue that there was still a way they could save Ardent.

But Fin whirled on her before she could say another word. "Oh no," he said. "Don't you get in the way again. You're the reason we're here in the first place, Marrill."

Her eyes went wide, her breath catching at the anger in his gaze. "Me?" she squeaked.

"I had him," he said, cheeks flushed. "I would have taken him out if you hadn't stopped me."

Marrill was thrown off balance by the attack. She'd rarely seen Fin mad about anything, and certainly never at her. "We haven't found the mirror yet," she sputtered. "The Dawn Wizard said we could still save him."

"This isn't *about* saving Ardent anymore," he snapped. "Look around!" He motioned with one arm at the lifeless expanse. "We could have saved the Stream, Marrill. We could have stopped *this*." He blew out a frustrated huff and stalked to the railing.

Marrill blinked, tears stinging her eyes. If she hadn't known better, she would have thought it was Vell pacing across the deck, not Fin. She sucked in a deep breath.

"What's the point of saving the Stream if we lose the people we love in the process?" The words burned in her throat as she spoke, and it was only after she said them aloud that she realized she wasn't just talking about Ardent.

She meant her mom as well.

Serth cut in, sparing her from Fin's response. "It matters little, regardless," he said. "We are where we are, which is outside the Mirrorweb. Using the Evershear here will only unleash the Lost Sun to finish the destruction the Master has begun."

"So now what?" Remy asked from behind the wheel. "Back to the Tallowtrees?"

Serth's expression turned regretful. "I am afraid that will not be possible. As with everything else in this world, the Tallowtrees will be iron. The way back in time is blocked to us."

Fin shot Marrill an accusing glare. She stood her ground. She wasn't sorry for interfering. They would still find a way to save the world, she knew it. And this time, they would save Ardent, too.

"Then where to?" Remy asked. "I'm not keen on trailing after a wizard who just tried to ram us out of existence, even if he used to be a nice guy."

Marrill glanced toward the Iron Ship plowing across the sky in the distance, the storm clouds a cloak it dragged in its wake. Ahead of it, Rose flapped furiously, heading toward far iron hills.

Rose. The missing piece to the Map to Everywhere. Suddenly, an idea clicked together in her head.

"We go after Rose," Marrill declared. "We get her first." The others stared at her, waiting. Marrill felt herself standing taller as she spoke. "With Rose, we can make the Map whole again, and open the Gate back to the Mirrorweb ourselves!"

Serth's lips twitched ever so slightly, the closest he ever came to giving approval.

"I hate to be a downer," Remy interjected, "but how exactly are we going to snag Rose out from under the Master's grasp? I mean, he's right on her tail. Suppose we catch her. No way we assemble the Map and open the Gate before he blasts us to ashes.

"Plus," she added, "he knows we have the Evershear now. We've lost the element of that surprise."

Marrill's heart sank. Remy was right. She chewed her lip, trying to figure out another solution.

Beside her Fin grimaced. "I think I know someone who can help." He sighed. The thought seemed to cause him physical pain. "We have to find Vell." He practically spat the name.

Marrill blinked, confused.

"Yeah, cause an evil twin helps any situation," Remy quipped.

Fin scowled. "Remember Flight-of-Thorns? So long as their Fade live, the Rise can't be taken by the Iron Tide." He gestured to himself. "Well, I'm Vell's Fade, and I'm alive so…"

Marrill's eyes widened with understanding. "So that means Vell's still out there, half-iron, somewhere in this wasteland."

Fin nodded. "Yup. And since he can't be defeated, that makes him the only person in this whole iron world who can truly stand up to the Master."

"Fin, that's brilliant!" Marrill cried, clapping her hands together excitedly.

"Me again," Remy interrupted. "The downer." She gestured toward their surroundings. "Everything looks the same. How do we find him?"

For a long while, they stood silently. Then Marrill's eyes fell on something—a distant plume on the horizon, far away to the port side. She smiled.

"We follow the smoke," she said, pointing. "Remember at Flight-of-Thorns? The Rise weren't the only ones able to survive the Iron Tide."

"The Salt Sand King," Fin groaned. "And what is Vell if not a loyal subject?"

Marrill nodded. "The smoke will lead us to the Salt Sand King—"

"And the Salt Sand King will lead us to Vell," Fin finished. They smiled at each other, forgetting their earlier tension for a moment.

"To be clear," Serth pronounced, "if we change course, we will no longer be following the Master and Rose. What we saw earlier confirms what I long suspected—the Master strikes from the Mirrorweb. He can pass through the mirrors to any point in time, any possibility." He shook his head slowly. His voice was loaded with warning. "If the Master recaptures Rose before we return, his power will allow him to travel back into the Mirrorweb and leave us stranded. *Permanently.*"

A chill stole down Marrill's back. Suddenly, grabbing Rose was more than just about saving Ardent. It was about saving themselves. She glanced between the smudge of smoke and the smudge of bird, trying to figure out which to pursue.

Rose dipped and spun. Always, always beyond the Master's grasp. Like the echo of her escape back in Meres, when she dodged the Master's cage.

In fact, Marrill realized, there was only one time Rose *had* been caught, at Margaham's castle. Just after the Master's fight with Ardent. *That whole time, he was really fighting himself,* Marrill thought. And just like that, she understood.

"Rose won't be caught," she told them. Her heart thundered in her chest. The more she thought about it, the more convinced she became. "The only reason the Master caught her at Margaham's castle was because he knew where she was going to fly before she did. Because he'd seen it happen before—as Ardent."

Fin poked out his lips, pondering. "Good call!" Marrill blushed, doing a little mock curtsy. "Plus, we have the rest of the Map," he continued, patting the thief's bag at his hip. "We know she'll come to *us*, because the Map wants to be whole, right?"

Marrill nodded. They'd learned that lesson the hard way, back when Rose had stolen the Face of the Map and taken it to Serth, who'd already collected the other pieces. She dared a slow glance at the wizard, but if he remembered any of this, he didn't show it.

Remy had taken off her bandanna mask and was shaking free her long hair. "Well," she said. "I guess I've heard crazier explanations since I've been on the Pirate Stream." She gathered her hair back into a ponytail, securing it with one hand while spinning the wheel with the other. The bow swung toward the smoky horizon.

Marrill took a deep breath. The smoke looked to be far

away. Finally, at long last, they had a moment to relax. As if on cue, Karny came trotting up from belowdecks, and she snatched him up, burying her face in his fur. He bonked his head against her chin and curled on her chest. Her shoulders loosened as his purrs rumbled through her.

As she settled into the journey she watched the world pass by below, the landscape frozen in iron. What had once been trees were now just chips of metal, flaked up as though someone had struck the ground with a sharp stone. It was beautiful and devastating at the same time.

She shook her head, imagining all the amazing things that could have lived there, now vanished beneath the tide of iron. "I wonder what world this was," she said aloud. "Before, I mean."

"You don't recognize it?" Serth asked softly behind her.

A chill stole up her back and she clutched Karny tighter. "Should I?"

"Unless you forget your friends so easily," he said.

Her heart spun into overdrive. She set her cat down on the deck and pressed herself to the railing to get a better look. It was an island, broken trees at the outer edges reaching up through what once had been the surface of the Pirate Stream but was now a stretch of sheet metal.

The island itself appeared unremarkable. No structures were visible, but there seemed to be hints that they once had been there. The suggestion of walls and ramparts, towers and bridges. A thick forest covered it, but cut off abruptly, giving way to a wide expanse of brambles. There were slashes throughout it all, swaths of land that looked barren—almost charred.

Marrill sucked in a gasp of recognition. "No," she whispered. The brambles coiled like barbed wire, their iron-coated thorns so sharp they practically glistened. She looked past them to what lay ahead. Already knowing what she'd find, but still not prepared for it.

A group of trees soared in the air, taller than anything else in sight. Their scorched canopies spread wide, every singed leaf rendered in exquisite, metallic detail. Marrill recognized each tree, knew each one's name. But her eyes sought out one in particular.

"Leferia," she breathed when she found it. This iron wasteland had once been the Gibbering Grove, where they'd first found the Face of the Bintheyr Map to Everywhere.

"A court of spies," Serth said, "transformed into trees, burned by fire, and now cast in iron. As I said, this is the inevitable end of everything."

He was omitting that he himself had started the fire, but that wasn't really relevant. Because for once, Marrill understood what the wizard was trying to say. For everything that had happened, for all that history, for everything that made the Pirate Stream unique—none of it mattered anymore. All things ended the same, in the iron world.

Unconsciously, one of her hands slipped down to her

pocket, tracing the sharp edge of the mirror shard. The broken piece of her perfect future, where her mother was safe and healthy and grown to a great old age.

Up ahead, the trail of smoke billowed high into the sky. Not *everything* would end in iron, she told herself.

Some fires, it seemed, would burn forever.

CHAPTER 16
Finding Friends in the Worst Places

In the past, traveling on the Stream had always been an adventure to Fin. But in the time of iron, it was drudgery. Below, no hint of life existed. No grasses swayed, no waves crashed, not even a breeze stirred. The only view was of destruction, an overwhelming reminder of just how much was at stake. It was hard to even know how much time had passed, as there was little difference between night and day here. Just a dim and a glow in the eternal dusk.

Onboard the *Enterprising Kraken*, the crew was growing

restless. The Naysayer hunched at the stern, glaring into the distance and grumbling about there not being any water to fish in. Remy slumped by the wheel, letting the Ropebone Man steer. Minutes trudged into hours, with no means of telling one from the next.

And then, finally, Marrill perked up from her perch on the bow and pointed. "I think I see it!"

Fin's mood jumped from bored to lively to tense. Up ahead, cast iron mountains scraped at the sky. At the heart of the range, five peaks towered above the rest, arrayed like the prongs of a savage crown. Smoke billowed from the tallest among them.

The world around the peaks danced in red light and shadow. Deep valleys that had never seen the sun were lit from within by waterfalls of molten metal pouring down from the high cliffs. Red-yellow rivers of flame sliced through sheer canyons, meandering out onto the plain beyond. Each peak was a volcano, somehow both dead and erupting all at the same time.

Fin felt his shoulders tighten at the thought of confronting Vell. Though it was the thought of having to ask for his help that made his stomach *truly* turn sour.

He didn't have much hope that Vell would willingly help them. He'd spent the trip trying to come up with a plan to persuade him, but so far he was drawing a blank.

Fin was about to suggest that they forget it. Then he saw the first of what looked like strange trees, scattered amid the

smelted rivers that oozed across the flat plain. He squinted. They were too small to be trees, he realized.

"Remy," he called. "Take us lower."

The *Kraken* swooped down, low enough for him to confirm his suspicion. He was right. They weren't trees. They were statues.

First, it was a man fleeing, glancing over his shoulder at whatever chased him. Then a woman, sheltering a child. Then more, and more. The closer the *Kraken* drew to the mountains, the more dense the statues grew, until they were all Fin could see.

Beside him, Marrill sucked in a breath. "They must have been running from the Tide," she murmured. "Those poor people." She turned from the railing, unable to look anymore.

Fin nodded mutely. But unlike her, he couldn't bring himself to tear his eyes away. Something about their frozen motions, something about their strides and postures, was all too familiar to him. These were not just random villagers escaping the Iron Tide.

His pulse ticked up, his insides twisting. A few moments later, the fleeing crowd gave way to columns of iron soldiers, all of them standing straight with their chins high, keeping rank. Their expressions, frozen forever in masks of metal, showed no fear or hesitation. No sadness or regret. No weakness at all.

"The Rise," he breathed.

His eyes skimmed back to the statues fleeing across the

plain, and his stomach sank. The Fade. It had to be. As the creeping iron had taken them, their Rise had become vulnerable, and they too succumbed to the Tide. Just like with Fig and her Rise, Karu.

He searched the Fade faces, wondering if in the possibility this world had once represented, Fig might be among them somewhere. If she might have been a nameless Sister Fade who'd never met him, never been given a name, never realized her strength and value.

"I'm sorry, Fin," Marrill said softly. "I mean, we knew it had to have happened, but it can't be easy seeing it."

Fin shook his head. "It's fine," he lied. His chest squeezed tight. His mind flew to all the things that could have been. His mother, the previous Crest of the Rise, had wanted to make the world a better place for the Fade. She'd told him that the Salt Sand King meant a chance to change things—a chance to make the Fade equals. He wondered if, somewhere in the Mirrorweb, there was a mirror that had shown that possibility.

He wondered what the world could have been like if Vell hadn't killed her. He wondered what it would have been like if he'd met her earlier. Or if the Master hadn't unleashed the Salt Sand King and Fin himself could have led the Fade to complete their revolution against the Rise.

All of that potential, all those possibilities were gone now. That was what the Iron Tide meant. That was what it took. The chance that things might be different. The chance that things might be *better*, someday.

"You sure?" Marrill asked. Her hand fell on his back.

He couldn't look at her. It was one thing, he realized, to witness the destruction of the worlds he'd known. It was another thing entirely to see the people in them robbed of any chance to make their lives better. It was almost unbearable to witness. And if Marrill hadn't stopped him from killing the Master earlier, it would already be over.

The Stream would be safe again, possibilities restored once more.

He shook her hand free. Resolve hardened in his chest, turning his tears to anger. Marrill looked hurt, but she said nothing. She just stepped away.

He hated this feeling. Hated fighting with her. But he couldn't spend his energy worrying about that. The frozen people on the plain were what mattered. They were why he needed to stop the Master of the Iron Ship. Regardless of the cost.

Carefully, Remy guided the *Kraken* higher again as they neared the mountains. The spaces between the peaks were dark, lost in perpetual shadow, and twisty like a maze. The *Kraken* plunged into them as she made her way toward the crown of flaming peaks. Steel cliffs and cast iron canyons surrounded them.

Fin was pretty sure he wasn't the only one who felt a chill run down his spine as the *Kraken* floated through darkness. Fountainheads of molten metal cut red slashes through it. The temperature plunged, then rose again as they passed by.

"Careful, Captain," Serth warned from the main deck as they threaded the gap beneath a soaring arch of what had once been stone. His dark robes blended with the shadows, making his pale face look like a mask floating in midair. "One touch, and the Tide will take us, too."

Fin shook the anxiety from his thoughts, focusing on the task to come. He was about to face the kid who had murdered his—their—mother. The thought twisted inside him, sharp and sure as the jagged mountains, hot as the molten rivers that poured out from them. He had to be ready.

Suddenly, Vell's voice broke the stillness, echoing through the sheer canyons.

"Welcome at last, Brother Fade!"

Fin's eyes jumped from cliff top to cliff top, hunting. He scoured the dark spots that could have been either caves or shadows. He couldn't find his double anywhere.

Marrill crossed her arms next to him, holding herself. "Where is he?"

Fin shook his head. The jagged landscape made pinpointing the sound impossible. "Take us higher, Remy," he urged.

"Working on it," she shot back. "This ship isn't exactly designed to move up and down, you know." The Ropebone Man creaked in agreement, the happy face drawn on his paper-plate head bouncing sadly as he strained on the sails.

"I've been wondering where you were," Vell's voice echoed from all around. "You had to be somewhere, or I would be a statue like the rest of our brothers and sisters."

Fin couldn't help the anger that boiled up inside him. Before he could stop himself, he shouted, "Funny thing, blood—we were *just* starting to think you'd done the world a favor and turned into a statue anyway."

Vell's laughter bounced around mountains, reverberated through gorges.

Marrill shushed Fin quickly. "We need his *help*, remember?"

Fin grunted. He wasn't so sure this idea was worthwhile. "We can't even *find* him," he shot back.

"He's definitely *above* us," Serth muttered. "But where…"

They were just passing between the first of the five big peaks, into a great round bowl of cliffs and high domes. A torrent of white-yellow metal poured down the middle of it, forming a pool of liquid fire below. The biggest peak towered far overhead.

There was nowhere to go but higher. The *Kraken* slowed to a halt, the rigging shifting in preparation. "This is going to take a minute," Remy said. "We're *really* not equipped to go *straight* up."

"Why have you come, Brother Fade?" Vell's voice asked from somewhere above.

Fin stepped forward, shouting to the air. "Oh, we're just here to…" He stopped himself on the verge of saying something nasty. Marrill's reminder floated in his head. "To…"

Serth's eyes flitted around the bowl, searching. "He is near. Keep him talking."

Fin swallowed, choking on the words even as they reached his mouth. He pushed them out in a single breath. "Wecamebecauseweneedyourhelp."

Marrill smiled at him. "Was that so hard?" she whispered. He nodded back forcefully.

"My help?" Vell seemed to practically choke at the thought. "*You* came for *my help*?"

Serth pointed one long finger. "There!"

Fin's eyes snapped to a scrap of barb-wire shrubs atop the cliffs. Almost as soon as he saw the figure there, Vell jumped. He twisted, jackknifed into a dive, and splashed straight into the pool of molten metal below.

Beside him, Marrill gasped. Fin shot her a look. "Sorry," she said. "I know, he's invincible. But still."

Serth leaned out over the railing. "We've lost him again, it seems."

Fin moved to the other side of the deck. Hot air blew up from the pool, drawing beads of sweat out of his forehead. The molten metal was so bright that he could scarcely look at it for long, let alone find where Vell had disappeared.

A tense moment passed as they hunted unsuccessfully for any sign of their quarry. Overhead, the rigging squealed, still reconfiguring itself.

"So what now?" Remy asked from the ship's wheel. She was looking at the peak towering above them. "The ship's ready to go up. But now it kind of seems like we need to go down?"

Fin scoured the boiling pool below. Maybe they *should* go down and get a closer look. Then again, Vell and Fin had an awful lot in common. And even though Vell hadn't grown up in the Khaznot Quay, he knew how to climb—almost as well as Fin himself. In the time they spent searching, he could head back to the top of the cliffs again, maybe higher.

"Come on, guys," Remy pressed. "Which way?"

Marrill spoke up quickly. "Rise!"

"You got it," Remy replied. The ship began to lift, hovering straight up.

Fin shook his head, unsure. He gripped the railing tight, squinting at the cliffs above. "Do you see him?"

"Rise!" Marrill said again.

"I *got* it," Remy snapped.

Fin looked over. Marrill was leaning out of the bow of the ship, looking *down*. Something wasn't right.

"Marrill?"

"Rise!" she cried again, stepping backward.

As Marrill retreated, another figure moved up, slinging himself over the rail. His feet made a thump as they struck the deck. His whole body was a folded knife, ready to snap out and stab them at any moment.

"Hello, Brother Fade," Vell said coolly.

CHAPTER 17
The King of Molten Metal

Marrill slow-walked backward across the deck. Vell, the heartless Crest of the Rise, rose to his full height before her. Behind him, the waterfall of melted iron highlighted his sharp figure. Then the waterfall and the cliffs surrounding it fell away as the *Kraken* lifted into the open sky.

"So," Vell said with a smirk. "You rabble have finally realized the superiority of the Rise and have come groveling for my mercy."

Marrill looked to Fin for help. He and Vell were the same person, after all, in a way. Even if they couldn't possibly have been more different.

But the smoldering anger in Fin's eyes was far hotter than the melting metal below them. Whatever Fin might say, it would only get them in worse trouble.

So she looked to Serth for help instead. He stood rod straight as ever, his face a demon mask in the forge light, his expression *almost* as arrogant as Vell's own. Marrill had a quick flashback to his parley with the Meressians at Flight-of-Thorns. Diplomacy, she reminded herself, was not the wizard's strong suit.

Neither of them appeared willing to bend to the Crest in any way. But if that's what it took to get his help, that's what she would do. Swallowing, she stepped forward, clasping her hands together to hide her nerves. And to keep from taking a swing at Vell. He'd killed Fin's mother, after all. Marrill didn't take kindly to people who messed with her friends.

"Um, yeah," she said. "Something like that?"

Vell nodded. "Good." He turned, throwing his arms wide just as the *Kraken* burst through a haze of smoke that ringed the summit of the highest peak. "Then bow before the Salt Sand King!"

Before them, the mountain summit jutted into the air. Atop it, cold and silent, stood the statue the Rise had carried to the siege of Flight-of-Thorns Citadel.

For all his power and ambition, the Salt Sand King wasn't a grandiose figure. He was small and hunched, his form wrapped in bandages so that the only things visible were his beak and glimpses of where his ember-like eyes would have been. Like his surroundings, every inch of him was covered in dark metal, utterly lifeless iron. But the ground beneath his statue glowed with a silent fire. Down below, somewhere deep inside the mountain, his heat must have been melting the metal, creating the burning rivers that poured into the valleys and lit the whole place like the inside of a forge.

Marrill had a bad feeling about this. "So…if we bow, you'll help us?" she asked. On either side, Serth and Fin scoffed.

"I am *not* bowing," they said simultaneously. Of course *now* would be the moment they took each other's side.

Vell turned back to them sharply. "Then you'll die," he said. He held out a hand. "Behold, he awakes!"

As Marrill watched, the glow beneath the statue spread upward. Blue at first, then an orangish red. It infused the entire mountain peak, seeping into the statue itself. The metal around its beaked visage began to glimmer, a sheen glistening across its surface.

Vell crossed his arms. "Are you so sure you won't bow?"

Marrill glanced toward Fin and Serth. Sure, it would be embarrassing. But if it got Vell to help them fight off the Master of the Iron Ship, what was a little embarrassment? "You *will* help, right?" she asked. "If we do?"

Vell laughed. "Of course not. I am the Crest of the Rise. *I* give the commands. And none but my king commands me."

"Oh, you've got to be kidding me," Fin spat.

The mountain peak snapped and bubbled. A jet of flame shot out over them, its heat so fierce that it buffeted Marrill's skin even from dozens of yards away. The *Kraken* was rising right into a full-blown inferno.

Fortunately, Marrill thought, dullwood was fireproof. Unfortunately, *they* weren't. "Uh, Remy?" she called. "You might want to put on the brakes."

"You know ships don't *have* brakes, right?" Remy responded. "It's called drift—we can't just stop. Ropebone, quick, modify the rigging. We need to sail!"

The ship came alive with movement—sails dropping, pirats scrambling, Ropebone screeching as they changed course. Serth muttered, his hands tracing invisible lines in front of him. The air cooled, but only slightly.

"I am not...ready for this," the wizard mumbled.

The captain glowered but said nothing as she spun the wheel hard. The *Kraken* began to bank. But it wasn't fast enough. The heat around the statue was so intense that it shimmered like water, turning the air into waves of glistening light. It was like staring into the base of a flame, colorless, with hints of blue flashing, giving way to a flickering yellow.

That's what the statue of the Salt Sand King was now, the heart of a flame that grew until its white tip snapped, whip-like, through the air. Two glowing embers appeared where his eyes would have been, piercing through the thin veneer of iron that still coated him.

His beak cracked, tearing a ragged slash in the metal. **"And what have you brought me, oh Crest of my Rise?"** he asked, voice raspy from disuse. He raised a hand, the fire around him answering his beckoning call.

Flames shot toward the *Kraken*, engulfing her in a burst of light. Fin threw his arms over his face. Remy was able to force the ship down, tilting them out of the worst of the attack, but the sails still caught the edges of it. Pirats scattered along the yards, using what they could to douse the small fires that broke out in the rigging.

"Do you know how long I've been waiting?" the Salt Sand King bellowed. **"My hunger growing, waiting for something to burn? Something to conquer?"** He raised his arms, and the mountains around him almost seemed to bend at his command. Then Marrill realized they actually were softening, sinking, as if the molten valleys were swallowing them whole.

"Uh-oh," Marrill said under her breath.

"What uh-oh?" Remy called from the wheel behind them, an edge of panic in her voice. "I can't see anything from here. What uh-oh?"

Marrill pointed. "I think the mountains are...uh... melting."

"What does that mean?" Remy asked.

Serth spun toward her. "It means we are leaving. Now!"

Behind them the Salt Sand King laughed, the sound echoing off the metal mountains. **"Do you think you can escape my wrath???"**

"Right. Leaving. Got it." Remy's cheeks glistened with sweat as she hauled at the wheel, turning them sharply.

Below them the liquid iron churned, forming waves that crashed against the dissolving hills, eating away at them like sand castles being swallowed by the sea.

As Marrill watched, the waves grew larger, more volatile, rising higher. Just ahead, one crashed into a mountain, sending a stream of molten metal spiraling upward. The tip of it splattered toward the *Kraken*, as if it were trying to bat the ship from the air.

Remy pushed them into a steep dive, just barely avoiding the volley. But this sent them even closer to the threatening tide.

"Where will you sail to, yunh? Where can you go? When all the Stream is metal, fire is the only life!"

The *Kraken* practically skated over the churning iron surface, bobbing and weaving as metal waves formed into hands, reaching for them.

Marrill screamed, wrapping her arms around the nearest mast to keep from being thrown overboard. Remy pulled back hard, slingshotting them into the air. But there seemed to be nowhere they could go to escape the roiling sea below.

In a molten world, the Salt Sand King was more powerful than ever before.

Throughout it all, Vell remained remarkably calm. Exasperatingly so. Beside Marrill, Fin's patience reached its limit. "Are you headsoft?" he shouted at Vell.

Marrill was having the same thought, but Vell didn't seem particularly swayed. "What Fin is saying is, if the Salt Sand King sets fire to the *Kraken*, then we'll all die." She leveled a finger at the boy. "*Including* you."

Fin growled under his breath. "Remember: I die, you die. So maybe you want to help out a little?"

Vell's icy exterior suddenly cracked. "Why do you think I'm not helping him kill you?" he snapped. But then he leaned back, shaking his head. Clearly, thinking for himself was not something he was used to. "I can't," he said. "I exist to serve the Salt Sand King. No matter what. If it is his pleasure that I die, so be it."

That's when it hit Marrill—they'd been going about this all wrong. Vell was nothing but a servant. He would never turn on the Salt Sand King. And even if they got away, he would never abandon the King. He would never help on his own.

Vell wasn't the one they had to convince. The Salt Sand King was.

Their only hope, she realized, was the one thing least likely to work. They had to talk the Salt Sand King into sparing them—*and* into helping them.

The burning figure at the heart of the maelstrom cackled as a massive iron fist formed nearby and swung toward them. The *Kraken* dodged, but the fist wound up for another shot.

"**Nowhere left to hide, troublesome fly,**" the Salt Sand King hissed. "**All the Stream may be metal, but you will still burn!**" The blazing fist shot toward them.

"Wait! Wait!" Marrill called. "We can save you! We can give you back your kingdom!"

The fist paused in midair, barely a few feet from the bow of the ship. Slowly, it unclenched, iron fingers revealing the figure of the Salt Sand King standing in its palm. Flames flickered around him, sending waves of heat across the *Kraken*'s deck.

Marrill swallowed, painfully aware of how close he was to the bowsprit. How easy it would be for him to leap on board and send them plunging to the valley of molten iron below.

"What are you doing?" Fin hissed under his breath.

"Trying to bargain," Marrill whispered.

"With what?"

Unfortunately, Marrill was still trying to figure that out. "Don't break my flow." She gulped. "But, you know, if you think of something, tell me."

Fin regarded her skeptically for a moment. Then he gave her a big grin and a thumbs-up. "This is my kind of plan!"

Marrill didn't feel terribly reassured by that. But it was all she had, so she decided to be encouraged by it. Slowly, she eased her grip from the mast and moved forward until she faced the molten avatar across from her.

"**My kingdom, yunh?**" the Salt Sand King asked when she approached. His voice, like his form, had shrunk. It squealed through the metal like a low whistle of steam. "**I have my kingdom. Look around you. Everything you see belongs to me.**"

"But what good is a land of iron?" Marrill countered.

The King's flames dimmed, morphing from blazing blue to a dull yellow. "**About as good as your empty promises.**"

"They're not empty promises," Marrill argued.

"**All promises are empty,**" the King interrupted. "**My existence is proof of that. The Dawn Wizard promised me three wishes and look what happened.**" He threw his arms wide. "**I am the ruler of nothing.**"

And then his hands fell to his side. His chin dropped. "**I am the ruler of nothing,**" he said again, almost to himself.

Marrill felt a stab of pity for the creature. "Help us and you can have it all back: your land, your army, your dreams."

"**You would save the Stream only to unleash my destruction upon it once more?**" the Salt Sand King snarled. He shook his head. "**I find that difficult to believe. You're just here to trick me like the Dawn Wizard.**"

Fin stepped forward. "The Dawn Wizard didn't trick you, King. He gave you what you wanted—he let you use your own ambition against yourself."

The flames pouring from the Salt Sand King's frame grew in intensity as his fists curled in rage.

But Fin pressed the point. "Desire and ambition were always your worst enemies. You cheated the Dawn Wizard in the first place because you wanted to rule everything. You fell for his trap because your desire blinded you to it. You destroyed your own kingdom in order to rule it. Now you have a chance to make up for that."

Marrill felt the struggle shifting. The Salt Sand King was listening for once. "The Dawn Wizard gave you an option long ago," she said. "Help someone else selflessly and be free. Help us now, and you live up to that." She swallowed as the flames danced along the molten sea. "Or," she said, "take our ship, complete your domination, and live eternally as the King of Molten Iron. Once we're gone, Vell will be, too, and you'll have *zero* subjects. Your choice."

Marrill watched as the Salt Sand King flexed, sending flames streaming in every direction. She dropped to the deck, throwing her hands over her head as heat singed the hair along her arms. She waited to hear the sound of the sails catching fire, for acrid smoke to choke her lungs.

But there was only silence.

Marrill peeked open one eye. Beside her, Fin was frozen in a crouch; Remy stared wide eyed.

The temperature had dropped; the crashing molten waves ceased. And the iron hand where the Salt Sand King had stood only moments before was now empty. The hot metal had cooled and solidified into dull iron.

There was no evidence of the King or his fire anywhere.

Except there was one thing. One small memento, forged from the iron, resting in the palm of the hand he'd been standing on. Marrill shuddered as Vell leapt the railing to pick it up. He sauntered back, as if he owned the whole world himself.

From his fingers, a lantern swung casually. The flame inside it flickered. He strolled to the center of the fore-castle and slowly held the lantern aloft. The Salt Sand King's voice sizzled from the tiny fire within.

"Meet your new captain," it said.

A cruel smile danced across Vell's lips as his eyes swept over the ship.

Remy let out a low growl. Serth shook his head. Fin just looked away. Marrill gulped, praying they'd made the right decision.

CHAPTER 18
Baby Steps

Vell seemed to relish the moment of shocked silence that surrounded him. Fin swallowed. A bitter taste had suddenly filled his mouth, and he wasn't sure how to get rid of it.

Not that long ago, Fin had stood up to Vell and turned his own people against him. Now Vell was taking over the *Enterprising Kraken* and was clearly enjoying it.

Like Fin, Remy was having none of it. She stormed

down the quarterdeck stairs, heading straight for Vell. "New captain?" she snorted. "I don't think so."

"You asked for our help," Vell said. "These are our terms."

Remy crossed her arms. "Then we officially unask. We don't need your help."

Marrill held up a hand. "Remy, wait," she said. "This is our only chance to save the Stream. We need them."

Remy whirled on her. "Coll left this ship in *my* care. She is *my* responsibility." Her voice cracked, and she swallowed several times. "I'm not letting someone else take his ship."

Fin looked to Serth. He seemed utterly uninterested in the argument. Instead his dark eyes were fixed on the lantern in Vell's hand.

The lantern that was made of iron.

"Uh-oh," Fin muttered.

Vell smirked. "You know what happens if I drop this?"

Fin waved his hand frantically at Marrill and Remy, who were getting ready to plunge into a full-blown argument. "Guys," he said. "Guys!"

"What is it, Plus One?" Remy snapped. The two girls paused, just long enough for him to motion to the lantern. It took them a second. Then their jaws dropped open.

"Oh," Marrill whispered. "The Iron Tide."

Vell nodded. If that lantern so much as touched anything on the ship other than Vell himself, the Tide would spread and take them all. "Now that we've established you are my hostages..."

Fin's anger boiled in his veins. All the hate he felt toward Vell rushed back at once, nearly overwhelming him. Being at his Rise's mercy was too much after all they'd been through. He couldn't deal with it.

But then, he didn't *have* to deal with it, he realized. He'd stared Vell down before. He wasn't going to stop now.

"Drop it," he said. Vell's eyebrows lifted, a strange mirror of Fin's own expression. "Go ahead," Fin pressed. He crossed his arms. "It'll kill me, but it'll kill you, too. So do it, if you think you're in charge."

His twin didn't speak. But the look of shock on his face was so priceless that Fin half wanted to snatch the lantern and turn them both to iron, just so it would be frozen there forever.

"Well then," Serth pronounced. "Now that we have established we are all *each other's* hostages, perhaps we can move to the next order of business?"

"Yeah, like where are we going?" Remy asked. "Not that I don't want to enjoy our time with Sparky and The Evil Twin, but we need a little bit of direction here."

Fin opened his mouth, then closed it. He had no clue where they were headed. "Rose was flying ea—"

"NOBODY BETTER SAY EAST!" Remy snapped. "I know she went east, that's why we're headed east. I need something more specific!"

Vell snorted approvingly. "That one is...tougher than I expected."

"Fiery," the Salt Sand King added from his lantern. Fin and Marrill let out a groan. "What?" the Salt Sand King asked. "What did I say?"

Marrill stepped forward. Fin had been waiting for this. He knew she would have a plan. Or at least, she would know how to make a plan.

"So," she said. Then she pivoted toward Serth. "How do we find Rose?"

"What an excellent question!" the wizard declared with a smile. It vanished instantly. His eyes jumped from her to Fin to Vell to the tiny lantern. "And I'm sure the four of you will work it out. In the meantime, I'll be in my cabin. The Naysayer and I have a card game."

And without another word, he blew right past them. The cabin door slammed behind him.

A moment later the main hatch popped open, and the Naysayer lurched out, Karnelius perched on one shoulder. He stopped halfway across the deck and eyed Vell. He looked at Fin. Then back at Vell.

"Oh, good," he said. "That replacement I ordered finally came in."

Fin felt a wicked smile cross his lips. He had long ago learned not to get offended by the Naysayer's jabs. And he couldn't *wait* to see how these two hit it off.

Vell puffed out his chest. "I am Vell, Crest of the Rise,

First Servant of the Salt Sand King and Marshal of the Army Unstoppable."

The Naysayer grunted. "This one's defective, too." He looked at Fin. "Must be a design flaw."

"Defective?" Vell scoffed. "You fool. I am Rise. I cannot be beaten. I cannot be harmed...."

As Vell droned on, the Naysayer reached up, slowly, with one thick hand.

"...*I* am invincible—ow!"

A fat Naysayer finger flicked right on the tip of Vell's nose. The creature rumbled with a low belly laugh, then made his way to Serth's cabin.

Fin laughed. Vell frowned.

"No one's immune to Naysayer snark," said Marrill. "Now if you guys are done, we have a bird to catch."

╫ ╫ ╫

A few hours later, with an uneasy truce struck, Marrill and Fin sat at a table on deck as the sun drifted low on the horizon. Across from them, the Salt Sand King's flame flickered in its lantern, dangling from Vell's fingertip. It cast sharp shadows across the ship as the crew discussed their next step.

Fin and Vell stared each other down. Both of them wanted to fight, but both knew better than to make the first move. Mirror images of each other, they were evenly matched, and both of them knew it.

At least, that's how Fin hoped it looked. In the privacy of his own thoughts, he was well aware that his other half was a soulless monster without fear or remorse, and utterly invulnerable to boot. Fin, meanwhile, was fairly soft and vulnerable to all manner of cutting, stabbing, beating, falling, burning, and general maiming. Not to mention emotional torture.

He snapped himself away from thinking of all the terrible things Vell could do without killing him.

"So to undo all of this," Marrill was saying, wrapping up an explanation about the Mirrorweb and how they intended to stop the Iron Tide, "we need to get back into the Mirrorweb, and uh…"

Fin caught her eye. She caught his. For a moment, they were locked in a silent battle of wills, struggling over Ardent's fate. "*Deal with* the Master," she said at last. "But to do *that*, we need to get Rose, and to do *that*, we need a way to occupy the Master. Which is where you come in."

"Distraction, then," smoldered the Salt Sand King.

"What happens to us when you do kill the Master?" Vell asked.

Marrill cringed at the use of the *k* word. Fin tried to smile reassuringly, as if to say maybe they *would* find this mirror of hers. But they both knew he couldn't promise that.

The problem was he didn't have an answer for Vell, either. He hadn't even thought about what would happen *after* this was over. He shrugged. "You can come with us into the Mirrorweb, I guess."

"Perhaps," said the Salt Sand King. "Perhaps I will find the possibility of raising my lost land so that I may conquer it once more."

Marrill shifted uncomfortably. Fin turned his head sideways, staring at the little flame. He remembered the devastation the Salt Sand King had wrought on his boundless empire. It burned to ash and then endlessly regrew, only to be burned down once again.

He sighed. The King had traded his kingdom, his people, and his humanity for the sake of conquest. Couldn't expect him to give up the habit all at once, he supposed. "At least you're not talking about burning the *whole* Stream anymore."

The little flame fizzled. "I only want to rule everything. Is that so wrong?"

"It's a little wrong," Marrill said quickly. Fin nodded his agreement.

Remy snapped her fingers from the ship's wheel. "Guys," she said. "Focus. You've been going at this for hours. There's *got* to be a way to figure out where Rose went."

But time passed, and nothing. Fin lay down, stood up, paced up and down the deck. Vell paced along the other side, a reflection of Fin but different in every way. Clothes, posture, demeanor. The way his black hair parted neatly across his forehead while Fin's hung disheveled.

Fin stopped at the port railing. He was too focused on his Rise. He needed to think about something else. He took a deep breath. The air here was cold, clear—it purged his lungs. Down below, the world was an endless sheet of gray. As though a storm had come through and washed the color straight out of it.

It reminded him of Rose in a way. Not of Rose, really, but of Annalessa. Fin had scarcely known her, but she had been full of color, full of life. That color had drained out of her, literally, when she drank Pirate Stream water and turned into the scribbled bird.

He pushed himself up. "Annalessa," he murmured. She was the key to everything.

"Marrill, I think I've got something," he said.

Marrill kicked herself up from the table where she'd been idly doodling on her sketch pad and half jogged over to him. Unfortunately, Vell heard, too—he was there just behind her, the lantern swinging lazily from his fingers.

Fin did his best to ignore his Rise. "So here's the thing," he said. "You know how Serth said the Master wasn't exactly Ardent, but he was *influenced* by Ardent's desires?"

She nodded.

He held out a moment for maximum dramatic effect. "What if Rose and Annalessa work the same way?" he said. "What if Rose wants what Annalessa wanted when she *became* Rose?"

"Which is?" Vell asked skeptically.

Marrill ignored him. "There was a letter," she said, following Fin's train of thought. "Annalessa left Ardent a letter, with the Sheshefesh...she said she couldn't stop the Meressian Prophecy, but she might be able to influence *how* it came true."

"Right," Fin added. "But how?"

"Did the letter say anything else?" Vell pressed.

Marrill bit her lip. "She mentioned she was being chased by a walking shadow of the man she once knew and that..." She trailed off, her eyes widening. "How did we not see it before?" she breathed.

Fin and Vell exchanged a confused look. Then Fin frowned. He didn't like being on the same page as his evil Rise.

"She was talking about the Master!" Marrill bounced onto her toes excitedly. "*You will see me again someday, though time and tide render us both unrecognizable.* That's what she wrote. She was talking about Ardent becoming the Master and her becoming Rose."

"You memorized the letter?" Fin asked.

Marrill blushed. "Just that part...I thought it was romantic." She lifted a shoulder. "But I'm still not sure what it means."

They were silent a moment, trying to think it through.

Vell rolled his eyes. "It means," he said, "that she *knew* Ardent would become the Master and that she turned herself into Rose because she knew he would always come after her."

Fin and Marrill both looked at him with wide eyes. Neither of them had expected Vell to contribute anything, much less something helpful.

He crossed his arms, jangling the little lantern as he did. "Likely to be somewhere that's special to both of them. Somewhere that will speak to the part of him that's still human. Somewhere that might cause that part to surface and beat back the parts of him that are pure destruction."

Fin stared at his Rise, unable to believe it. Vell had solved the mystery. Vell, the arrogant jerk who only thought about himself and his precious Salt Sand King, had broken the code.

"Well, I'm not stupid," Vell said.

Fin rubbed the back of his neck, feeling sheepish. "I didn't think you were," he said. "It's just…you had to think about how people feel for one another to come up with that, and I didn't think you had it in you." He looked straight at the other boy. It really was like seeing another version of himself. "Maybe we're more alike than I thought."

Vell blinked. "Most people are weak, and their emotions are weaknesses. If I were Annalessa, I would have used that to manipulate my enemies to force them to do what I want."

Fin slapped his hands together. That spell was broken. "Yeah, we are nothing alike," he said. "I don't really know what I was thinking on that one."

Marrill waved her arms, refocusing their attention. "Boys, please. We have a job to do. We have to figure out where Rose would take Ardent to remind him of his humanity. A place that would be special to both Annalessa and Ardent." She nodded with self-satisfaction. "And I have no idea where that would be." She deflated with a sigh.

But now Fin had a challenge. Something that really motivated him: showing up Vell. He wasn't about to let that opportunity get away. "Fortunately," he said, "we know someone who knew *both* of them really well." He looked toward Ardent's cabin.

"You want to interrupt the Naysayer's card game?" Marrill asked with a wink.

Vell shook his head quickly. "Leave me out." His eyes darted around. The look in them wasn't exactly fear. But it wasn't exactly *not* fear, either.

Fin grinned. Mission accomplished; they'd finally successfully ditched Vell. "Come on," he told Marrill. "They're probably both cheating, anyway." Together they approached the wide door. Cautiously Fin knocked.

The door cracked open. On the other side, Fin expected to see chests leaking various forms of gasses or sounds, the desk piled to overflowing with books and papers, bookshelves dripping with thick tomes, bizarre ornaments, things few people even dared imagine. That was how Ardent had kept the cabin: a perpetual mess.

Now, however, everything had been put away. The bed was made, the nightmare shield polished. The floor had been swept and swabbed, the shelves reorganized. Karnelius lounged on a pillow by the window, though the Naysayer seemed to have vanished.

It looked almost normal...well, as normal as any wizard's chamber would be. And it felt entirely wrong. Like the spirit of Ardent had somehow been purged, though his belongings remained.

The only spot still in disarray was a corner by an elaborately carved bookcase. The shelves had been emptied, the dusty tomes that once occupied it stacked precariously in a semicircle around Serth.

Fin immediately recognized the massive, ancient book he cradled in his lap. It was a volume of Serth's own words, the ones he had spoken after drinking Stream water. The ones that had foretold the coming of the end of the Pirate Stream.

The mad Oracle was leafing through the Meressian Prophecy.

CHAPTER 19
Remy Gets a Tattoo

Looking around, Marrill felt a stab of sorrow. The cabin was yet another reminder of how everything had changed. Was still changing. Without the clutter and junk, Ardent's cabin felt abandoned. As though Ardent would never be returning.

Because maybe he wouldn't be.

"Poor Ardent. Trying to make sense of my madness," Serth said, snapping the book closed and tossing it with the others. "Using the Prophecy as a means to escape his own problems."

Marrill frowned. Though a small part of her still cringed at the sight of Serth, she'd really started to get used to him. To like him, even. Maybe trust him.

But for *Serth* to talk about *Ardent*'s problems? Serth, the wizard whose actions had torn Ardent and Annalessa apart in the first place? That was more than Marrill could ignore.

"All his problems were because of *you*," she said, mustering the courage to defend her former mentor. "He was trying to figure out a way to stop you."

"*All* his problems? Really?" Serth arched an eyebrow. "You think *I* made him join the Wizards of Meres? You think love of *me* led him to divine the rituals I used to contain and drink the purest waters of the Stream? No, much like the Salt Sand King, Ardent's biggest problem was his own ambition. Why else do you think he became obsessed with the Prophecy?"

Marrill threw up her hands in exasperation. "So he could stop you from releasing the Lost Sun!"

Behind her, Fin cleared his throat. "Um," he said, "not to interrupt, but…what happened to the Naysayer?"

Serth shrugged. "He left an hour ago. Said something about seeing you in the Mirrorweb later. Peculiar things, those old creatures. Did you find Rose yet?"

Marrill's mouth was still open to continue their argument, but Serth's quick shift of topic threw her. "Sort of?" she offered.

"We think Rose is leading the Master somewhere that would help him be more human," Fin said. "Somewhere that both Ardent and Annalessa would know, somewhere that would be important to them."

"Makes sense." His eyes snapped back to Marrill. "And you think I would know such a place?"

She nodded, hopeful, but kept her arms crossed, still angry at the wizard.

Serth moved forward, sitting on the edge of the big desk in the middle of the room. "Well then, I suppose now would be a good time to speak more about my old friend."

His expression was almost sad. Like he felt sorry for her. She scowled at him. She didn't want his sympathy. Besides, sorrow on him looked far too much like menace.

"I wasn't joking about the reasons Ardent studied the Meressian Prophecy," Serth explained. "He studied it because he wished to *control* the future. The Prophecy was a test. If the Prophecy was fulfilled, then it was proof that the future could be predicted—could be made certain. It was, in a way, a precursor to the Iron Tide."

Marrill felt the blood drain from her face. "That's not true," she breathed. "He didn't *plan* the Iron Tide. He was trying to stop *you*."

"Was he?" Serth tilted his head slightly, his eyes unwavering. "Ardent Squirrelsquire was the smartest and most powerful wizard the Stream has seen since the Dzane. He may not have planned the Iron Tide as such—I don't imagine the thought of destroying the Stream even entered his mind. That part's all the Lost Sun's doing. But certainly a wizard as powerful as Ardent could have found a way to thwart a simple prophecy if he'd truly wanted to." He spread his hands over the stacks of books. "Everything he needed to know was here. The key to defeating me was in these pages. How could he fail?"

Fin shook his head. "You're making about as much sense now as you did back when you were spouting prophesy," he said.

Serth leaned toward him, eyes narrowing dangerously. "And I was right then, too. Everything I said in these pages came to pass, did it not?"

"Fine," Marrill said. "So why did he care so much about the future?"

Serth eased back and tented his fingertips beneath his chin. "Because he was scared."

Fin snorted. "Yeah, right."

Marrill nodded her agreement. She'd never seen Ardent truly frightened. "You said yourself he was the most powerful wizard on the Stream. What was he afraid of?"

"Himself," Serth answered simply.

Marrill rolled her eyes. She was about to give up on the conversation when Serth added, "You didn't know him before. What he was capable of, back when he was called Ardent the Cold."

Marrill shook her head in protest, but it was half-hearted. She glanced toward Fin, who'd slumped into a chair. He seemed just as stunned as she did. She took a seat next to him.

"There was a time when Ardent and I were comparable in power, but we were never equals. His strength was in study—he read and learned and practiced. My strength was my brashness, my willingness to embrace the magic."

"He said *you* were the more powerful wizard," Fin broke in.

Serth smiled and tapped his fingertips together. "Untrue, unfortunately. I was just less constrained. I was willing to do the things he wouldn't. Take the risks. Push the envelope." He shook his head. "We were the ones who understood each other best. We urged each other on. And in many ways, we were each other's nemeses as well. It was a constant game of brinksmanship, of finding that line the other wouldn't cross."

Marrill thought she knew where he was going. "That line was drinking Stream water."

Serth nodded. "He was never willing to risk it all. That was his saving grace. In the old days, everything was about the magic, the quest for power and knowledge. We put that ahead of other people, ahead of what others might call right, or wrong. Back then, Ardent often seemed—and at times was—incredibly cold. Callous, even. But the truth is, he had a conscience, where I often did not. He had a heart."

He moved to the window. Outside, the night was black. No stars. No moon. No lights on the horizon. Marrill realized just how accustomed she had become to the soft golden glow of the Stream. In the world of iron, it had all been extinguished.

"Annalessa was that heart. Or so he saw it. And with her gone, the last restraint on his unimaginable power has fallen away. That's who the Master is. Ardent unbridled. Ardent the Cold, deprived of his one source of warmth."

"You make him sound just like the Salt Sand King," Marrill said, her voice a whisper. "Destroying everything through his desire for power. But that's not who he was. You don't just forget to have a heart." She swallowed. "Ardent had a huge one."

The cabin was quiet as the words settled around them. Marrill stared at the corner of Ardent's empty desk, trying to understand how it had come to this. How a man who'd once seemed so kind, whose heart had been so full, could now be so empty.

"True," Serth said at last. "We would likely be in a different place if it wasn't. If he were heartless, Ardent would never have given in to the power of the Lost Sun contained in that wish orb. If he were heartless, he would never have unleashed the Iron Tide."

Marrill looked at him quizzically. "What are you saying?"

Serth's eyes locked with hers. It was still difficult to

meet his stare, even after all they'd been through. "Those without a heart do not bleed," he replied. "I am saying that I believe Ardent's pain at losing Annalessa is what drove him to encase this world in unfeeling metal. So that all the Stream might be just as numb as he is."

Marrill thought back to the way Ardent had lashed out in the end, when he found out Annalessa was gone.... That was definitely in line with what Serth was saying. But to destroy the whole Stream?

"Also, he's infused with the essence of elemental destruction," Serth added. "So that's probably a factor, too."

The cabin fell silent once again, everyone's thoughts stuck in the past. "So how does that help us figure out where Rose would lead him?" Marrill asked.

Serth rose up before her. "I can only think of one place that would fit. His tower."

Fin clapped. "Great! Let's get a move on!" He turned and headed for the door.

"There is a problem," Serth added.

Fin froze in his tracks. "Of course there is," he sighed.

Serth let out a long breath. "I am still not ready to do battle with the Master. But it seems I will have little choice."

Marrill looked up at him. For the first time, she noticed the deep bags beneath those black-tear trails. The gauntness underneath those pale cheeks. Serth was not doing well, she realized.

Until that moment, it hadn't hit her how much she'd come to rely on him. And how much it scared her that he might fail them all. But not because he might still be evil. She didn't worry about that anymore. What worried her was that he simply might not be strong enough to save them.

"Can you...stop him?" she asked.

Serth twisted his lips. "Yes, of course," he chided. "I was just waiting for this one dramatic moment to reveal that. Sorry for the delay, but I do so love a good statuary."

Marrill crossed her arms sternly. "No one likes a smart aleck," she told the dark wizard.

"Fair enough," he said, the corners of his mouth lifting into the smallest of smiles before flattening again. "But no, to answer your question. I cannot stop him. With the help of our new friends, I may, however, be able to slow him down enough for you to collect Rose and get back to the Mirror-web. That will have to do."

There was a deep sadness about him as he glanced toward the stack of books. The pages and pages of Prophecy he spouted over the years in a magic-induced insanity. Perhaps this, Marrill thought, was what the Meressian Oracle had been crying about all that time.

"The end has already been written," Serth said. "Ardent knew that. In a certain respect, we both knew it would be this way. Us against each other. And we both knew that when that day came, Ardent would win."

The deck was nearly empty when Marrill and Fin emerged from Serth's cabin. The Ropebone Man steered the ship, the world around them silent as they cut through the twilight. Vell lounged on one of the yards, back to the mast, lantern dangling from his finger. Marrill couldn't tell if he was asleep or ignoring them; either was fine by her.

Fin yawned and headed belowdecks, but Marrill wasn't ready to go to bed quite yet. Instead she sat on the steps to the quarterdeck and stared into the gloom.

She pulled the shard of mirror out of her pocket. The Salt Sand King's lantern, glowing amidships, cast just enough light for Marrill to catch the edge of her mother's reflection. Still alive. Still healthy.

Still waiting for her to come home.

"What you got there?" Remy asked, descending the stairs behind her.

Marrill sighed, slipping the shard back into her pocket. "Nothing," she said quickly. "Just...a reminder of home, you know?"

The older girl settled in beside her. "Yeah," she said. "Home."

They sat quietly for a long minute.

"I need to tell you something," Remy said at last.

Marrill's eyes perked up. "Oh boy," she said. "If *I* said something like that, you'd be asking me if I got a tattoo."

Remy's laugh was forced. "Funny you mention it," she

said. "Because...I did." She rolled back the cuff of her sleeve, revealing a knotted rope drawn in ink. It stretched across the smooth skin of her forearm and snaked around her elbow.

Marrill's heart stopped. She recognized the design. It was the same as Coll's. The living tattoo that traveled over his body, guiding him from port to port. The tattoo that made him immortal. The tattoo that meant he could never stay in one place for long.

"No," she whispered.

Remy gave her a sad smile. "Sorry I didn't tell you earlier, kid. Back at the Sheshefesh, remember, one of the spines was about to strike you? And I pushed you out of the way?"

Guilt washed over Marrill. She felt tears threatening. She swallowed thickly. "It got you instead." She closed her eyes. "Oh, Remy, I'm so sorry."

Remy scoffed. "Sorry for what?"

It wasn't the response Marrill had been expecting. "That because of me you got the mark of the Sheshefesh?"

The older girl waved a dismissive hand. "You didn't make us go to the Sheshefesh, Marrill, and you certainly didn't ask to be attacked by a massive ink monster. And if there's one thing I know as northern Arizona's best babysitter, you do *not* let your charge get tattooed. Not on my watch."

"So *that's* why you're so good at sailing all of a sudden," Marrill declared.

Remy arched an eyebrow. "I'm *also* a fast learner, I will

have you know. I was going to *kill* the ACT." She shrugged. "This is cooler, though." She narrowed her eyes. "But don't think for one second that means learning isn't cool, young lady."

Marrill laughed. They sat in silence for a long minute. "What does it feel like?" Marrill asked at last. "How does it work?"

"Itches," Remy said. "A *lot*. And it can tickle when it shifts along my ribs or behind my knee. It went totally bananas in the Mirrorweb, like having poison ivy in your eyeballs."

Marrill shuddered. At least that explained the full-body cover-up.

"As for how it works?" Remy shrugged. "No idea. It moves, and I just know where we are. Pretty neat, eh?" She dropped her sleeve and leaned against the railing.

Marrill nodded. But there were a few things Remy hadn't mentioned. Like the whole bit about how she was bound to the Sheshefesh and could never stay in any one place for long. "But the curse...?"

Remy's jaw clenched. "Don't worry about it."

"But—"

Remy hauled herself to her feet. "I'll be fine, Mare," she said with a wink. "Now get some sleep." It was pretty obvious Remy wasn't keen on discussing the Sheshefesh any longer.

As the teenager—the captain—walked away, Marrill's

hand dropped back to the shard in her pocket. Already, it seemed, her actions on the Stream had changed things forever. Remy would never be coming back to Arizona.

She wouldn't let her mom down the same way. So long as she held on to this shard, she had a way to make her mother healthy and safe again. A possibility that she could turn into reality. They just had to beat the Master, undo the Iron Tide, and set everything to right again. *Then* she could embrace the world where her mother lived to be old and gray.

Marrill patted the pocket, feeling the mirror edge within. So long as it was with her, she never had to be afraid.

CHAPTER 20
The Lightning Net

In the wan light of what passed for morning, Fin watched from the ship's bow as Ardent's tower came into view. He hadn't known what to expect, but it certainly wasn't this. He'd seen a whole lot of towers in his time on the Stream, from the waving towers of Jellyfurrow to the Great Upside-Down-and-Around-Again of Saint Baslington's Stoop. But none of them compared to Ardent's.

It thrust up directly from the Stream, with no evidence that it actually sat on any land at all. Its base was made of rounded stone, the surface worn smooth by time and the swirling currents of magic.

Several hundred feet in the air the stone branched like a tree, each arm constructed of different material: feathers and clouds, whispers and words. How a structure could be comprised of such things, Fin had no idea. Now, of course, it was all consigned to the Iron Tide. But there were still hints of what had once existed underneath.

Each branch, he realized, was a hallway, leading to a different set of chambers, like leaves on the tree. Some led to mazes of flowers, others to spheres or stars. Others twisted around one another until he couldn't tell what came from where. It was massive and beautiful and overwhelming, all at once.

"It used to be a living thing," Serth said, moving up beside Fin as they drew closer to the tower. "Every branch was dedicated to one of his passions, a different arm of his study. In the day, it would shift depending on Ardent's mood. At night, it would shine like a beacon."

"It sounds amazing," Marrill said. Fin could hear the ache in her voice, the desire to disembark and run down the corridors, exploring the mysteries within. He felt the same way. But that would have been suicide—the iron would take them before they managed a second step.

Fin squinted. "I don't see the Iron Ship. Or Rose."

"But the Master is here," Serth said. "I can feel his power on the wind." He turned away, but not before Fin heard what sounded like a wistful sigh. "He'll be in the central tower, the one at the top."

It took Fin a moment to determine exactly which one he meant. Because unlike the rest of the elaborate structure, the central tower was fairly normal—so much so that it almost disappeared in the grandiose nature of the whole. "Why that one? How do you know?"

Serth tapped one of his long fingers against the railing a moment. "It's where Annalessa chose to stay, when she lived here."

Marrill practically choked. "Wait, Annalessa lived there? With Ardent?"

"In a manner of speaking. After Meres, when I was ill, they brought me here. Annalessa, in the hope she could help mend my addled brain. Ardent, in the hope he could learn the secrets contained in said addled brain."

"Yeah, well, it didn't work," Fin said, pointing out the obvious.

"No," Serth said simply. "It did not. That is how I know Ardent will be in the tower. Because it is the one place he could have turned the tide of the future, if only he'd been willing to look beyond himself." He gave Fin a knowing glance.

Fin shrugged it off. "The longer he stays up there, the better for us, anyway. Let's find Rose, fast."

It was Marrill who answered. "She's up there with him." She pointed. Fin saw it now. A scribbled smudge, circling above the tower. Marrill took a deep breath. "We were right about her luring him here."

"Great," Fin said with a smile. "Now all we have to do is get her to meet us in the middle. Bring us higher, Remy!" he called to the captain.

"Aye, aye," she shouted back. The *Kraken* shifted, tacking a path up through the air.

"I have a bad feeling about this," Marrill said as they moved closer. The lowest limbs of the tower were practically on them. "She has to know we're here. Why isn't she coming down?"

Fin shrugged. "I don't know," he said. "It's not like there's anything keeping her up there...."

"Yes," Serth said. "Something keeping her from..." He suddenly sprang into motion. Alarm filled his voice. "It's a trap! Get down, children!"

As he dove to the deck, the hairs along Fin's arms and neck stood straight up. His skin tingled; his teeth hummed. A millisecond later, the sky above the ship exploded in a web of red.

Lightning streaked between the branches of the tower as a massive net of electricity burst into existence. He heard cracking as bolts struck the ship, shattering the dullwood masts. The accompanying thunder wasn't so much a sound as a force that rolled through him, shaking his bones.

In a heartbeat, everything was chaos.

The ship listed downward. Overhead, the rigging was a tangled mess of ropes and splintered wood. The top half of the mainmast leaned at an impossible angle. Rigging squealed as Ropebone strained to keep the debris from crashing to the deck and crushing them. Pirats scrambled everywhere, trying to fix what they could.

Serth still stood at the bow, legs braced, pushing upward with all his might. Overhead, the net of red lightning flexed and lifted off them.

Vell stalked across the deck. Debris rained down on him, but it bounced off, leaving him unscathed. "A trap," he spat, leveling a finger at Fin. "Your enemy set a trap, and you ran right into it."

Fin jumped to his feet. His angry response was cut short when he was forced to duck as a shower of splintered wood fell from above.

Marrill intervened. "It's not a trap for *us*," she yelled. "It's for Rose. Another way to keep her caged."

Fin slapped his hand against his forehead. Of course. The Master couldn't catch her on his own. But he could hem her in. "Great," he said. "Now we've got a rescue mission on our hands."

He thought for a second, taking stock of the damage and trying to figure out their next move. They had to get through that net somehow if they were going to free Rose. He looked up. High above, a motionless figure stood on a balcony, one hand stretched downward, pushing against Serth. Fin couldn't see the blue eyes behind the visor, but he knew they were watching him.

The Master was holding the net in place, he realized. Suddenly, a plan came together.

"Come on!" he shouted, motioning to Marrill and Vell. He scrabbled across the deck, dodging and weaving as the shattered rigging fell apart around them. He looked back as he reached the stairs to the quarterdeck, waving the others on.

Marrill was practically there already. At first, Vell paused, apparently uncertain at the very concept of following Fin's orders. But at a hiss from the Salt Sand King in the lantern dangling from his fingers, he joined them.

"Okay," Fin said quickly, ushering them over to the wheel so Remy could join the conference. "Here's the situation. If we can distract the Master, the web will go down. We'll go up, and Rose will come to us."

Remy's knuckles were white as she gripped the wheel. "Super plan, Plus One. Now how do we distract the Master when that lightning will incinerate anything that touches it?"

Fin looked at Vell. Vell looked back.

"Not anything," they said together.

"Keep your ship steady," Vell ordered Remy.

A flash of fire blazed in her eyes, but the captain stifled her grumbling as she bent over the wheel. The muscles in her arms strained as she fought to bring the ship under control.

Grudgingly, the *Kraken* stabilized. Vell clambered his way up the broken rigging. Fin had just started up the mizzenmast after him, when someone grabbed him, dragging him down and shoving him to the deck.

It was Remy. Marrill crouched beside her, her face a mask of concern and fury. "What do you think you're doing?"

He held up his hands, protesting his innocence. He had no idea why she was so angry at him.

"Vell is the invincible one," Marrill hissed. "And more to the point, we need him to stay that way." She poked him roughly in the chest. "So no more risks! *Your* part of this job is to stay out of sight and safe while *he* goes and gets Rose."

Fin bristled at being told what to do. He was starting to feel more and more sympathy for Vell every second.

"Get me closer." He heard his voice shout from above.

Rubbing it in, he thought.

Marrill narrowed her eyes at him. "Look, I'd throw you in the brig if I didn't think you'd escape it in ten seconds flat."

"Brace yourselves," Remy mumbled. The *Kraken* shifted upward, another loud splintering accompanying it. Remy groaned, squinting up at the rigging. "This isn't looking good."

At the very top of the fractured mast, one of the great branches of Ardent's tower came perilously close to brushing the ship. One graze against the iron would spread the Tide and mean death to them all.

Just beneath it, Vell coiled. The lightning net crackled mere inches from his face.

He leapt, lantern still clutched in his fingers. Lightning snapped, sparking across Vell's exposed skin. But as Fin well knew, his Rise was truly invincible. Vell landed on the branch, balanced, then raced along it toward the tower.

They all tensed, watching. There was still no guarantee Vell wouldn't go rogue and turn on them. Or that their plan would work at all.

Marrill's hand slipped into Fin's, squeezing tight. Reminding him that despite everything else, they were still in this together. It gave him courage as he steeled himself for what came next. "Ready, Serth?" he called.

At the bow, the wizard rolled his shoulders, flexing his long fingers before curling into fists. "Ready," he yelled back.

Fin watched his Rise shimmy up a narrow iron branch, sneaking closer to the Master's balcony. It was impressive, Fin had to admit, that Vell had made it that far without the Master turning on him. But that wouldn't last for long.

Not that they needed it to.

"Ready, Remy?" Fin asked.

Remy nodded, squaring her shoulders as she gripped the wheel.

Overhead, Vell pulled himself onto a branch just below the Master's balcony, directly in the wizard's line of sight. At first, the Master barely even seemed to register Vell's presence. Then his hand came up quickly. A blast of energy smashed into Fin's twin, sending him flying.

But not before Vell sent off a volley of his own.

Fin could just see the small black object soaring through the air. He could just see the flame within, flickering and growing.

He held his breath, watching, waiting.

Marrill's hand squeezed his tightly.

And then the lantern smashed against the face of Ardent's tower.

The fire burst free instantly, as though it had been starving and they'd just laid out a feast before it. With a cackle and a crackle, the Salt Sand King raced across the metal, spreading flames everywhere. It roared toward the Master.

"Let's give that fire some fuel!" Fin shouted.

The tall wizard spread wide his black-robed arms. "Wind!" he called. "Take your revenge!"

The tips of Fin's hair began to drift around his face as a breeze struck up behind them. It quickly grew to a hurricane, tearing shreds of sails from the yards and snatching the air from their lungs.

Remy struggled to keep the ship from capsizing or being dashed against Ardent's tower. A task made even more difficult by having to keep her eyes shut against the punishing gale.

The wind howled, almost gleeful, as it swept around them. Fin watched as it ravaged Ardent's tower, battering the Master so forcefully that he threw his hands up against it, even stumbling back a step under the onslaught.

The flames exploded, raging up and down the face of the tower, transforming it into a tree of fire. The web of lightning flickered, then vanished.

Serth, meanwhile, seemed to exist in his own bubble of calm, not even the hem of his robe ruffling. With a twitch of his fingers the bubble expanded, and the wind's assault on the ship ceased.

"Let's go!" Fin cried, tugging at Remy's sleeve.

"On it," she said. The *Kraken* soared upward through a blaze of limbs, threading between fire and iron to retrieve the Compass Rose.

Marrill clapped Fin on the back. Remy grabbed his shoulder and shook it. "Great plan, Plus One!"

Fin stood up, taking a bow, then leaned his head over the side of the railing, trying to see where Vell had fallen. It was a long way down. Even for a Rise, that had to hurt.

"That was for Mom!" Fin shouted through his cupped hand. He turned back to Marrill. "We'll have to remember to go get him," he said with a laugh.

It was short-lived, though. Because a second later, a blast of red lightning smashed through the center of the *Kraken*, nearly shearing her in half.

CHAPTER 21
Friends Who Were Enemies Fight an
Enemy Who Was a Friend

"N o!" Remy shrieked as the *Kraken* lurched to one
side and began to drop. There was a tremen-
dous, inhuman roar as the Master threw his
arms wide.

Lightning seemed to come from everywhere, striking
the *Kraken* in a dozen places at once, and then a dozen more
and a dozen more after that. Wood burst into pulp next to

Marrill. The railing exploded. She scrabbled to keep from being bucked overboard.

Suddenly, everything was going wrong.

Marrill struggled to keep the panic at bay. The great tower was burning, and the Master was furious. He lashed out at the *Kraken* with waves of red lightning, threatening to tear her clean from the sky.

It was a threat that he might well make good on.

"You want a duel, old friend?" Serth shouted. He threw up a shield of energy as the Master blasted him with streaks of crimson. He was barely able to get off a volley of his own before he was forced again to repel the Master.

Beneath them the ship was breaking apart. The Rope-bone Man struggled to keep her in one piece, but there was only so much he could do. Only so much rope he could use to lash the hull and the masts in place, to keep the decks from flying apart.

To make matters worse, the fire was burning too hot. The entire tower had begun to sink. Branches melted and crashed down. Limbs of hallways fell away, smashing into the roiling expanse of iron so far below.

The *Kraken* dodged and wove through the falling debris as best she could, but it was only a matter of time before something struck her. And when it did, she would be smashed to pieces, or petrified, or both.

At this point, Marrill realized, there wasn't anything anyone could do to keep them from crashing. The only question was whether they'd get the Gate open and escape to the Mirrorweb first.

"Hold it together, Remy!" Marrill yelled. "We just have to get to Rose!" She scanned the skies, hunting for any sign of the bird.

"I'm trying," the older girl said. She strained to control the ship, but nothing seemed to stop its slide. "She's too damaged," Remy said, clenching her teeth as she hauled at the wheel. "I can't get her rudder to move."

It seemed to Marrill that the rudder was the least of their problems. The entire ship was breaking to pieces as the onslaught continued without pause. A white-hot branch of tower collapsed in a shower of sparks, moments before the *Kraken* would have smashed into it.

"Rose, where are you?" Marrill whispered, as much to herself as to anyone.

There was only one thing she could think of that would draw the Compass Rose near. "The Map wants to be complete," she repeated to herself. "The Map wants to be complete." She turned to Fin. "Quick, give me the Map!"

In a moment, Fin had scoured his thief's bag and produced the mended Map to Everywhere. Without a second thought, Marrill raced to the bow, where Serth was soaking up the Master's wrath.

He'd been right, Marrill realized. Serth wasn't a match for the Master of the Iron Ship. He was barely able to deflect the majority of the Master's assaults, let alone return any of

his own. The *Kraken* shuddered as a streak of red crashed against the hull, punching a hole through it.

The wizard was clearly exhausted. His body trembled, his robes soaked with sweat. He collapsed to one knee. He wouldn't hold up much longer.

She had to act now. Marrill took a deep breath. Then she leapt from behind Serth, into the open, hanging off the tip of the tilting bow. With all her might, she thrust the Map into the sky.

"ROSE!" she screamed. "ROSE, THE MAP IS NEARLY COMPLETE!"

For a long moment, there was nothing. Then, with a victorious cry, Rose came wheeling through the burning tree.

She was a beautiful sight, her scribbled wings unfurling against the sky, stretching wide as she soared and banked.

The Master let out another roar, another storm of lightning. Serth leapt, just in time to block it from hitting Marrill. The force of it lifted him off his feet, smashing him against the foremast. Rose screeched, spiraling up and away.

Marrill scrabbled on her hands and knees over to the wizard. The deck groaned and twisted beneath them.

"Smart," Serth croaked. He reached a hand to her shoulder, using her strength to stand. "Go," he told her. "Save the Stream, if you can."

"We need Rose," she told him.

"She'll come to you when you need her." His voice was weak.

"What about you?"

He looked down at her, and she saw that the black grooves down his cheeks were once again filled with tears. Her heart squeezed at the pain so clearly evident in his eyes. He placed a hand over hers. "I did not need a prophecy to know it would come to this."

She realized then that Serth had known this ending all along. When he saved Fin and her at the tower of Meres, when he brought them safely to the *Kraken* and offered to help them save the Stream. At every point he'd known he was marching closer and closer to his own death at the hands of his closest friend.

And yet he'd never wavered. So many times he could have led them astray, could have lied or kept himself locked in Ardent's cabin, refusing to help. But he hadn't.

He'd known from the beginning that helping them likely meant sacrificing himself, and he'd done so willingly.

He squeezed her hand and then nudged her shoulder. "Go," he told her again.

"But—" she began to protest. But they'd already lost, she wanted to tell him.

He shook his head. "No regrets," he said. "It has already happened."

"Serth, I—" Her voice cracked. She didn't know how to put into words what she was feeling.

"I know," he said. His lips trembled into a smile. "I've seen the future, remember?"

Without thinking, Marrill threw herself at him, squeezing her arms around his waist. She heard him gasp. Then felt his hand touch against her back in a brief hug.

"Thank you," she whispered against his black robes. Then she turned, racing toward Fin and Remy. She pressed a hand against her pocket, feeling for the outline of the mirror shard, letting thoughts of her mother give her strength.

"We need to open the Gate now!" she called as she bolted up the stairs to the quarterdeck. She reached the top in an eruption of sparks, another lightning blast forcing the ship to dodge through a tangle of burning branches.

Suddenly, she was thrown from her feet as the *Kraken* lurched to a stop. She landed against Fin, letting out an *oof* in the process. Remy lunged toward the railing as they untangled themselves. Her face paled. She turned back to the bulkhead and slid down until she was sitting.

"What happened?" Marrill asked.

Remy's eyes were empty; her voice was hollow. "The keel..." she said. "The keel just struck the tower."

The tower covered in iron. The creeping metal of the Iron Tide.

Remy raised a slow finger toward the bow. Sure enough, tendrils of gray were already climbing the railing and oozing across the deck.

"Oh no," Marrill whispered. This was it. The ship was the only thing left in this world that *wasn't* iron. There was nowhere else to go.

Up on the forecastle, Serth stood his ground, either oblivious or uncaring. But one thing was certain, once the iron took him, no defenses would be left between them and the Master.

She whipped the Map to Everywhere from her pocket. "We have to hurry!"

"The stern," Fin said. "It'll give us more time." He started aft and Marrill chased after him. It took her a moment to realize that Remy wasn't behind her.

She spun. "Remy, let's go!"

The babysitter pushed herself up and squared her shoulders. But she didn't move toward them. Instead, she planted her feet, her knees slightly bent as Coll had taught them both. The edge of her tattoo coiled furiously, barely visible under her collar.

"I'm not leaving," she said. "The captain doesn't abandon her ship."

"Marrill!" Fin called from the stern.

"This isn't real anyway, right?" Remy said. "It's just one possibility. That's all." She was trying to be reassuring. But her voice quaked with fear.

Marrill froze. She didn't know what to say. This was one possibility she never thought she'd have to face.

"Marrill Aesterwest, as your captain and your babysitter, I'm ordering you off this ship!" Remy shouted. "And take Plus One with you!"

Marrill glanced past Remy. The Iron Tide was sweeping

toward Serth's feet. He didn't falter, didn't backtrack or retreat. Even as it caught the hem of his robes, climbing across blazing white stars, burnishing them with iron, he continued to fight.

The Master strode toward them, his assault as furious as ever. There wasn't time to argue.

And Marrill never could win an argument with Remy anyway.

She didn't know what to do other than touch her hand to her forehead in a salute, tears flooding her eyes. "Captain," she whispered, her heart breaking too hard to speak.

Remy nodded and turned back to the wheel.

Marrill choked on a sob as she spun and chased after Fin. He'd pulled the Key from his thief's bag and cleared a space on the deck. He knelt, holding the sun-shaped knob in his hand, ready. She dropped next to him and unfurled the Map.

Marrill cupped her hands around her mouth and shouted for Rose. The bird banked toward them, diving through a cavalcade of exploding lights, streaking between the dueling wizards at the bow.

The Iron Tide had reached Serth's waist, pinning him in place. Still he fought, doing everything in his power to give them time to escape.

"You are more than this, my friend," Serth wheezed, the metal streaking up his torso. He let forth one final volley, his arms freezing in place as ragged energy shot from his fingertips.

"Ardent—" he breathed.

And then the Tide swallowed him completely, his friend's name frozen on his lips forever.

Marrill pressed a hand over her mouth to keep from crying out and drawing the Master's attention. But it didn't matter. Of course the Master knew where they were. Knew what they were doing.

With Serth gone, there was nothing between them and the powerful wizard. He charged toward them now, relentless in his pursuit. His magic tore at the sky, blasting at Rose in an effort to scare her away from completing the Map.

"Rose!" Marrill cried. The few remaining rumor vines took up the call.

roseroseroseroserose

The Iron Tide washed toward them. It crashed against Remy, who didn't so much as flinch. The newest and last captain of the *Enterprising Kraken* kept her hands clasped on the wheel, her gaze held on the horizon. Marrill's lungs squeezed at the sight of it, so tight she was afraid she might never draw air again.

If they didn't succeed, if they didn't make it into the Mirrorweb, then this was the end. This was their last chance.

Rose dove. The Master charged. Fin gripped the Key in his hand. Marrill reached her fingers around his, holding tight.

The scribbled bird smashed into the unfurled Map in a blaze of light. Fin and Marrill slammed the Key down after her.

The Tide had nearly swallowed the entire ship, pulling them down as though they were sinking into a sea of unfeeling metal. Beneath their hands the Map buckled and bucked. The parchment bent, shifting, morphing.

The Master was yards away and closing fast. He reached for them, lightning dancing across his fingertips.

The Gate yawned open. Marrill dove through it, dragging Fin along with her.

CHAPTER 22
No Reflections

Fin landed hard and rolled to his feet, hand on the hilt of the Evershear, ready for anything. He waited for the crash of the Master shattering through a mirror, for the flash of red lightning crackling in the air around them.

Nothing came. He let out a slow breath, allowing his shoulders to relax.

"Marrill?" he called, almost afraid of what response he

might receive. There was no echo. The word seemed to be absorbed into space, as though the air itself were solid.

Or as though it refused even the possibility of sound.

"Here." Her voice came close behind him. He turned to find her pushing slowly to her feet. A slightly panicked look tinged her eyes.

His heart tripped. "You okay?"

She frantically shoved her hands into her pockets, as if searching for something. Then she let out a long breath and nodded. "Yeah, I think so." She bit her lip as she took in their surroundings.

Fin did the same. His horror grew with every moment. Mirrors towered over them, so tall their tops were lost to distance. But their surfaces didn't glimmer with light and possibility. All of them were dull and gray—frozen in iron. Each mirror was a story waiting to be written, and every single one had its ending cast in metal.

The scope of it overwhelmed him. For as far as he could see, there was no light. No color. No life.

Behind him, Marrill let out a tiny whimper. He spun to see her standing before a tall mirror. His eyes slipped past her, to the image captured within. Every last bit of air felt like it was sucked from his lungs as he took in the scene.

It was the *Kraken*, frozen in iron. Her sails were carved sheets of metal, tiny statue pirats frozen midstride along the yards. Remy stood on the quarterdeck, feet planted, hands grasping the wheel, the expression on her face fierce as she commanded her ship. Near the bow stood Serth, his mouth still forming his friend's name, his arms raised in a final defense.

But the enemy he'd been facing, the Master of the Iron Ship, was gone. A wraith of the Stream, the embodiment of the Iron Tide itself, he'd already slipped from that iron world and into another.

Where he'd gone, they couldn't know. For those he'd left behind, however—for the crew of the *Kraken*—that mirror was their forever. The Iron Tide had won. And if Fin and Marrill failed, they would never escape.

Beside him, Marrill choked. Tears glistened on her cheeks, and her chin trembled. He could feel his own body threatening to crack, his own heart threatening to break. But he couldn't let that happen. He had to keep the panic at bay.

He rested a hand on her arm, pulling her into a hug. "We'll get them back," he told her. He hoped he sounded more confident than he felt.

She nodded and pressed her face against his shoulder a moment longer. Then she drew a deep breath and stepped back. He could see her struggling to rein in the fear and despair. She clenched her hands in her pockets and tried a smile, her chin still wobbling. "So saving the Pirate Stream falls to the two of us. Again."

He waggled his eyebrows. "What could possibly go wrong?"

Marrill rolled her eyes. "Seriously?"

He shrugged. "I mean, that hasn't already?"

"Good point." She chuckled, pulling her hand free so she could swipe at her tears with her knuckles. "So what now?"

Fin took a deep breath. "Now," he said, "we find the Master."

Marrill winced at the hard edge to his voice. He braced for her to argue. But instead, the color drained from her face.

"Or he finds us!"

Fin spun. In the distance, fingers of lightning danced along the Mirrorweb in a wave of red sparks. His heart seized. The Master was coming. On instinct, he prepared to run.

But then he stopped himself. The time for running had passed. It was time to stand and fight.

"Come on!" Marrill called, plucking at his sleeve.

Fin shook his head. He planted his feet. This was it. He'd come to kill the Master. To save the Stream. Now was his chance.

The lightning grew in intensity, so powerful that his bones seemed to vibrate with it. He squared up.

"Fin! What are you doing?" Marrill hissed.

"What we set out to do." He drew the Evershear from the sheath at his hip. "Piercing through the armor to reach the man underneath."

Marrill sucked in a breath. "No!" she breathed. She grabbed his arm. "Come on, we still have some time. We can still find the mirror that will save him."

"Are you *kidding*, Marrill?" Fin shouted, shaking himself free. "After he just turned every last person we've ever cared about to iron, you're still trying to *save* him?" Already, he could see the shadow of the Iron Ship moving through the lightning. In moments, it would be on them. And Fin couldn't hesitate.

He *wouldn't* hesitate.

The blade of the Evershear trembled slightly as he held it before him, the bone handle biting into his palm.

"Ardent's in there," she said. "Deep down, somewhere. You'll be killing him." Her voice cracked.

Fin's gut twisted. He hated the thought. But he shook his head. Maybe the Master wasn't entirely Ardent. But he was partially Ardent. And he was fully Ardent's fault.

"There's nothing of the Ardent we knew left," he told her. "Don't you think if there were, he'd be fighting against the Lost Sun? Don't you think he'd be trying to stop all of this?"

Marrill didn't respond. He flicked his eyes toward her. She was looking past him, toward the mirror with the *Kraken*. "Is that Rose?" she asked, pointing. "What's she doing here?"

He followed her finger to a smudge of darkness perched along the mirror's edge. The smudge shifted, wings spreading wide, flapping once before settling to stillness. It *was* Rose.

The scribbled bird let out a cry, the sound reverberating through the Mirrorweb.

Marrill cringed. "Shhhh!" she hissed at the bird. "He'll hear you."

Fin blinked, a thought occurring to him. "What if that's what she wants?"

Marrill scowled at him. "You think she *wants* to be caught?"

It seemed so obvious to him now, so clear. "She's leading the Master right to us so we can save the Stream."

As if to prove his point, the red lightning intensified its dance across the mirrors. Any moment the Iron Ship would come crashing through it, bearing down on them. Fin dropped into a fighter's stance.

"But that doesn't make sense," Marrill argued, still standing beside him as if their worst enemy wasn't about to rain destruction down around them. "Rose always took *us* where *we* needed to go, not the other way around."

"Right," he said. "And she's the one who brought us here. She opened the Gate for us." He lifted the blade. "It all makes sense, Marrill. This is our chance to end it all and save the Stream."

"But Rose wouldn't want Ardent to die!" Marrill snapped. "If there was any way to save him, she would...." Her voice trailed off as she watched the bird take flight, wheeling in a circle above them. "That's it," she breathed.

She spun toward Fin. "Rose can lead us to the mirror. She'll show us the way to save Ardent." Behind her the

Mirrorweb sparked and hummed, lightning crashing and burning between the mirrors.

Fin gritted his teeth. "It's too late, Marrill. Too much of the Stream has been destroyed. We have to end this now."

The tip of an iron bowsprit carved through the crimson lightning. Fin braced himself for the Master to appear.

But then Marrill was in front of him. A hair away from the tip of the Evershear.

"A long time ago," she said calmly, "you asked me to trust you. It was on the deck of the *Black Dragon*, remember? When Serth first tried opening the Gate?"

Fin let out an aggravated sigh, trying to move around her. The rest of the ship broke into the Mirrorweb. But he had to nod. He remembered.

She pushed herself back in front of him. "Well, now I'm asking you to trust me." She looked him straight in the eye.

"Please."

Then she stepped to the side, clearing the path between him and the Iron Ship, the Master astride her bow. Giving him the choice.

He could strike the Master and save the Stream, killing their old friend Ardent in the process. Or he could trust that Marrill had figured out another way.

He sought the blue eyes through the slit of the Master's iron helmet, searching for any hint of Ardent. He saw none. But when he looked at Marrill, her eyes gleamed with hope.

It was possible, he realized, that they could save Ardent. And if he struck now, that possibility would be gone. Just like all the potential swallowed by the Iron Tide. Only *he* would be the one destroying it for Marrill.

Fin wasn't sure he could live with that. Slowly he lowered the Evershear, slipping it back into its glass sheath. "Lead the way," he told her.

She jumped toward him, pulling him into a ferocious hug.

"And, uh, we should probably hurry," he added.

Together, they turned and ran.

+⊦ ⊦ ⊦+

Marrill took the lead, chasing after Rose, Fin on her heels. The Iron Ship crashed behind them, the Master at her helm. There was no way they would be able to outrun him. He was the most powerful being in existence; he could move in and out of the mirrors at will. They were in *his* world now.

And yet, Fin and Marrill still managed to elude him. Being on foot meant they were able to duck through narrow corridors, finding shortcuts under mirrors the Master had to go around or navigate through.

They stuck to the tight passages, keeping as many obstacles between them and the massive Iron Ship as possible. "This way!" Marrill shouted, running faster. All at once, she dropped to her knees and skidded under a particularly low mirror.

"Nice one," he said, sliding after her. She flashed him a smile, then jumped to her feet and kept running.

It reminded him of days in the Khaznot Quay when the other kids would race through the city. Fin always raced alongside them, pretending they might remember him at the end. Pretending he had friends.

Now he didn't have to pretend. Marrill always remembered to look back to make sure he was with her. She automatically cupped her hands to boost him up when they reached a wall they had to climb.

And even if they didn't save the Pirate Stream, even if the last possibility turned to iron and everything he'd ever known was gone forever, at least he had this. At least he had Marrill. Her friendship was worth more to him than anything else in existence.

He was about to tell her so when she skittered to a stop ahead of him. She threw her arms out to either side, teetering on the lip of a sharp drop. "Whoa!" He pulled up short behind her and grabbed her shirt, yanking her back to more solid footing. They stood at the edge of a sheer cliff, a wide chasm separating them from the next metal mirror. Ahead of them Rose banked and spun, circling the canyon, waiting.

"How do we get across?" Marrill asked.

Fin chuckled. "I'm surprised you even have to ask," he said as he pulled the strings on his skysails.

She bit her lip. "But we won't make it with the two of us. It's too much weight." She turned to face him. "You should go on. Follow Rose, find the last mirror, figure out how to save Ardent."

He waited for her to laugh, but she didn't. "Wait, you're being serious?" he asked.

She nodded. "You don't need me. If the last mirror doesn't work, our only option is to use the Evershear. You have to be there. I don't."

He blinked at her, incredulous. "There's no way I'm leaving you here."

Crossing her arms, she lifted her chin. "I can figure out a place to hide. I'll be totally safe."

He shook his head. "Marrill, it's not about that. I'm not facing the end of the world without you. It's always been you and me together, and it always will be."

Her eyes glistened, and she smiled. "Thanks," she said.

"Plus, the Evershear is incredibly easy to use," he added. "I mean, it just slices through stuff like it isn't even there!" He made little swoops through the air with his arm, getting carried away with how awesome the blade was.

Marrill cleared her throat. "That's great," she said. "But it still doesn't help us get across."

Fin grimaced. There was *that*. But then the more he watched, the more he realized Rose wasn't actually *on* the other side of the canyon. She was circling right above it.

Dipping down, even, halfway through her flight pattern, always at the point directly over the middle of the drop.

"Maybe we don't have to make it to the other side," he said. "Maybe we're not supposed to cross this chasm *at all*." Marrill raised an eyebrow. He spun, offering her his back. "Hop on," he said, folding his hands behind him in a makeshift step. "Quick, before we get a bad case of the red lightnings."

Without hesitation, she climbed onto his back, clinging tight around his neck. Fin threw out his arms. "Hold on!" he called as he leapt into the void. As before, the lack of wind in the Mirrorweb made skysailing a challenge. There were no air currents to ride, no drafts to bank against.

But all Fin really needed was to control their fall a bit, and his skysails worked perfectly for that. He aimed them toward a mirror tilted away from them at a 45-degree angle. "Brace yourself, there's going to be a bit of a drop," he warned. Then he pulled his arms to his chest, and they plummeted.

They hit the face of the mirror with an *ooof* and a tangle of arms and legs. Almost immediately, they began sliding, skidding down the steep slope of the mirror face. Perhaps, Fin thought, he should have warned Marrill about his plan.

His fears were blown away when she threw her arms up and let out a loud "Wheeeeee!"

Their laughter seemed to fill the iron surroundings.

When they reached the bottom, Fin tucked and rolled, letting his momentum carry him forward. Marrill did the same, and a few moments later, they found themselves stumbling to a stop near the entrance to a narrow tunnel of mirrors.

Fin glanced at it uneasily. It looked dark. And ominous. And really, really scary.

But that didn't stop Rose. She winged past them, diving into the tunnel with a whoosh. Behind her, there was a crackle of energy—the sound of lightning striking iron. The Master was on their tail.

They had no choice but to follow the bird. Fin looked at Marrill, and she nodded. Together they plunged into the tunnel after Rose. The mirror walls were close, arching low overhead. The only sound was their pounding footsteps; the only confirmation Marrill still trailed after him, the echo of her ragged breathing.

They ran and ran. No other tunnels branched off. There were no gaps between the mirrors. The only option was to continue forward. Wherever they were going, there would be no retreat, not with the Master behind them. Fin dropped his hand to the hilt of the Evershear, ready to turn and do battle at any moment.

And then, suddenly, the tunnel opened up. The walls swung in a wide circle, the ceiling arching into a dome overhead. They were standing inside a mirror ball. The shock of it ground them both to a halt.

Fin gaped at his surroundings. It wasn't the space that surprised him, though.

It was the light.

Because the mirrors along the walls still shone with possibility. Though most were already growing dull as the Iron Tide leached from the tunnel, oozing its way around the chamber, slowly eking out whatever life remained.

"The Tide's coming in from all sides," Marrill said. Despair was heavy in her voice.

Fin understood why. The Tide had already swept across the rest of the Mirrorweb and was converging on this point. This was the last bastion of the Pirate Stream.

They glanced at each other. Marrill held out a hand, and Fin took it. Together they slowly walked toward the far wall. There, one mirror waited, still shining bright with possibility—untouched by the Tide.

Rose perched on its corner, preening her scribbled wings.

They'd found the final mirror.

CHAPTER 23
Black Mirror

Marrill's heart thundered as she approached the final mirror. This, according to the Dawn Wizard, was her only chance to save Ardent. As long as this one possibility remained, so too did they all.

She had assumed that she would just know what to do once she found it. That's what the Dawn Wizard had promised. But as she drew closer, as the vision within it became clearer, the answer grew less and less so.

She wasn't sure what she'd expected to see in the last

mirror. Maybe a vision of her saving Ardent. Maybe a world where she and Ardent stood together on the *Kraken*, like they had so many times in the past.

She was positive there was one thing she *hadn't* expected to see here. She tilted her head to the side, sure she couldn't be seeing right.

"Is that...the Naysayer?" Fin asked. "Wearing a tuxedo? And is he dancing with—"

Marrill nodded. "Yup. Pretty sure."

Fin grunted. "Well, that's not a possibility any of us wants."

She wanted to laugh, she really did. But the sound that came out was more of a sob. She didn't understand. *This* was the final mirror? How was *this* the answer? It didn't make sense.

She moved closer, pressing a hand against it. Wondering if that might make a difference. But the surface was smooth and cold beneath her touch. Just like every other mirror.

There was nothing special about this possibility at all. Unless you counted the Naysayer looking dapper. Which she didn't.

She spun toward Fin. "What are we supposed to do?" she asked. Even she could hear the edge of panic in her voice. He said nothing, only stood there stricken, watching as the Iron Tide spread across the surrounding mirrors.

Clearly, he didn't know, either.

Marrill's pulse tripped, her breathing growing strained. She realized now what this meant. She'd been so sure that if she found the last mirror she could save Ardent. The Dawn Wizard had told her!

And then a horrible thought caused her stomach to plummet. "The Dawn Wizard is a trickster. He told us that himself." She ran a hand down her face, pressing it against her chest, where her heart ached so hard she feared it might actually break.

What had she done?

"I trusted him," she breathed.

She looked back to Fin. "And you trusted me."

This was all her fault. She had to find some way to fix it.

Her eyes dropped to where Fin's hand still rested on the hilt of the Evershear. Hope sprang to life inside her. She lunged toward him. "You can still get the Master," she said, pushing him toward the door. "If you run, you can get to him before it's too late. Before the Tide takes the last possibility."

He dug his heels against the ground. "What are you doing?" she cried. "Go!"

If she strained, she could hear the soft clank of the Master's iron boots in the distance. His steps were slow, purposeful. As if he was taking his time, now that he knew he could. Now that they were trapped with no way to stop the Tide.

"It's too late," Fin said, confirming the words her heart already knew. Even if he sprinted in a collision course, he would never be able to strike before the Master blasted him to cinders. Let alone before the final mirror vanished into iron.

Gently, Fin placed his hands on her shoulders, turning her toward the mirror.

The edges had begun to tarnish, the vivid purple of the Naysayer's hide leaching of color. "No." She shook her head. "No, no, no, no! This isn't how it's supposed to end," she shouted, suddenly angry.

She ran to the mirror, slapping her hands against it as if she could somehow physically hold back the Tide. But of course she couldn't.

In the final possibility, the debonair Naysayer twirled his partner past the edge of the mirror and then turned, as though aware of his audience, and executed a bow.

And he remained like that. Frozen in iron for all eternity.

Marrill's legs gave way. She sagged to the ground, staring down at her empty hands, unable to meet Fin's gaze. "I was so sure," she whispered. "This mirror. It was supposed to save Ardent. It was supposed to save us all."

They'd failed.

No, she realized. *She'd* failed. Fin had the opportunity to strike down the Master and save the Stream, and she'd stopped him.

Because of her, the Master of the Iron Ship had won. Destruction ruled. Every mirror had turned to iron. All possibility had been destroyed. The fight was over.

The Pirate Stream was no more.

"I'm sorry," she breathed. Tears leaked down her cheeks. Above her, Rose flapped her scribbled wings but remained perched on the mirror.

After a moment Fin muttered, "I don't get it."

She looked up at him, confused. "Huh?"

His forehead furrowed in thought. "What happens to us now?"

She shrugged. It hadn't occurred to her to think past the end of the Pirate Stream. "I guess we're trapped here forever. Or at least until the Master arrives." She held her breath, listening for him. His steps still echoed in the distance, slow and steady like the heartbeat of a venomous reptile.

Fin smiled. "Exactly."

She had no idea why he looked so happy. "I think you've lost me."

He dug into his pocket, doing a little spin before crouching next to her. He held both arms tucked behind his back. "In one hand I'm holding a tentalo. And in the other, nothing," he told her. "Pick one."

Her first thought was that now wasn't the best time for a magic trick. But then she figured, why not? It was either choose a hand or lament the end of the world.

He grinned. "Pick the right one, and you get to eat it. So which is which, Marrill Aesterwest?"

She let out a breath of laughter. "Well, you did just give me the answer...so I guess I'll go with the right one."

"Excellent choice," he said, wriggling his shoulders. But then he hesitated. "Though, before I show you...is it possible it could be in my left hand instead?"

She rolled her eyes. "Of course. You're basically presenting me with a fifty-fifty chance."

"Exactly." Ever the showman, he drew his hands from behind his back and presented them to her. His right held a bright yellow fruit with six squiggly growths coming off it. The other was empty.

Marrill gave a wry smile. "Finally I get to find out what a tentalo tastes like."

Fin made quick work of peeling it and held a section out to her. She plucked the fruit from his palm and took a big bite, slurping the juice from her fingers.

Her tongue shriveled, her eyes crossing when the sour aftertaste hit her full force. It almost knocked the air from her lungs. She gasped for breath.

Fin laughed. "I probably should have warned you about that."

"All this time..." Her words trailed off as the bitter sour gave way to the sweetest, most delicious flavor she'd ever tasted. She let out an appreciative "*mmmmmmmmm.*"

"Right? That's the best part of the tentalo. The *after* aftertaste."

She swallowed, reluctantly, and smacked her lips.

"So what do you think would have happened if you'd chosen my left hand?" Fin asked, offering her another segment of fruit.

She popped it in her mouth and braced herself against the arresting sour, almost choking from the force of it. "I don't know," she finally managed. "I probably would have whined until you let me have a taste."

"Exactly," Fin said again. "You could have chosen differently. There was another possibility." He looked at her pointedly.

Marrill sucked in a breath and jumped to her feet. "Not everything is certain yet." Her mind spun as she thought it through. "So the Iron Tide *hasn't* taken everything."

He beamed. "Yup. There must be another mirror somewhere. One that the Tide missed. And the Dawn Wizard said that so long as there is one possibility, there are all possibilities." He looked toward the tunnel. "We just have to find it."

And then understanding hit her with such force that she practically staggered under the weight of it. *Another mirror.* She thrust her hand into her pocket, feeling the sharp edges of the shard press against her palm. *Every piece of a broken mirror was a mirror in and of itself.*

Her heart sped up, pounding painfully against her ribs. "You're right," she said. "There is another mirror."

She pulled the shard free, glancing at the possibility of her mother, alive and healthy. She traced a finger across her mother's smile before tilting it so Fin could see. "It broke off when I tried to cut free the mirror with my mom in it."

His eyes met hers, and she could see confusion. "You've had that all this time?" There was a note of betrayal to his voice.

Heat flooded her cheeks. "I didn't mean for it to be a secret, I just—" She wasn't sure what to say. How to explain why she hadn't told him.

"Remember when you used the Map to see your mom? When everyone thought you'd destroyed the Key?"

Fin nodded.

"I get why you did that now." She cradled the shard in her hands. "Sometimes there are things so important that you're almost afraid that if you say them out loud, they'll no longer be real." She swallowed, trying to find the courage to explain. "I was saving this possibility for the end. I thought we could save the Stream, and then I could use this to—make it come true. And then my mom would live, and everything would work out."

She blinked, allowing the tears to trail down her cheeks. "It's the only way I can save her." She clutched her fingers around the mirror, obscuring its face. "But I don't know how to make it real. And I'm afraid..." Her voice cracked and she drew a trembling breath. "I'm afraid I can't save her after all."

Fin sighed and placed his hand over hers so that they both held the shard together. "Maybe you can't, Marrill."

She closed her eyes against the words, emptiness swelling inside her at the thought of losing her mom. She shook her head. "But that's why I came on the Stream. That's why I stayed."

Fin tugged her hand, forcing her to look at him. "You stayed because you were also running from the possibility of her death." His tone was gentle, even if his words weren't.

"I wasn't running away," she argued.

He lifted a shoulder. "Maybe you and Ardent aren't all that different this way," he said. "Rather than facing the loss of Annalessa, rather than face his own heartache and guilt, he decided to tear the world apart. He was faced with losing the person he loved—and all of a sudden, he could only see one possibility."

She stared at him, unable to speak. She wanted to protest. She wanted to tell him that he was wrong. That she and the Master were nothing alike.

But she couldn't.

She pulled away from him, stumbling back. She stared at the shard in her hand, the images inside blurry from the tears in her eyes.

She'd have torn apart the Stream if it meant saving her mom. How could she blame Ardent for doing the same?

"Here's where the Master's wrong, Marrill," Fin said.

"And here's where you're wrong, too: Love outlasts death."
He let that sink in. "I know because I lost my own mother,
but I still love her. We lost Coll and Fig, but they still matter to us. Life isn't about loss. It's about joy and sharing and
friendship and love."

He spread his arms to the iron mirrors surrounding them. "It's about possibility. Yes, that means the possibility of pain and heartache. But it's also the possibility
of something good. Of something unexpected. You and I
would have never met without it. Remy would have never
ended up on the Pirate Stream and learned to sail. The
Naysayer"—he grinned—"well, maybe some possibilities
are left unexplored."

She let out a watery laugh. He stepped forward, cupping
her shoulders.

"You're not giving up on your mom, Marrill," he told
her. "You're just facing reality. She's sick. Running away
from it can't fix it. The only thing you can do is love her and
spend time with her and live your life knowing that there's
the possibility her illness gets worse and the possibility that
she gets better and a hundred possibilities in between."

His words caused a mixture of pain and sorrow, happiness and hope, to swirl through her. She nodded, feeling the
truth of it in her heart. "You're right," she told him, voice
cracking.

He met her eyes. "So long as there's one possibility,

there's every possibility." He took her hand again, wrapping his fingers around hers, both of them gripping the final shard. "Which means so long as *this* mirror exists, we can still save the Stream."

A red glow came from the tunnel, turning the air around them crimson. The air crackled with energy as the Master drew close.

"But you have to be willing to let go of Ardent," Fin added softly.

She knew what he was saying. He was really telling her that she had to let go of her mom. Let go of the certainty of her future. He was right, but it still hurt to nod. To give up on the known to leap into the unknown.

"You're right," she whispered. "We have to save the Stream." She swallowed, her throat thick with tears. "You have to use the Evershear."

Lightning careened around them, crashing against the iron mirrors, causing the hair along her arms to rise. Fin spun. They stood shoulder to shoulder as the Master finally reached the end of the tunnel. He stepped slowly into the room and stood, feet planted wide, arms crossed over his chest. As though he had all the time in the world.

Perhaps he did.

Marrill's heart pounded, her entire body trembling. Fin glanced her way. Slowly, he drew the Evershear. She could see the regret in his eyes. The pain of what he had to do.

But the Dawn Wizard hadn't given them much of a

choice. He'd told Marrill that if she couldn't save Ardent, she should not hesitate to strike him down. And whatever tricks he may have played about the mirrors, she knew he had been deadly serious about that. She clenched her teeth.

"It's the only way to save the Stream," she murmured.

Fin nodded. Then he stepped forward to face the Master.

Marrill didn't want to watch. Couldn't. But she'd stood by Fin's side through everything else, and she refused to abandon him now. She gripped the shard by her side, holding it so tight that the sharp edges bit into her palm.

Her emotions roiled inside her like a wild storm, tossing her heart like a ship lost at sea. She thought about the Dawn Wizard, angry at him for giving her hope. For making her believe. How he must have laughed as he'd sat there, his whiskers twitching, telling her lies about how to save Ardent.

Cut through the metal and reach the man, he'd said. *A bit literal for my tastes, but it should do the trick.*

He'd been a trickster from the beginning until the very end. Always playing games and twisting words.

Marrill's heart skittered. She sucked in a breath, her stomach plummeting as though the floor had given way beneath her.

A bit literal for my tastes.

The room seemed to tilt as the pieces locked together. They'd been wrong. The Dawn Wizard *had* told them how to save Ardent. They'd just misinterpreted it.

They needed to reach the man underneath the metal. But not with the Evershear. Not in a physical sense. They needed to reach Ardent, the wizard they'd loved. The one who'd loved them. Who liked to tell meandering stories and recite esoteric facts. The one who continually tripped over his robe and tugged on his beard when he was lost in thought.

He was still in there. He was a part of the Master.

That was why Annalessa had become Rose, knowing it would drive Ardent to become the Master. Because she'd known the Prophecy would come true. She'd known the Lost Sun would destroy the Pirate Stream. But if there was a part of Ardent mixed up with it, then...there just might be a way to bring the Stream back.

All they had to do was reach the man beneath the iron. The one man who could reduce the world to a single possibility, then turn it back into everything all over again.

Fin stood in the center of the room, the blade clutched in his hands. He began to lift it as red lightning vibrated along the Master's fingertips.

"Wait!" Marrill cried. Fin's shoulders tightened as he held the blade high. He could have ignored her. He could have stepped forward and swung the Evershear against the Master, but he didn't. Instead he hesitated.

"I know how to save him." She laid her fingers on his arm, her touch light as a feather. "It's the Master's heart that's coated in iron, Fin. I can see it now. That's what we have to reach. Not the flesh—the real person. *Ardent*."

He still seemed uncertain. "Are you ... sure?"

She nodded. "If all possibilities exist, then we have to believe in the possibility we can save him."

Slowly he lowered the blade. "Okay." That's all he said. All he needed to say.

He trusted her. Believed in her. The same way she believed in Ardent.

Drawing a deep breath, she turned to the Master. Lightning cracked from his fingertips and spread across the iron mirrors surrounding them.

She refused to be afraid. Refused to back down. She took a step toward the enemy, her hand trembling as she extended the shard containing the one thing she'd wanted more than anything else. Fin joined her, standing with his shoulder against hers, lending his support.

The Master stared down at them, the room glowing red, bristling with energy and power.

He could end it now, touch them both and turn them to iron. He could take the shard and destroy it, turn the one remaining possibility to certainty. Add it to the infinite web of iron surrounding them.

The Master stared at them, cold blue eyes flashing. Ready to strike.

"This is *your* possibility," Marrill told him. "You can

make it anything, or you can turn it to iron and throw it away. No matter what you do, we love you, Ardent."

Fin grabbed her free hand and squeezed.

The Master reached for the shard. She turned it so that it would reflect his own image back at him. His fingers hesitated, millimeters away. And then the sharp tip of his gauntlet clicked against the hard surface of the mirror.

CHAPTER 24
Headwaters

Fin braced himself as the Master's finger brushed against the mirror shard. This was it—the *real* last possibility. If it turned to iron, the Pirate Stream would be lost forever. *They* would be lost forever. His heart hammered in his chest. Beside him Marrill trembled. He squeezed her hand tighter.

At least if this was the end, they were facing it together.

Fin prepared himself for the cold embrace of iron.

But it wasn't metal that engulfed them. Instead, the mirror began to glow. Softly at first, then brighter.

Marrill gasped, dropping the shard. She stumbled back, dragging Fin with her. The mirror struck the ground in a shower of golden sparks. They illuminated the room, beating back the darkness, banishing the red streaks of lightning.

Fin clutched Marrill as the gold from the shard spread, expanding across the ground to the surrounding mirrors. It washed across them like a tide.

Not a tide of iron. A tide of light. Of possibility.

In its wake, the iron mirrors softened. The dull gray gained color, growing vibrant. As he watched, the frozen Naysayer bloomed purple. He rose from his bow, clapping, as though applauding Marrill and Fin.

"It's...amazing," Marrill whispered, her eyes open wide as she craned her neck, taking it all in.

Around them possibilities burst to life. With color. With sound. With light and energy.

Fin returned his focus to the Master, keeping the Evershear at his side, still gripped in his hand. Just in case.

The metal-clad figure began to glow as the golden tide overtook him. Brighter and brighter, until Fin and Marrill were almost forced to look away. The Master held a hand aloft. His armor seemed to melt, to flow off him, coalescing into an orb cradled in his outstretched palm.

By then, the new tide had gained momentum. It struck

against the mouth of the mirrored tunnel, rippling into the darkness, turning it bright with possibility.

Still the Master stood there, shining like a star as the world burst to life around him.

The iron swirled toward the orb in his hand, uncovering the purple robe, the wrinkled skin. Even the helmet receded, revealing a long purple cap beneath. In a moment, only the metal face mask remained. In one smooth motion, he pulled it away.

It was Ardent. At least it looked like Ardent. He wore the familiar purple robes, his beard a riot of white across his chest. Fin couldn't be sure until the wizard smiled, eyes now full of warmth instead of cold, a smile twisting his lips.

"Ardent," Marrill breathed. She raced toward him, throwing her arms around his waist. He wrapped his free arm around her, his other hand still clutching the molten orb of iron that had once been his armor.

Fin still held back a moment. Ardent looked at him. *Straight* at him. Fin stepped back, stunned. Ardent had never noticed him, never remembered him before.

The wizard's eyes dropped to the Evershear still gripped in Fin's hand. He had no idea how much Ardent would remember from his time as the Master, but he seemed to understand how close Fin had come to using the blade against him.

"Thank you," Ardent said. And then his forehead

furrowed a bit, and he tilted his head to the side. "Fin, isn't it?"

A lump formed in Fin's throat. "You...remember me?"

The wizard smiled, a soft, gentle smile. "Oh, my boy," he said. "If I'd had a choice, I would never have forgotten you in the first place."

Fin dropped the blade, warmth flooding over him as he threw himself at the wizard, joining Marrill in the group hug.

A moment later Marrill pulled back. "What happened?" she asked. "What was all of that?"

The wizard glanced around the chamber, at the endless sea of glowing possibilities. "That was the Pirate Stream being born anew," he told her. "And this." He held aloft the molten orb. Where before it had appeared solid metal, now cracks of light had begun to show. "This is the Lost Sun. It is contained now, momentarily. But that won't last. We should probably lock it away before it can cause any more trouble."

Fin frowned. "How?"

Ardent's eyebrows danced. "We leave it where we found it: here, in the Mirrorweb, imprisoned in the Pirate Stream." He knelt and placed the orb gently on the floor. "It will come back again, of course," he said. "In some form, in some way. Just like it did after the Dzane first locked it here. It always will, you know. The Lost Sun and the Pirate Stream are two forces forever in balance—it can never truly be defeated."

He stood, staring down at it. "But," he said, "based on how long it took for it to get out this time...I daresay we shall all be long gone before it bothers the Stream again."

And then he kicked it. Hard, sending it ricocheting around the room. "Never did like it much," he murmured. Then he tossed aside the hem of his robe and started toward the tunnel entrance.

At a wave of his hand, the maw of the tunnel began to widen. The light of the web beyond grew brighter, larger. Every mirror a new dawn ready to break. A fresh story waiting to be written.

And then the tunnel entrance was nothing but light. Ardent reached into it and grabbed something Fin couldn't see. He heaved against it. There was a loud creaking sound and a heavy door swung inward.

Just beyond, Fin could see the deck of the *Kraken*.

"It's the Gate!" Fin realized.

Ardent nodded. "Indeed," he said. "And hopefully this will be the very last time we or anyone we know ever uses it." He offered his arms to Fin and Marrill. "Come," he said. "The Pirate Stream awaits."

Fin and Marrill exchanged a laugh and they leapt forward, threading their arms through Ardent's. Together they strode toward the light.

Just before they crossed the threshold, however, there was a loud *caw*. Ardent froze, his back going straight. Slowly he dropped their arms and turned back to the chamber. Rose lifted from her perch on the Naysayer's mirror and wheeled overhead, banking and soaring.

Fin held his breath, waiting to see what Ardent would do. If the reminder of Annalessa would be too much.

A smile touched the wizard's lips. His eyes glistened. He held out a hand. "Let's go, old friend," he said. The scribbled bird took one last turn around the Mirrorweb, and then, with a flutter of wings, she settled on Ardent's shoulder.

Once more Ardent offered them his arms. Together, they strode through the Bintheyr Map to Everywhere, and into a world full of possibility.

CHAPTER 25
The Last Port

M arrill leaned out over the railing, the breeze brushing her hair from her face. Overhead, the sails popped and sang with wind. Below, the hull of the *Kraken* cut her way through the golden water, throwing sprays of whispering magic into the air.

It was a beautiful day on the Pirate Stream. The water was wide open and perfect before them. Alive again, fresh and new.

Reborn.

And Marrill was about to leave it all behind.

Tears stung her eyes. She closed them, trying to memorize this moment so she could carry it with her. The chittering of pirats as they scampered through the rigging, the squeal of the Robebone Man hauling lines through the tackle. The sun sending golden reflections to dance against her eyelids, wrapping her in warmth. The smell of possibility and the hum of raw potential tingling her skin.

Behind her, Remy called a command, her voice carrying across this ship. The deck swayed under Marrill's feet as the *Kraken* changed course. She leaned into the movement without thinking, her knees soft, her body naturally attuned to the sway and tilt of the ship.

On the main deck, the tip of Ardent's cap snapped in the wind. He leaned over a giant tome spread open on the table before him, tapping a page as he passionately argued the finer points of some obscure magical theory with Serth. Serth mumbled something under his breath, and Ardent tilted his head back, laughing. Serth's lips twisted, a chuckle escaping him as well.

At the stern, the rumor vines echoed a twining symphony of ornery grunts and contented purrs as the Naysayer tended his prollycrab traps with Karny perched on a shoulder.

And beside her: Fin. His arm brushed hers as the *Kraken* slipped between waves. She could feel the warmth and steadiness of him. Could hear the slight hitch in his breathing and knew he was thinking the same thing she was.

This was good-bye. Again.

"Will you come back?" he asked.

"I don't know." It was an honest answer. And a better one than the last time she'd left the Stream, when she'd felt certain she'd never return. Only now, she had no idea what she was going home to. What her disappearance might have done to her mother's health.

"I want to, but..." She sighed, the thought trailing off. She didn't know how to explain that she would spend the rest of her life on the Stream if she could. That a part of her wanted to tell Remy to turn the ship around and set a course for anywhere *but* home.

But she would only be running away. And she knew now that running wouldn't help. It wouldn't fix her mom. Nothing would. It was time for Marrill to face that.

And once she went home...well, now she knew better than to think *never* when it came to the Stream. But coming back was unlikely, to say the least. After all, it was the Master of the Iron Ship who'd created the storm surge that had brought her to the Stream to begin with. And it was the Master of the Iron Ship who'd started the Syphon of Monerva and brought her back, when that should have been impossible. With him gone, not only were there no more Master-induced storms—there was no one left spinning evil plots behind the scenes to bend the forces of creation.

Fin didn't ask her to finish the statement. He understood without her having to explain.

After a moment, he lifted his eyes to hers. "Are you scared?"

She bit her lip. More tears burned their way up her throat. She nodded. "I really thought I could save her," Marrill said, her voice cracking.

Fin shifted his hand over hers on the railing, his fingers slipping into place between hers. "I'm sorry, Marrill."

She pressed her lips together, trying to hold back the fear. "What if I've made everything worse?"

He pulled her into a hug. "You're going to be okay, Marrill. Whatever happens." He held her a while longer before pulling back, his hands still on her shoulders. "Do you want me to go with you?"

Her eyes widened with surprise. "And leave the Pirate Stream?"

He shrugged like it was no big deal. "You're my best friend."

"But you might never be able to come back!"

He laughed. "I just said, 'You're my best friend.' What more do you need?"

He said it so simply that she couldn't help but laugh. But she would never ask him to leave. Nor did she want him to. The Pirate Stream was his home. It was where he *belonged*.

She squeezed Fin's arm. "You're my best friend, too, you know. Which is why there's no way I would want you to leave this awesome place." She looked off toward the horizon, watching for her world to appear soon. "Besides, you faced losing your mom. It's time for me to face the possibility that I might lose mine."

"Yeah, but I had a friend by my side to help me get through it. You're having to face it completely alone."

She smiled at him. "No," she said. "I'm not." He frowned in confusion. "You may not be with me in person, Fin. But you'll still be with me—in my heart."

His grin turned wobbly. She leaned her shoulder into his. Growing up, it had always just been her and her parents. She'd never stayed in any one place long enough to make friends, so saying good-bye and moving on had never been a problem.

Now, though, the thought of leaving Fin and the rest of the crew behind caused a hole to open in her heart. One she wasn't certain she'd ever be able to fill.

Especially since the one person who should have been coming with her wasn't. "The *Kraken* needs a captain," Remy had said. Her smile had been genuine, but a hint of sadness dusted the edges of her eyes.

The reality, of course, was that Remy *couldn't* go home. Not with the Sheshefesh tattoo. Staying in one place too long would be deadly. She was now cursed to a life of wandering, same as Coll had been.

A wave of guilt had hit Marrill at the announcement. After all, it was her fault Remy was even on the Stream in the first place. "Maybe I should stay and help you find a way to break the curse," Marrill had suggested.

"No way. Northern Arizona's best babysitter is getting you home," Remy had told her, fluffing her hair. She'd then turned, eyes on the horizon, and added softly, "Besides, I have some loose ends that need tying up."

Marrill hadn't asked more. She'd known from Remy's expression that the older girl wasn't likely to elaborate.

Marrill cleared her throat, forcing her thoughts back to the present. "So, what's next for you?" she asked Fin.

A small smile lit his face. "Sailing on with the *Kraken*, of course! Where else am I going to find an entire crew who remembers me?" He cast a quick glance at Remy. "Well, more or less, anyway. But hey, Remy even asked me to stay on as crew. I'm officially First Mate Plus One!" He scrunched up his face. "Which I'm pretty sure makes me a second mate, but that seemed like a demotion, so who am I to argue?"

He was cut off by Remy calling, "Land ho!"

Marrill looked up. She could just see the dingy ROSE-BERG'S sign, see the stores in the abandoned strip mall near her subdivision. And it was much, much closer than she'd expected.

Her breath hitched. She was almost home.

Ardent came to stand beside her. The old wizard's eyes fell on the bird perched on the very tip of the bowsprit. She spread her scribbled wings, letting out a sharp cry before taking flight and banking toward the parking lot.

Rose. Forever leading the way.

He let out a small sigh. His eyes shone with a tangle

of emotions. Grief. Adoration. Pride. Regret. Confusion. Acceptance. Love.

Marrill understood them all because they were the same feelings knotting her own heart.

She braced herself for the keel to run aground, but the ship continued crashing through the waves. The *Kraken* soared across the asphalt, swinging gently in an arc before coming to rest against the row of abandoned shops. Waves lapped gently at the concrete walkway bordering the water-filled parking lot.

Marrill's eyes widened. The last time she'd come home they'd floundered several hundred yards away, the Stream not deep enough to carry the ship all the way into her world. And the only reason they'd gotten that close in the first place was due to the storm surge caused by the Master.

She spun, scanning the horizon behind them for hints of clouds, but the sky was clear as far as she could see.

"You wouldn't know it took me four times to pass the parallel parking part of the driving test," Remy said as she swaggered across the ship to join the group at the bow.

"How were you even able to get us this close?" Marrill asked.

Remy shrugged. "Ask the wizards," she said, nodding to Ardent and Serth. "I don't explain the Stream. I just navigate it."

"Yes, well." Ardent twittered his fingers together. "Do recall that for a time I was one of the most powerful beings that ever existed. I may have controlled the Lost Sun of Dzannin, but I also controlled the Pirate Stream. I may have...er...made a few slight changes to things before relinquishing control."

Serth barked out a laugh. "Show-off," he coughed under his breath.

Ardent scowled at him, but that just made Serth chuckle more.

Hope caused Marrill's heart to soar as possibility thrummed through her veins. "Does that mean the Pirate Stream now touches my world all the time?" she asked excitedly. "We can come and go as we want?"

Ardent cringed. "I'm afraid not."

"Oh." Disappointment crushed her insides.

He tugged on his beard. "Of course I still have to work out the timetables for the tide, what with the currents and the whatnots. Factor in the gravitational alignment—"

"Don't forget the time disparagement facsimile quotient," Serth interjected.

"No one's listening, old men," the Naysayer grunted as he lumbered up the stairs toward the group, Karnelius on one shoulder. "Wizards, and your need to sound all impressive and everything. Cutting to the chase, they're saying the Stream'll crash into that parking lot every 12.0012948 months with a slightly smaller after-tide three months later."

Ardent readjusted the cap on his head. "Well, I think you may be off by a decimal point or two."

"But more or less, yes," Serth added.

Marrill glanced between the three with wide eyes. "Are you saying I'll be able to come back to the Stream?"

Ardent laughed. "Of course!"

"Only if you bring this guy," the Naysayer said, stroking a protective hand down Karny's back.

Marrill looked at Fin, her heart so full she thought it would burst. His expression of surprise and excitement mirrored hers. She grabbed his hands. "I get to come back!" she squealed at the same moment he shouted, "This isn't good-bye!" They jumped up and down in celebration.

There was only one other thing that would be better than knowing she could return to the Stream again. She glanced toward Ardent. "Are you sure I can't take anything back to save my mom?" She said it as a joke. Mostly. Even so, her heart broke a little at the resignation in his eyes.

"Your mother doesn't need Stream magic. She needs you." He wiped a tear from her cheek with the pad of his thumb. "Whatever happens, Marrill Aesterwest, you will make it through." He pulled her into a hug. "You are the one who taught me that," he said softly. He held her long enough for her to catch her breath and swallow back the worst of her tears. When she let go, he continued to cup her shoulders.

"Thank you for having faith in me, Marrill," he said. "I'm sorry for"—his eyes drifted to the scribbled bird soaring far overhead—"disappointing you."

"Also ya nearly destroyed the Stream and killed everything that ever existed, but yeah, disappointing a little girl, that's the part you regret," the Naysayer grunted. "Least ya learned to prioritize."

Marrill swallowed a chuckle. A smile played around Ardent's mouth as he straightened. "That too." He gave her shoulders one last squeeze. "See you soon," he said before stepping back.

Then Serth stood awkwardly before her. Black scars still marred his cheeks, but they were tempered ever so slightly by the wrinkles of laughter creasing the edges of his eyes. His smile still looked more like a tortured grimace, but it was progress.

"You didn't have to help us save the Stream," she told him.

He lifted a shoulder. "One could argue otherwise. If the future is set—"

"It wasn't, and you know it," said Marrill, laughing. "It was your choice, and I'm glad you made it." She gave him a hug. "We couldn't have done it without you. Thank you."

"Well, that's true, certainly." He cleared his throat. "I . . . I'm glad I made that choice, too," he said, stepping back.

Remy was next. She clutched several intricately folded sheets of paper, and her hand trembled as she held them out to Marrill. "For my family." She cleared her throat, her eyes red. "To explain. Tell them"—she took a deep breath to steady herself—"tell them that I love them and I'll see them again. I just don't know when."

Marrill took the letters and folded her babysitter into a hug. She could feel the older girl's shoulders shaking as she struggled to control her emotions. "They'll understand," Marrill told her. "I'll make sure of it."

Remy gave her a watery smile. "I should check the..." She waved her hand aft and turned to go, tears spilling down her cheeks.

The Naysayer held Karny with all four arms, and the cat purred loudly, bonking his head against the lizardy creature's chin. After another moment, the Naysayer let out a huff and thrust him into Marrill's arms. He opened his mouth, then closed it. He frowned and swallowed several times.

"Good-bye, monster," he finally said, his voice rather gruff. He spun and stalked off. A moment later she thought she heard the rumor vines sniffling.

Then it was time to say good-bye to Fin. Though it was a little easier knowing she might see him again, there were still no words. She was afraid that if she opened her mouth, that if she said anything at all, she might start crying and be unable to stop.

So she simply pressed a thumb to her heart. He did the same. They were best friends. No matter where they were, together or apart. And they would be forever.

With a watery nod, she raised a hand and a line dropped from the rigging, snaking securely around her waist. "Good-bye," she whispered to them all. And then Ropebone Man swung her out over the railing and lowered her gently to the ground below.

A deep grumbling came from within the hull, a groaning of dullwood as the sails filled and the massive ship pulled away from the row of empty stores. Marrill stood on the concrete sidewalk, Karnelius clutched in her arms, watching as the *Enterprising Kraken* sailed toward the sun, the glow of the Pirate Stream turning the entire world golden.

When the ship was no longer in sight, when she could no longer hear the calls of her friends shouting good-bye, when the world stopped shimmering and the endless lake returned to a cracked asphalt parking lot, Marrill took a deep breath and finally started for home. She had no idea what she would find there or what her future held.

Anything was possible.

Epilogue

Marrill turned the bone over in her hand, squinting against the glare of the Arizona sun blazing overhead. She was standing in a barren stretch of desert just past the culvert that bordered their Phoenix neighborhood. "No question—it's a dragon bone. Probably from a scythetooth if I had to guess."

The three Hatch brothers eyed her suspiciously. Tim fisted his hands on his hips with a scowl. "That's what you said last time."

"I know. And I was telling the truth last time." She grinned, hoisting the bag slung over her shoulder. "But this time it's even *more* true."

Tom's scowl matched his brother's. "I'm not sure there is such a thing."

"As dragons?" Marrill asked, feigning surprise at their skepticism. "Sure there is. In fact, I have it on good authority that the Peruvian Dragon Research Center is considering designating this area as a former dragon hunting ground."

Tom rolled his eyes. A habit the triplets all seemed to have acquired when they turned ten the month before. "Dragons aren't real, Marrill. We're not kids anymore. You don't have to make up stories to entertain us."

Marrill smothered a smile and shrugged. "That's unfortunate. I told the master dragonologist that I knew a few budding paleontologists who were free this summer and might help with the search. But if you're not interested..."

The Hatch brothers weren't convinced, but Marrill could see they still wanted to believe. "You really think there might be dragon bones around here? For real this time?" Ted asked.

"Without a doubt." Marrill waggled her eyebrows, just the way Fin did when he was going for maximum showmanship. "I have proof." She dropped the bag she'd been carrying and pulled out a Y-shaped piece of bone she'd smuggled home from the Pirate Stream. At first glance there wasn't anything extraordinary about it. But on second glance, it shimmered slightly, its edges a little blurry as though it were vibrating at a very high intensity. She felt a tingle start in her palm and travel up her arm as she held it.

"This is a Dragon Divinationator." She could tell she had their attention now. "It only vibrates like this when there are dragon bones nearby. I got it for you because I thought you might be interested in hunting for dragons this summer. But if you're not..." She started to put it back in the pouch.

As one, their eyes went wide. "Well, if you already got that for us..." Tim began.

"Yeah, I mean, we don't want to be rude...." Tom continued.

"What they mean is, that looks totally awesome, and we'd love to use it," Ted finished.

Marrill laughed and tossed him the bag. "Good luck!"

Ted clutched the bag while Tim and Tom waved. "You're the best, Marrill!"

She was still grinning as she jogged toward home, but when she turned on to her street, the feeling morphed into a fluttering of nerves in her stomach. After waiting all year, the day had finally come for them to leave.

"Today's the day!" she shouted when she threw open the front door. "Everyone ready?" She paused, frowning at the sight of her suitcase standing alone in the middle of the front hall. It had been there for weeks (no matter how many times her parents tried to move it). Her excitement was just too overwhelming to wait. But her parents' bags were nowhere to be seen.

"Mom? Dad?" She raced into the kitchen, ready to drag them to the car if need be. She found them sitting casually at the table clutching steaming coffee mugs. Karnelius lay on his side between them, batting at his leash.

Her lungs tightened, flashbacks of a similar scene from years before hitting her like a punch in the gut. "What's wrong? Why aren't you packed? We're still going, aren't we?" Her heart hammered painfully in her chest as she eyed her mother, trying to see if she'd missed any signs of sickness returning. But she looked as healthy as ever.

Her mother laughed. "Of course we're going, sweetheart." She reached out and patted Marrill's arm. "But we have three hours before it's time to leave."

Marrill slumped into the third chair at the table and let her head fall forward, her relief instantly replaced by impatience. Karny batted at her ponytail, and she frowned, prying it from his claws. "I just want to be there already."

"I know, Petal," her father said. "Would it make you feel better if we left a little earlier?"

Marrill raised her head. "Now?" She knew she was pushing her luck, but she couldn't help it.

Her parents exchanged a glance and smiled as they nodded. Marrill jumped up and pumped a fist in the air with excitement.

An hour later, they were squeezed in the back of a taxi, their luggage stuffed in the trunk, with another case tied to the roof. Marrill tapped her fingers impatiently against the lid of Karnelius's carrier as they zoomed through the barren desert outskirts of Phoenix.

As they approached the abandoned strip mall, the driver glanced between the GPS on the dash and the stretch of empty storefronts. "Are you sure you have the right address?" he asked, pulling to a stop in the vacant parking lot.

Marrill already had the door open, spilling out in the Arizona sun. She spun, scanning the horizon. No sign of storm clouds yet.

The driver helped unload their luggage, but he seemed reluctant to leave them all alone in the middle of nowhere. Marrill could understand. It was a bit odd. But at the same time, if he didn't move his car before the storm came . . . well, it wouldn't be a car for very long.

"Our ride should be along soon, don't worry," her father reassured him, promising they'd call for a pickup if they ran into problems. The taxi drove away, the driver looking back at them as though they'd just escaped a mental institution. Finally, it was just the three of them, Karnelius, and a pile of luggage waiting in an empty parking lot.

An hour passed. Then another.

Then another.

The afternoon sun beat down. The air was still and quiet.

Sweat dampened the back of Marrill's shirt, and she didn't have to see the glances her parents exchanged to know they'd started to grow concerned.

Their ride was late.

Her father cleared his throat. "Maybe we should call the driver back? We can recheck our calculation and try again tomorrow." The words were barely out of his mouth when a breeze stirred the hair at the base of Marrill's neck. She straightened. The wind grew stronger, tossing the tip of her ponytail.

She jumped to her feet, grinning, just as a massive ship hove out of nowhere and into the handicapped parking spot in front of them. Instead of coming to a stop, however, it continued to crash forward, the hull tilting from one side to the other as if it was out of control.

Marrill heard someone shout. Tiny creatures frantically raced along the yards and up the masts. The ship began to turn, but it was too late. With a wrenching clatter of twisted metal and shattering glass, the bow plowed into one of the abandoned storefronts.

Finally the ship came to a stop, listing slightly to one side, the shop's sign dangling from the bowsprit. Everything seemed frozen for a moment. Marrill tensed, her eyes wide, waiting to see how extensive the damage was.

"You said hard to lee!" a voice shouted. She smiled, recognizing Remy.

"I said it was hard to *see*," another voice countered. "And it's much harder now, I might add. Just wreckage everywhere." Marrill laughed—definitely Ardent.

The two continued to argue, but Marrill ignored them. Because a familiar face had appeared at the railing. The minute his eyes fell on her, he grinned widely and waved. "Marrill!" he called.

Marrill's heart exploded with joy. "Fin!" she cried. Forgetting her parents, her bags, and even Karnelius, she leapt from the sidewalk and splashed across the water-covered asphalt, not even waiting for the pirats to lower the gangplank before scrambling up the rope ladder slung over the side of the hull. Big-eyed barnacles waved their feathers at her temptingly as she passed, but she knew better than to give in and touch them.

When she reached the top, a pair of hands grabbed her, pulling her onto the deck. She tumbled into her best friend's arms. They squeezed each other in a massive hug, jumping up and down with excitement.

She pulled away, grinning so hard it almost hurt. Fin beamed back at her. Marrill couldn't help noticing that in the past year he'd definitely grown older. His face was a little less round, his features a bit more pronounced; his shoulders were wider. He'd probably grown close to a foot taller as well. But his hair was just as disheveled as ever, and his eyes still sparkled with mischief.

"Glad to see you're in one piece," she told him.

He lifted a shoulder. "A few close calls. Nothing the Master Thief of the Khaznot Quay couldn't find a way out of." He waggled his eyebrows and Marrill laughed.

Someone behind her cleared her throat, and Marrill spun. "Remy!" she squealed. She was immediately enveloped in another hug, and she squeezed her former babysitter tightly. "I've missed you so much!" And then, in a lower voice so that no one else could hear, she added, "Are you doing okay?"

"Never better," Remy told her. And when she pulled away, Marrill could see the truth of it in her friend's eyes. Remy had also changed in the past year. Though she hadn't aged, her hair was longer, twisted now in twin braids that fell over her shoulders. Her skin was a deep tan from spending so much time outside, and her arms were lean and muscular from the work of steering the ship. Marrill could just glimpse the edge of the rope tattoo peering out from under the shoulder of her sparkly pink tank top.

As usual, Marrill felt a stab of guilt at the sight of the ink. Remy must have noticed the shift in Marrill's mood because she planted her fists on her hips and scowled. "Oh, don't worry about that," Remy said. "Tattoo or not, the Stream is my home now. And besides...things have changed a little recently." Her eyes flicked past Marrill, and her features softened, an almost swoony smile tugging at her lips.

Marrill turned to see what she was looking at. A familiar figure loped down from the quarterdeck. Her jaw dropped.

It was Coll.

It had been years now since she'd last seen him, snatched away as they escaped from the Sheshefesh. They'd nearly made it when the giant squid had swiped Coll from the deck, dragging him back into the depths of its cathedral, trapping him there forever.

"What?" Marrill sputtered, shaking her head. "How?"

Coll grinned widely and opened his arms. She raced toward him and gave him a quick hug before pulling back and searching for his tattoo, wondering if he'd somehow gotten rid of it. If Remy, too, might be able to escape the curse.

But no—it was still there, dancing across his shoulder in exactly the same spot as Remy's. "But how in the world are you here?" she asked.

He laughed and patted her arm. "I'm afraid that's a story for another day."

"Let's just say the Dawn Wizard gives good secrets," Remy added, chuckling. "Even if they take a while to pan out."

Marrill was about to ask more, when she looked past his shoulders and saw Ardent.

Everyone else seemed to have changed in the past year. But he hadn't at all. His white hair still tufted out from under a limp purple cap and his beard still tumbled like cotton candy down his front. His skin was softly wrinkled, especially around his eyes. They glittered with mirth and wisdom.

Marrill's breath hitched. She hated the moment of doubt she felt. The slight hesitation as she searched his eyes to see if any remnants of the Master were hidden in their depths. Despite everything they'd been through, she didn't know if she would ever be able to shake that moment of uncertainty. She wondered if she could ever trust him so completely again.

But, she realized, perhaps that was just a part of life. People messed up. Even wizards were human, and all humans made mistakes. It wasn't fair to judge a person based on their worst actions alone. People were more complicated. Everyone should be given the chance to change.

Just look at Serth. If they hadn't been willing to trust him, they might not have saved the Stream.

Ardent smiled gently, as though he saw the moment of hesitation and understood. "Welcome aboard, Deckhand Aesterwest."

She fell into his arms. He may have appeared frail, his long purple robe practically swallowing him whole, but when he hugged her back she could feel his strength and warmth. She could feel he was still the gentle Ardent she loved.

"We're glad you're back," Ardent said softly. Marrill smiled. So was she.

She glanced behind him. "Where's Serth?"

Remy shrugged. "He's going to meet us at the next port. Said something about needing to plant some trees, then walked onto the Promenade Deck, and we haven't seen him since."

Ardent frowned. "He actually said, 'I have business with trees, those that time burned down and those that burn with time.'"

Worry knit Marrill's brow. "That sounds...ominous."

Ardent snorted. "Oh, I wouldn't worry about it. That's just the problem with oracles, you know. Once they get in the habit of speaking in prophecy, they want to do it for everything. Last week, he called his bed 'that place where night-born visions dwell.'"

They were interrupted by the sound of a giant splash followed by a wave of angry chittering. Turning, she found a gaggle of pirats gathered at the top of the gangplank. They didn't look pleased. Marrill raised an eyebrow in question.

Ardent cleared his throat, pressing his fingertips together. "There've been some...ah...negotiations over the return of Karnelius."

"One side, one side, quit yer fussin', will ya?" The Naysayer pushed his way across the deck toward her. Draped over one of his shoulders was a lanky tortoiseshell cat, a gift from Marrill and her family the summer before. Marrill grinned and started to say hello, but he just continued past her as if she didn't exist.

"Good to see you, too," she grumbled at his back as he stepped over the cluster of pirats without ceremony and thumped down the gangplank, his thick purple tail trailing behind.

He reached the parking lot and splashed his way toward Marrill's parents and their collection of luggage. They straightened, grinning in greeting. "Mr. Naysayer, so lovely to see—" her mother began.

"Not interested," the Naysayer cut in. It was the only acknowledgment he gave to their presence as he swiped at Karnelius's carrier and flicked it open. An orange ball of fur leapt free, scrabbling up the Naysayer's arm. When the cat reached the lizardy creature's opposite shoulder, he bonked his forehead against the Naysayer's jaw and began purring loudly.

The Naysayer let out a contented sigh and retreated back up the gangplank, balancing both cats the whole way.

Ardent strode past him, approaching Marrill's parents with open arms and a welcoming grin. "Mr. and Mrs. Aesterwest, we're so pleased you could join us again." He shook her father's hand, turning it so he could get a better look at his wrist. "Good to see that the side effects wore off from that...*unpleasantness* last time. Sometimes they don't, you know."

Marrill's dad pushed up his glasses. "Last time you said they *always* wore off."

"Yes," Ardent muttered. "I probably did, I probably did. Nasty little creatures, at any rate." He quickly turned to Marrill's mom, taking her hand. He held it for just a beat longer than necessary. "How are you feeling?" he asked, his face folded with concern.

"I'm well, thank you. I still need to take care not to overextend myself. The doctors have said there are no guarantees." She smiled. "But there never are, are there?" she added with a wink.

Ardent nodded. "No," he said, with just a touch of sadness in his voice. "There never are." Then he spun, kicking aside the hem of his robe, and held out his elbows for them to take. "Adventure awaits!" he exclaimed as he escorted them on board the *Enterprising Kraken*.

+ + +

That evening, Ardent snapped his fingers, and hundreds of tiny lights burst to life around them. It was like the fluffiest snow caught in the gentlest breeze, except instead of snowflakes, they were soft fuzzy motes dancing in the rigging overhead, illuminating the darkening deck. Around them, the Stream stretched out to the horizon on all sides, shimmering with a soft golden glow.

A large table in the middle of the deck was piled high with buckets of prollycrabs. The Naysayer was ensconced at the head, already elbows deep in his own mess of food. Every few bites he alternated between dropping a hunk of meat for Karnelius, who sat purring in his lap, or tossing a bite to his other cat, who lounged on one of his shoulders.

The rest of the crew sat trading stories from the last year and laughing. Fin updated her on Fig and the Fade's declaration of independence form the Rise, and Ardent expounded at length on the truce he'd negotiated with the Salt Sand King.

Then it was her turn. "Mom, Dad—tell them about your news," Marrill prodded.

The crew quieted, turning to Marrill's parents. Her father adjusted his glasses and cleared his throat. "As you know, when Marrill first told us about the Pirate Stream, we were a bit…ah…skeptical." Beside him, Marrill's mom chuckled at the understatement and threaded her arm through his. "But it's difficult to deny the possibility of magic when confronted with a bedside table that follows you around the house like a dog, demanding to be petted."

"Plus," Marrill's mom said, "we *wanted* to believe such a magical place exists. So when Marrill suggested we actually travel here and see the Pirate Stream for ourselves, we jumped in with both feet." She winked at Marrill. "And we're so glad we did."

Marrill's dad nodded. "Of course, once we returned from our first trip on the Stream, we did what we always do after an adventure: We documented it. And then, on a whim, we decided to try publishing it."

Her parents exchanged a grin. "Turns out we weren't the only ones who wanted to believe in the Pirate Stream."

"Understatement," Marrill said. "It's one of the bestselling series right now, and everyone thinks they made it all up when it's actually all true!" She dragged her bag onto her lap and pulled out a stack of books to pass around. *Welcome to the Pirate Stream!* was printed across the top, above an image of a towering ship with a wizard in purple robes standing on the bow, his arms wide open to the reader.

Ardent took a copy and fanned through the pages with a look of interest. "Well, if you need additional source material for inspiration, I'd be happy to tell you about the time I accidentally invented an entire species of..."

While Ardent launched into another long-winded story and Marrill's parents sat listening, enraptured, Marrill slipped a bundle of letters from her bag. "From your family," she said, handing them to Remy.

Her former babysitter's eyes widened and instantly glistened with tears. "They all miss you and send their love," Marrill added.

"Thank you," Remy said, holding the packet of letters to her chest. Coll draped an arm across her shoulders. She leaned in against him.

Marrill let out a sigh of satisfaction as she looked around the table. She could think of no other place she'd rather be and no other crew she'd rather be with. Happiness bubbled up inside her. She stood and lifted her glass. "We should toast," she announced.

Everyone else stood, except for the Naysayer, unsurprisingly. Marrill turned to her parents. "You go first."

"To good health," Marrill's dad said, squeezing her mom around the shoulders.

Her mom smiled. "To family," she said, pulling Marrill into a side hug.

Coll went next. "To the wind at your back."

"To love," Remy said with a grin. Marrill could have sworn she noticed the older girl's eyes dart to Coll, and his cheeks flush.

It was Ardent's turn, and he cleared his throat. Marrill braced for a rambling speech. But instead he said simply, "To Annalessa." A hint of sadness filled the air as he lifted his eyes to the scribbled bird perched on the yardarm above. She let out a cry and took to the air, soaring through the glittering lights.

The moment was broken rather quickly, however, by a loud belch from the Naysayer. "Heh," he chuckled. Then he raised a goblet, joining their toast. "To me."

Next was Fin. He turned to face Marrill and placed a thumb against his heart. "To friendship."

Marrill's heart swelled as she touched her own thumb to her chest in response.

"Who is that young man?" her mother asked politely.

Coll scowled. "I thought we rounded up all the strays and threw them into the brig."

"He's Fin," Marrill said proudly. "He's my best friend."

Then it was her turn to raise a glass. There was so much she was grateful for, so many things she could toast. But in the end she chose the one thing that brought them all together. "To the Pirate Stream."

"To the Pirate Stream!" the others at the table echoed.

Overhead, the Ropebone Man squealed happily in his rigging. The pirats all let up a cheer. The rumor vines took up the call from the stern, echoing it until the night was filled with laughter and merriment.

And through the dark, the *Enterprising Kraken* sailed onward, toward the distant horizon, charting a course for possibility and wonder.

ACKNOWLEDGMENTS

A list of all the people and creatures who helped us on our journey would be as long and magical as the Stream itself. And all the thanks in the world are not enough to recognize the gifts they have given us. But for this last book of the series, it is you, dear reader, who we would like to thank the most.

You are the one who makes the Pirate Stream possible; you are the one whose thoughts bring magic to life. It has been a privilege and a joy to share our world with you. We hope that someday, in the near future or the far future or the many futures between, when you are standing in line somewhere, or trapped by something tremendously boring, your mind may drift down eddies of wonder, and you will find yourself looking at some nearby object and wondering, *What would happen if I dropped that into the Pirate Stream, right now?*

And you will smile.

We hope that on the edge of sleep, just as dark creeps beneath your eyelids, you may drift off on some foreign tide to far-off worlds filled with fantastical creatures and endless magic.

And you will spin those imaginings into your own stories.

We hope that you will daydream. That you will imagine. That you will wonder and question and believe. In magic. In friendship. In yourself.

And you will remember: At its truest heart, magic is imagination and imagination is magic.

With that in mind, it seems only fitting to end this series where it began (in our minds, anyway), with the words of Ardent Squirrelsquire:

From *The Manufacture of Enchanted Artifacts and Implements*
By Ardent Squirrelsquire, VVM, XQR, TLZ, etc., Wizard
"Thus, I draw this epistle to its close, with this simple reminder: items acquire magic as a fuzzy sweater acquires shock. It may come at once, or it may build over eons beyond reckoning, but this is the truest type of enchantment, the type which never, ever wears off. While your common artificer may lay an enchantment upon an item temporarily (this is oftentimes the nature of the magic potion), this is as a thin film on a running mare, quickly washed away.
True enchantment comes not from spells, but from lives."

Live your lives in true enchantment.

Sincerely,

The Authors